Samuel Booth, John Jorden Upchurch

The Life, Labors and Travels of Father J. J. Upchurch

Founder of the Ancient Order of United Workmen

Samuel Booth, John Jorden Upchurch

The Life, Labors and Travels of Father J. J. Upchurch
Founder of the Ancient Order of United Workmen

ISBN/EAN: 9783337207236

Printed in Europe, USA, Canada, Australia, Japan

Cover: Foto ©Raphael Reischuk / pixelio.de

More available books at **www.hansebooks.com**

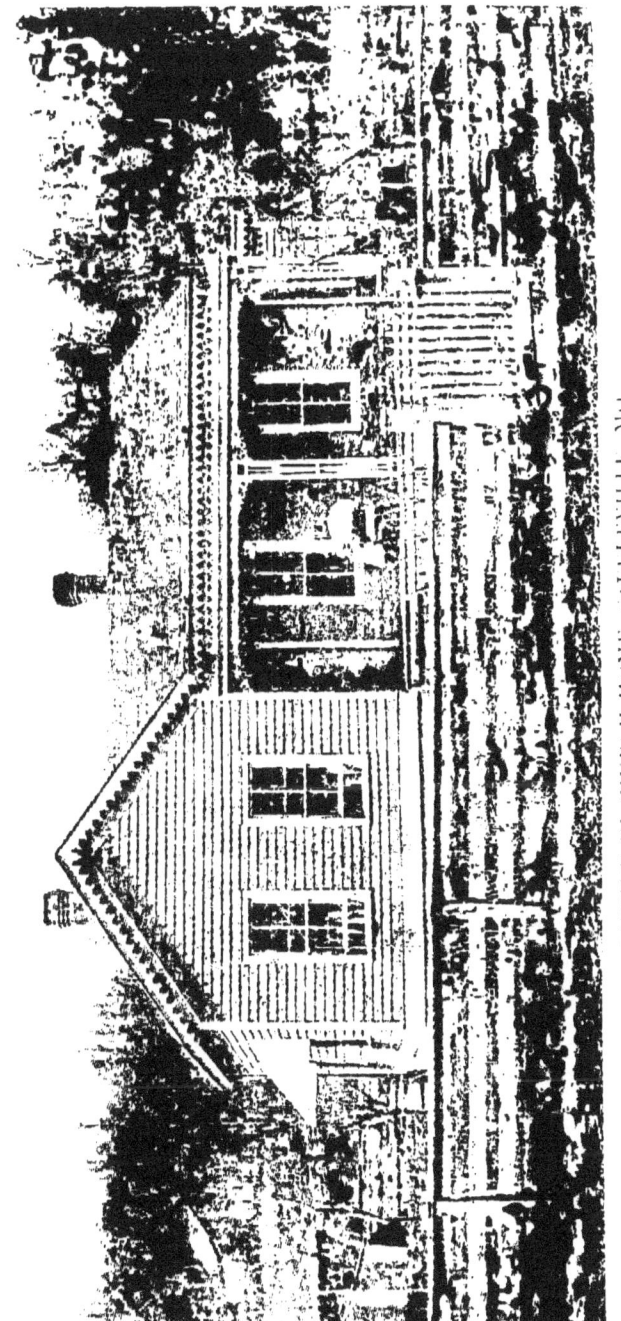

FATHER UPCHURCH HOME, STEELEVILLE, MO.

THE

LIFE, LABORS AND TRAVELS

OF

FATHER J. J. UPCHURCH,

FOUNDER OF THE

ANCIENT ORDER OF UNITED WORKMEN.

WRITTEN BY HIMSELF.

———

TO WHICH ARE ADDED

POEMS & EULOGIES BY PROMINENT MEMBERS OF THE ORDER.

REVISED AND EDITED BY

SAM. BOOTH, P. M. W.

———

A. T. DEWEY, PUBLISHER,
OFFICE OF THE "PACIFIC STATES WATCHMAN,"
SAN FRANCISCO, CAL.
1887.

Sold for the Benefit of Widow Upchurch and Family.

A "FATHER'S" BLESSING.

STEELVILLE, Mo., August 30, 1886.

To My Children of the Ancient Order of United Workmen:—

*A*S *I grow in years my heart seems to expand with gratitude to the Creator that I should be selected before all others to promulgate and put in practice the principles of our noble Order.*

I am truly thankful for the thought that has been the means of organizing an Order that has carried relief to thousands of the widows and orphans of our deceased brothers. Poverty and degradation have been driven from their doors, and the standard of Hope and Pro-tection erected in their stead.

Men are made better by assembling together in our Lodge rooms, where the true principles of fraternity are taught. We meet on a common platform of equality as all brothers should, and try to instill into each other's minds high and noble aspirations.

Now, let me, as the Father of the Order,—and it may be for the last time,—make an earnest request that all arouse from the lethargy we have fallen into. Let us go to work with renewed energy in building up our beloved Order to that standard she is destined to attain, both in numbers and acts of charity.

Let me impress upon your minds the importance of using every honorable means to induce good and true men to unite with us in protecting the widow and orphan from the cold charities of a heartless world.

Let us try to educate them to look forward to a high and noble purpose.

Do this, and you have, in a great measure, fulfilled the noble design of the Creator in placing man upon earth.

This work has been written, believing that my fraternal children would like to know more of my early history, trials, etc.

It has been my earnest wish to produce a work both interesting and entertaining, that when I have passed away my children can take up the book and say, " This is the record of our Father, the founder of our noble Order."

I have tried to make a true statement of facts, and I trust and believe that the members of the Order generally will read and not judge too harshly this, my humble effort.   Your Fraternal Father,

INDEX.

ILLUSTRATIONS.

GENERAL CONTENTS.

EDITOR'S NOTE.

IN looking over the material for the following pages, two courses
seemed open to the Editor's choice, to rewrite the manuscript, clothing the substance of the narrative in language of his own, or taking it
as he found it, to add the sub-headings, smooth out a wrinkle here
and there, snip off the ragged edges, and put in a stitch or two occa-
sionally, but leaving it substantially as it was left by the writer himself.

In the former case the work would have been that of the compiler;
in the latter it would retain its originality and be what it purported to
be, the work of the Founder himself. Believing that the latter course
would be the one most acceptable to those who will be most interested
in it, *i. e.*, the members of the great organization of which he was the
founder, and that being the one most in accord with his own inclinations,
he adopted it. The reader who comes to the book expecting to find a
literary and intellectual gratification will undoubtedly be disappointed,
except as it may be found in the glowing periods of his panegyrists.
The hands of both Author and Editor were hardened by the handling
of heavier tools at rougher handicrafts than the use of the pen and
Authorship; and in attempting to solve the more serious problems of
life, they had but little leisure to master the art of elegant literary com-
position. To the brethren, therefore, of the Ancient Order of United
Workmen and kindred organizations, whose beneficent labors received
their inspiration from his first efforts, as a legacy from a father to his
children, this little book, with all its imperfections, is commended by
their brother and friend.

SAM BOOTH,
P. M. W., Excelsior, No. 126, A. O. U. W.

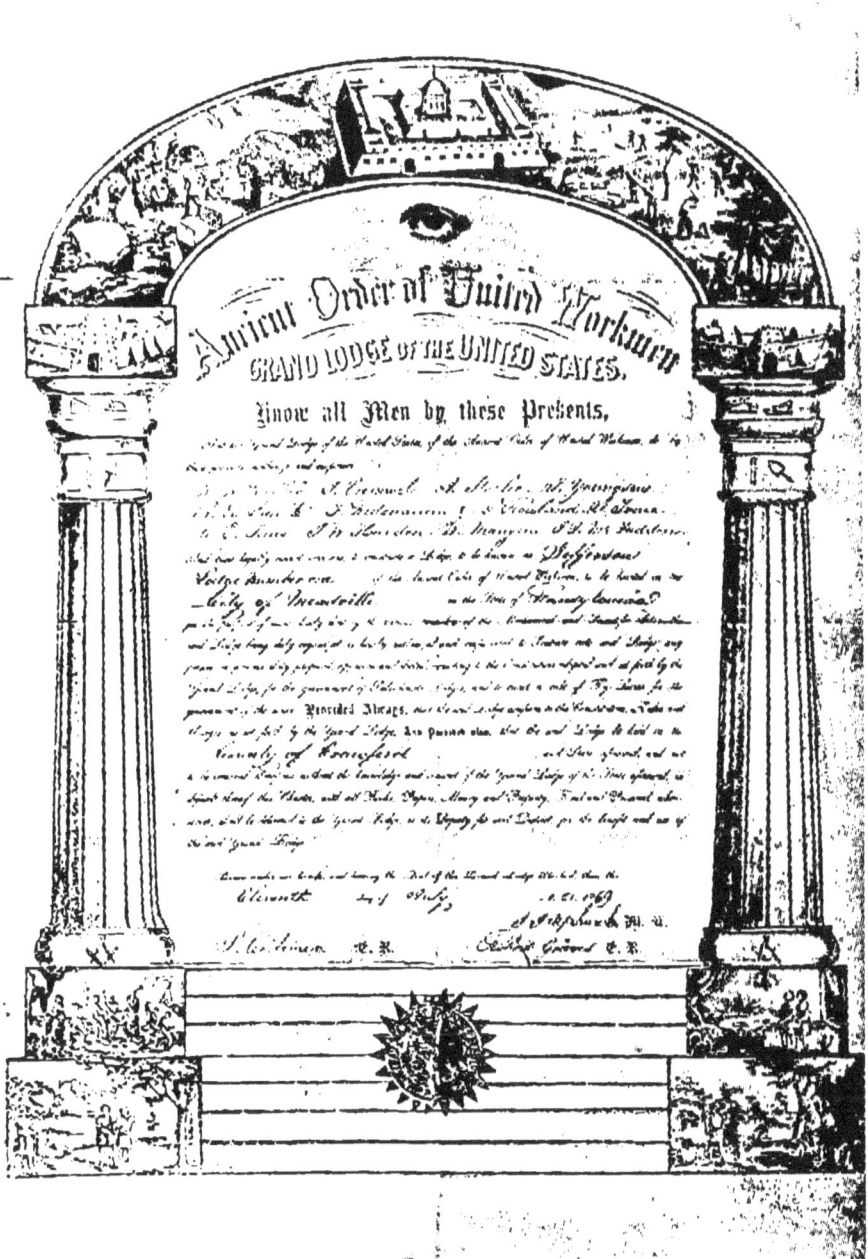

CHARTER ADOPTED BY THE FIRST GRAND LODGE A. O. U. W.

The views bordering this engraving picture some of the scenes alluded to in the lessons taught by the old Ritual, the ceremonies of which were not by any means as simple as those adopted later.

LIFE, LABORS AND TRAVELS

FATHER J. J. UPCHURCH.

——— ⁘ ———

HIS BIRTH AND FAMILY.

WAS born in Franklin County, North Carolina, March 26, 1822.

My father, Ambrose, was the only son of John Upchurch; my mother, Elizabeth, was the only daughter of Hon. Henry Hill. All of Franklin County.

There were of our family, two boys and two girls. My father followed the business of farming.

DEATH OF HIS FATHER.

In 1824, my father was shot and killed by a man by the name of Wright, who married the half sister of my mother. What the difficulty was about, I was too young to comprehend. Wright fled the country, and it was said went to Arkansas, while that State was held by Mexico; at any rate, his family followed some time after.

(13)

I well remember the circumstance of three negroes and three hundred and fifty acres of land being taken from us, which led me to believe that property was the cause of the murder.

SCHOOLING AND EARLY PRIVATIONS.

My mother was forced to resort to the needle to support herself and children. Educational facilities were few.

When I was eight years old, I attended school for six months and made fine progress. Commenced to read in Webster's Spelling Book. Had to walk three miles, night and morning, to and from school.

My Grandfather Upchurch took us children to live with him and sent us to school as opportunity offered. That was not often, and only of short duration. We went four miles on Sunday to attend Sabbath-school.

EMPLOYED AS CLERK.

In 1834, I left the farm, and was employed as a clerk in a country store, by a man by the name of Lawrence, who afterwards married my eldest sister. I again went on the farm in the winter of 1834–35, and remained there until the summer of 1835, when my Grandfather Hill purchased and gave to my mother a small farm.

LEARNING A TRADE.

She then took her children to live with her. I remained with my mother on the farm until the spring of 1837, when I went to learn the trade of a millwright with Thomas Duke. I remained with him until the fall. •My health being poor and the work heavy, I could not stand it, and left him and entered as an apprentice with William and Edward Allen, house-carpenters, as I thought the work would be lighter.

I ran a water-power saw-mill for William Allen for a

month or two, and then went with them to put up a saw-mill on the Tar River, for a man named Kenaday.

I remained here until the work was completed. The contractor had taken several buildings to put up at Henderson. a station on the Raleigh & Gaston Railroad, where quite a village had sprung up. I went with them and remained until one of the buildings was nearly completed.

CLERKING AGAIN.

One day, Charles Allen, the foreman, said to me, that as I was not strong enough to follow the business, he could get me a situation as clerk in a store, and advised me to take it. I consented to do so, and went to work. In a short time, Prof. E. A. Jones bought the store and opened a wholesale and retail grocery in the building.

GETS MARRIED.

I remained with this house until June 1, 1841, and then went to Raleigh and married Miss Angelina Green, daughter of Salome Green, of Bethlehem, Pennsylvania. She had gone South with John Zeigenfuss, an uncle, who was a contractor on the Raleigh & Gaston Railroad.

OPENS A HOTEL.

On getting married, Mr. Zeigenfuss and myself opened a hotel in Raleigh, North Carolina. We carried it on in the usual way, with a bar attached, until the winter of 1841–42, when the Washington Temperance Society was organized there. We both united with it, and opened what was said to be the first temperance house south of Mason and Dixon's Line.

We were in advance of the times. The people had not been educated up to this point.

In 1843, an old tramp, an Englishman, named James

Wood, came to the house with a pack on his back and in-
quired if we had any kettles to mend or silver plate that we
wanted marked. I handed him half a dozen spoons. In a
few minutes he had them engraved in good style. He then
wanted five cents with which to get a drink of whisky. In the
morning he was sick, and remained so for two or three
weeks. Although not confined all the time to his bed, he
could not walk, and claimed that he had the royal gout. I
soon made up my mind that his disease was brought on by
excessive use of intoxicants.

Some orders for engraving came in, which he executed.
In the meantime I would not allow him to have anything to
drink. So finally I got him sobered up, when he joined the
temperance society.

He then said if I would give him a place to work, he
would teach me the business of engraving and die-sinking.
I liked the idea, and rented a shop and bought what tools
were necessary, when we went to work. I made fine progress
in the art, but the old man began to drink alcohol, bought
for making varnish for cleaning plate, etc., until he was
finally carried away by delirium tremens in such a way as I
I never wish to see again.

RAILROADING.

The business at the hotel had been falling off, until we
finally had to close out. Mr. Ziegenfuss returned to Pennsylvania, and I ran the shop until 1844, when I accepted
the situation of assistant depot agent in the Freight Department of the Raleigh & Gaston Railroad. When not employed here, I was in the shop. I held this position until
the winter of 1844–45, when one of the engineers on the
passenger train left. The Superintendent, Wesley Hollister,
put me on the road in his place.

GOES TO CHARLESTON, SOUTH CAROLINA.

I remained on the road until December, 1845, when I left and went to Norfolk, Richmond, and Petersburg, Virginia; but could get nothing to do. A fellow-engineer accompanied me, and we concluded to go to Charleston, South Carolina. When we reached Wilmington, North Carolina, we were divided in opinion; he wanted to go by stage to Cheraw, South Carolina, and there take the railroad; I wanted to go by steamer, as I had never been to sea.

He finally consented to go by steamer; however, I regretted it afterwards, for as soon as he saw the waves rolling, thirty miles before we crossed the bar, he was the sickest man I ever saw. I remained up all night with him. We landed at Charleston, and put up at the Mechanics' and Planters' House, on Church Street, and searched all over the city for work. The only thing I could get to do was to work on a new saw-mill that was being erected.

HORSE TAMING.

I worked here some time with the intention of going somewhere else. I had but little money; my friend persuaded me to buy "Rarey's Horse-taming Process," which I did, having only six dollars left. I went to the superintendent of the Charleston & Augusta Railroad, showed him my letters, and he gave me a pass to Augusta, Georgia. Here I opened up the horse-taming business; sold one recipe for ten dollars, and then crossed the river to Hamburg; stopped there several days, selling recipes at almost anything I could get for them—feeling that I must have money to go further.

From here I went to Edgefield, in South Carolina. My money was short; I found I had to have some printing done, which would take nearly all the money I had. I, however,

2

had a few posters struck off, when I gave an exhibition in the jail-yard, where I took a vicious horse and subdued him to the satisfaction of all present. From this I raised money to pay my hotel bill and stage fare further on. I worked in this way until I reached Granville, South Carolina. I stopped there until I owed two weeks' board and had but fifty cents left. Money I must have. I sold recipes from one to five dollars each, and paid my board and stage fare to the next county town.

I finally reached Rutherfordton, in North Carolina. Here I undertook to subdue a horse that would run away. He ran away with me, tore the wagon to pieces (which I had to pay for), and threw me into a stone pile. When I came to, I was surrounded by a number of ladies (with the all-healing camphor-bottle) and men who had come from the town, a distance of a quarter of a mile. However, I was not seriously injured.

From there I traveled from place to place, following the court circuits until I reached Charlotte, North Carolina. Here business was better than it had been at some other places. I bought a horse four years old, and gave a recipe and twenty-five dollars for him. When the bargain was made I did not have the money. However, I raised the amount next day. I traded a gripsack for an old saddle and bridle, and then went on my own hook.

At Statesville I got a set of silver-plated buggy harness for teaching a man how to tame horses.

I put them in a sack and strapped them behind my saddle. I then went to Lexington, where I procured the assistance of a stage-driver. We hitched up my horse. My assistant was nearly frightened out of his head. The horse was as gay as a peacock, and proved a fine racer. A candidate for the office of sheriff got the stage-driver to try and trade for him. I asked fifty dollars to boot, and finally got thirty dollars and a much better horse for myself.

RETURNS HOME.

Next morning I bought an open buggy, hitched up my horse, and went independent. Reaching home I had a horse and buggy worth one hundred and fifty dollars, and two hundred dollars in cash. I had done pretty well.

STARTS FOR PENNSYLVANIA.

I traveled around the country trading and taming horses that summer. On October 1, 1846, with my family (wife and child). I started for Pennsylvania. Reached Philadelphia on the 3d by steamer from City Point, *via* Norfolk and Baltimore.

On the morning of the 4th, we took stage for Bethlehem. I could get nothing to do there. Tried making corn-shellers, but they would not shell the small, hard corn of the North. In February, 1847, I got a situation as superintendent of a large flouring and saw-mill at Lock Haven, in Clinton County, Pennsylvania, with a man by the name of Myers. When I reached there, the owners had sold the mill to a man by the name of Sterret, of Harrisburg. The purchasers wished to retain me as superintendent, but were going to have some extensive repairs made, and would not be ready for me for three months; but they wished me to go with them to Harrisburg, where they would get me work until such time as the mill would be ready.

Mr. Myers paid my expenses when we took stage for Harrisburg. We were caught in a snow-storm, and it took two days and nights to get through. On Saturday morning I called on the purchasers of the mill. We canvassed the city for work, but could not get any. I then concluded to go to Reading, and promised Mr. Sterret that I would in form him where I located, so that he could notify me when the mill was ready.

GOES TO READING, PENNSYLVANIA.

I went to the stage office and learned that the stage would not leave again until Monday morning. The Legislature was in session, board was high, and as twenty dollars was all the money I had, I concluded to leave. The livery man wanted ten dollars, and I to pay expenses. I thought if I could get out into the country, I could go for less. Ten miles out they wanted the same. I walked on and made twenty-two miles that afternoon.

I was tired and foot-sore, and in the morning very stiff and lame. Here they wanted six dollars to take me to Reading. I thought as I had made twenty-two miles in half a day, I certainly could make thirty in a whole day, which would be good wages. I started out and walked all day, but only made twenty miles. I came up with a gentleman with a buggy going to Reading, and paid him one dollar to let me ride with him to the city.

AT WORK IN THE RAILROAD SHOPS.

The next day I called on the master mechanic of the Philadelphia & Reading Railroad, and got employment in the shops until such time as a vacancy should occur on the road. About this time one man a day was being killed there. I concluded that I would remain in the shop, which I did for two years. I then got a situation and moved to the Catasauqua Iron Works, in Lehigh County. Previous to this we had been in the habit of living up to my income.

SAVING, AND OUT OF WORK.

I finally made up my mind that, as soon as I was paid, I would lay by ten dollars and that I would not spend it as long as I could help it. My wife thought that it could not be done; however, we concluded to try, and we got along about as well as before, except that we did not buy so much nonsense. I remained with the Iron Company and saved one hundred dollars. I then got out of work and traveled around the country for some time. I finally got a situation on the Mine Hill & Schuylkill Haven Railroad, Geo. W. Glass, Master Mechanic, and R. A. Wilder, General Superintendent.

APPOINTMENT AS MASTER MECHANIC.

After I had got moved my hundred dollars was all gone; still I adhered to the ten-dollar-a-month system. Two years from this time, the master mechanic resigned, and David Clarke was appointed to succeed him. I then acted as foreman for a year, when Clarke resigned, and I received the appointment of master mechanic, which I held for thirteen years.

ORIGINATING THE ANCIENT ORDER UNITED WORKMEN.

The circumstances which caused me to think of a plan by which working people would be benefited, and their families protected in case of the death of the husband and father, were as follows:—

In June of 1864, while I was master mechanic of the Mine Hill & Schuylkill Haven Railroad, the train hands demanded an advance of fifty cents a day in their wages. Engineers were then getting three dollars and sixty cents per day. I notified the President of the road of the demand, and he directed me to give them an ad-

vance of forty cents per day all round, which would give
engineers an even four dollars a day.

The proposition was received with great derision. They
said to me that their union had directed them to demand
fifty cents and take nothing less, and unless that demand
was acceded to, they would go on a strike.   •

I was very forcibly impressed with the injustice done to
men by any order or society which thus assumed to direct
in matters of such vital importance, while they (the society)
could not possibly know much, if anything, about the circumstances under which the difficulty had arisen between
the employer and employé, as was very evident in the
present difficulty.

The men went on a strike. They were out two weeks, ·
when the Secretary of War sent on a corps of engineers
and firemen, put them in my charge, and I operated the
road for two weeks in the interest of the Government.

At the expiration of that time, the men were ready to
return to work at what I had offered them before the strike
took place.

These men had lost a whole month's wages that never
could be regained, and some of them were not able to lose
four days in the month without depriving their families of
some of the comforts of life.

The inquiry arose in my mind, " What right has any man
or set of men to dictate to others what wages they should
receive? What right has a society to order that men
must not work unless the demands of the society are complied with? Who gave them power to take away or control the will of workingmen? "

As I thought over the subject, I saw more and more the
injustice done not only to capital, but to laboring men,

whom they profess to befriend. I was thoroughly convinced the way these societies were managed, that they exercised a baneful influence upon the business relations of the country.

I was convinced that something should be done to try to harmonize the two great interests of our country, capital and labor. They, being equal, should receive equal protection.

There was such an impression made upon my mind that something should be done, that I finally made up my mind to do all in my power to accomplish this great object, and if possible unite employer and employé into an organization and obligate them to the same great principles, of "the greatest good to the greatest number;" and I am happy to say that where this has been done there has been no trouble between the employer and employé.

I went to work on the great task allotted to me, and when an idea struck me I would write it down.

OIL SPECULATIONS.

In the latter part of 1864, the oil excitement became rampant. I got a pretty heavy dose. I had saved some money and thought I would soon make a fortune. I was told by my friends in Pottsville that if I would take three thousand shares of stock in the Martin-Binchoff Petroleum Company, they would appoint me as their superintendent, with a salary of two thousand dollars per annum. I resigned my position on the road to take effect January 1, 1865.

I then went to the oil regions and opened an office in the Washington McClintock House, Petroleum Center. The winter was very severe and we could do nothing until spring opened. I then saw that more money was made by speculation than by sinking wells.

While here, I got in conversation with Capt. Francis J. Keffer, on the trouble that was then agitating the business relations of the country between capital and labor, and I disclosed to him my plan of uniting them in one grand organization. I thought if it was carried out in good faith, it would obviate those difficulties and benefit both employer and employé.

Brother Keffer thought the object was a good one, and encouraged me to perfect and introduce the work; and I am proud to say that he showed his faith by uniting with the Order at the first opportunity and became a Grand Master Workman.

I got the refusal of two thousand seven hundred and sixty acres of land on the Tionesta; I was to pay sixty thousand dollars for it when sold. I took the papers to Philadelphia and put them in the hands of a broker at two hundred and fifty thousand dollars. I was to give the broker twenty-five thousand dollars for stocking; and I subscribed twenty-five thousand dollars to the capital stock. When the war closed, a committee was appointed to view the land and report when the money would have been paid in.

On peace being declared, everything like speculation closed. That summer and fall I put down two wells, which did not produce oil enough to pay for the pumping.

GOES TO ALABAMA.

In December I received, through M. W. Baldwin & Co., the appointment of master mechanic of the Alabama & Florida Railroad, headquarters at Montgomery. I sold out, and on the 1st of February, 1866, after shipping my goods by vessel, I took my family and started South. I made but slow progress, and had to lie over every night after leaving Washington.

VISITS HIS MOTHER.

At Franklinton, North Carolina, I stopped off to visit my mother. We could get no conveyance except a large farm wagon, drawn by four scrawny mules, and had to go eight miles into the country. I found my mother well. I had not seen her for twenty years. Here one of my children was taken sick, which detained us several days. We finally bade them farewell, and again took the train, stopping at Thomaston a few days to see a niece, a Mrs. Pleasant.

On leaving here, we passed through Salisbury, which was in a very dilapidated condition, from the effects of the war. We finally reached the end of the road, twenty-seven miles north of Columbia, South Carolina, it having been torn up by Sherman's army. The country was completely devastated, and we had to take stage for Columbia, twenty-seven miles; fare, seven dollars each, large and small; stopping at Columbia overnight.

In the morning we took the train for Augusta, *via* Branchville, where we changed cars. In the afternoon we came to the end of the road again. There were a good many passengers and only six ambulances to carry us twenty-four miles to Johnson's Siding; fare, seven dollars each. We had considerable amusement, notwithstanding. The ambulances were drawn by old, broken-down mules, and we made about three miles an hour. The beating those poor animals had to take, will never be forgotten. There was a conductor who carried a sea-shell, that he would blow every few minutes; he said to keep his train together. He was a jolly, good fellow and created a great deal of fun; but the worst had to come. It was as dark as a black cat, and the rain pouring down like fury. Amidst all this, he discovered that the ambulance that we were in was about to follow the example of the mules,—break down.

One ambulance was full of negroes. The conductor stopped them, when we changed ambulances, baggage and all, in the rain, the scene being lit up with one tallow candle in a lantern. However, the change was made and we proceeded, and finally reached the station in time for the train. I have heard nothing from the ambulance or negroes since.

REACHES MONTGOMERY.

We proceeded with no mishap until we finally reached Montgomery, February 13. This trip cost me four hundred and sixty-five dollars, and, pretty well worn out, we stopped at the Exchange Hotel. In the morning I reported to Sam Jones, the superintendent, who wished me to take charge at once, but I had to find a place for my family. Board at the hotel was six dollars per day. I secured board at a private house at forty-seven dollars a week for the family. I wished I was back in Pennsylvania, and if I had not been ashamed to return so soon, I would have returned at once. Everything was unnecessarily high—the people had not forgotten Confederate prices. I, however, entered upon my duties.

The ship on which my goods were loaded got into the ice and had to return to Philadelphia for repairs. In six weeks she finally landed in Mobile. I was notified of the fact and that a salvage bill was charged against them amounting to thirty dollars, which I got refunded from the Insurance Company.

TAKEN SICK.

About a month after my arrival here, I was taken sick, most of the time not being able to attend to business properly. The doctors finally told me that if I remained there the following summer I would die, which I was not ready to do.

Having been solicited to take the superintendence of putting down some oil wells in St. Stephen's County, I concluded to resign, and on October 1, sent my family back to Pennsylvania, thinking that I would remain with the oil company until spring. I employed men to put the wells down, but in a short time I was prostrated with what was called the "break-bone" fever, and came to the conclusion that that was not the country for me. I resigned November 1, and started North.

RETURNS NORTH.

I got as far as High Point, North Carolina, where I stopped off to visit a sister. Here I was taken sick with diphtheria. I had the best of attention from my sister and niece. At this time one of my children was sick with typhoid fever at home. I can assure you that I was very anxious. One day my niece played "Home, Sweet Home" on the piano, and as I lay upstairs, I shed tears like a baby. Do not laugh at me, I could not help it.

HOME AGAIN.

As soon as I was able to get out, I again took the train for home, where I arrived very weak and jaded. I remained at home a few weeks and then went to the Baldwin Locomotive Works at Philadelphia. The firm told me to go into the shop, and when I felt like working I could do so. I remained with them until April, 1867, when I got a situation in the shops of the Pennsylvania Railroad, at Altoona, but was not able to do much. What money I had when I went South was expended, and work I must. I continued to improve, however, aided by the mountain air, and by October 1 I felt pretty well again. I was given the position of die-sinker for the company, which was a pretty easy job. I remained here until April, 1868, when I got a situation in the lathe shop of the Atlantic & Great Western Railroad, at Meadville, Pennsylvania.

AT MEADVILLE, PENNSYLVANIA.

Soon after my arrival I was informed that a society had been organized there, which was called "The League of Friendship, Supreme Mechanical Order of the Sun." I was told that this was the Order for the protection of the workingmen. In June I was proposed and elected to membership in the Order. I was but a short time in making the discovery that the Lodge was groping in the dark. We could get no information whatever from the Grand Council, unless we invested more money and took what was called the "Knight of the Iron Ring" degree, which required a further payment of five dollars. I came to the conclusion that the whole thing was rotten to the core, gotten up for the purpose of fraud, and therefore unworthy the confidence and support of workingmen. I made known to the members what I thought of it, many of them agreeing with me.

IS ELECTED MASTER.

I was elected Honorable Master of the League. I to'd the members that I had a plan that was calculated to benefit the working people more than anything that I knew of. I explained its principles to them as far as possible and redoubled my efforts to inculcate in their minds the objects contemplated in the plan which I had been working up. At a meeting of the League held on September 29, 1868, the following resolutions were offered and carried:—

ATTEMPTS AT REFORM.

"*Resolved*, That a committee of seven be appointed to revise and remodel the work of the Order, together with the Constitution and By-Laws; and that the committee correspond with all the other Lodges and with the Grand Council asking for their approval.

"*Resolved*, That if the Grand Council will not approve of the revised work, we will return to them our Charter, moneys, etc., and at once proceed to organize a new Order.

"*Resolved*, That the Honorable Master be the Chairman of said committee."

The following brothers were then appointed as the Committee on Revision: J. J. Upchurch, Chairman; J. R. Umberger, W. W. Walker, M. H. McNair, H. C. Deross, A. Klock, J. R. Hulse.

The committee met at the house of the Honorable Master, on the evening of October 11, 1868, and expressed their willingness to leave the work in the hands of the chairman.

As soon as I had written out the first degree and the Constitution, I notified the committee of the fact. A part of them met, and after hearing the ritual and Constitution read, they all expressed their approval, stating that they were perfectly satisfied with the entire work.

On October 27, 1868, I reported to the League that the Constitution and the first degree were ready. Report accepted and committee continued.

THE NEW ORDER.

After the Charter, etc., of the League was removed, I read the Constitution, which was adopted by sections. I then administered the obligation of the first degree to thirteen persons besides myself, viz.:—

J. J. Upchurch, A. Oaster, P. Linen, T. F. Upchurch, W. C. Newberry, W. S. White, J. R. Hulse, M. H. McNair, H. C. Deross, J. R. Umberger, S. Rositer, P. Lawson, A. P. Ogden, and J. R. Tracy.

Thus dates the organization of the Ancient Order of United Workmen.

TRIALS AND DIFFICULTIES OF THE NEW ORDER.

On the morning of the 28th several of the members came to me and demanded that the words " white male " be stricken from the Constitution, which I refused to do. The Recorder then refunded to each man his entrance fee.

On November 3, the second meeting night, I went to the hall, not knowing whether there would be anyone there or not, when six of the thirteen came forward and paid their initiation fee the second time, including, viz.:—

A. Oaster, P. Linen, T. F. Upchurch, H. C. Deross, and J. R. Umberger.

During the fall and winter I taught two classes in machine drawing.

In the fall of 1869, I was sent to Leavittsburg, Ohio, to take charge of a shop there, which I held for three years. The shop was then closed and I returned to Meadville and went to work in the shop.

UNCONSTITUTIONAL PROCEEDINGS.

While in Leavittsburg, I was notified by the Grand Recorder that on December 10, 1870, a meeting had been called by Keystone Lodge, No. 4. It was believed that an attempt would be made to institute an opposition Grand Lodge. I made it my business to be present at the opening of this meeting.

The Master Workman stated that the meeting had been called for the purpose of conferring degrees. I informed him that he had no authority to confer degrees at a special meeting, without a dispensation from the Grand Master Workman, and as a dispensation had not been applied for, none had been granted. The Lodge then closed. Immediately after closing, Bro. George Jeffery was called to the chair, and W. W. Walker appointed Secretary.

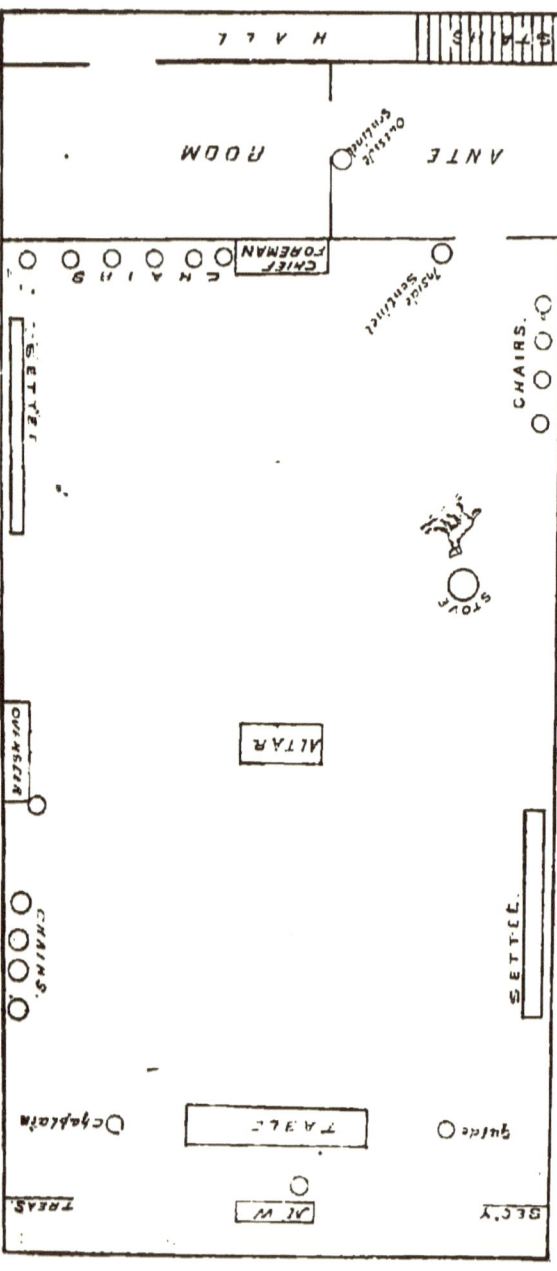

PLAN OF HALL ORIGINALLY USED BY THE ORDER.

The accompanying diagram shows the position of the officers' chairs, the disposition of the furniture, etc., of the Lodge-room in which the Order was cradled. In those early beginnings of the organization, before the pioneers of the Order began to realize the benefits which were to flow from it, or the dimensions to which it was destined to grow, there were often occasions when it was hard to get a quorum at the meetings for the transaction of the necessary business, and Mr. Upchurch relates that on one memorable occasion, when there was business of some importance to transact, there was one Workman short of the requisite number, and they were at their wits' end what to do for another member to make a quorum. Some one suggested counting the dog in, belonging to one of the members present. It was accordingly done. The meeting was called to order, and no one questioning a quorum, the business was transacted and the difficulty thus got over. Such conduct will not do as a precedent, however.

The Chairman stated that the object of the meeting was to call a convention to form a State Grand Lodge, to take the place of the Provisional Grand Lodge, announcing the fact that there were now six subordinate Lodges in Pennsylvania, and as they had a constitutional right to form such Grand Lodge they would proceed to do so as soon as possible. I, still being in the hall, protested against the proceedings as being unconstitutional, irregular, and uncalled for.

If the present Grand Lodge was only provisional (which I most positively denied), the proceedings of this meeting were irregular and unconstitutional, for the proper way was to notify the Grand Master Workman, when he should issue the call for the convention to meet and form the Grand Lodge.

I stated to them that the article from which they claimed to have received their authority, did not apply to Pennsylvania, but to those Lodges in other States working under the Grand Lodge of Pennsylvania; and further, if I, the Grand Master, was in error in the matter, and if the members were dissatisfied with the present Grand Lodge officers, they could elect such brothers as suited them, as it was only a few days until the next election would take place, it being the last meeting night in the month.

SECESSION.

The meeting then adjourned, without taking any definite action, re-assembled in another hall, and passed resolutions seceding from the original Grand Lodge; when I immediately revoked the Charter of all Lodges which participated in the secession.

At a meeting of the Grand Lodge held in Meadville, Pennsylvania, in January, 1871, J. O. Rockwell, of No. 3, was elected as Grand Master Workman. I was created the Provisional Supreme Master Workman.

3

The two wings of the Order having made two attempts
in the Grand Lodges to compromise their differences and
again become united, and failing, the idea that I would try
what I could do to accomplish the desired object struck
me. I approached W. W. Walker, the Grand Master of
the secession wing, on the subject of a union. He thought
the object could not be consummated, as the attempt had
been made without success. My reply was that all former
attempts were illegal. I, as Provisional Supreme Master
Workman, had given no authority for such proceeding, but
I thought that I had a plan, which if he, as Grand Master
Workman of his wing of the Order, would agree to, the
object sought could and would be brought about.

RECONCILIATION.

My plan was as follows:—

That each wing of the Order appoint five representatives,
to meet in convention to be held at an early day, to try and
accomplish the desired object; each representative pledging
his sacred honor to abide by and support the decision arrived at by said convention and to do all in his power to
induce his Lodge to acquiesce in the same.

This convention met in Meadville, Pennsylvania, January
14, 1873, and was composed of the following brothers:—

From the original Grand Lodge: J. J. Upchurch, Provis-
ional Supreme Master Workman; Jas. M. McNair; Joseph
Morehead, Grand Master Workman; J. H. Williams, and
Robert Greaves.

From the secession Grand Lodge: W. W. Walker, Grand
Master Workman; Jas. M. Bunn, M. W. Sackett. H. G. Pratt,
and Jas. McCandless.

The object for which the convention was called was happily consummated.

ELECTED PAST SUPREME MASTER WORKMAN.

The first Supreme Grand Lodge convened at Cincinnati, Ohio, February 11, 1873, with eleven members from Pennsylvania, Ohio, and Kentucky. At this meeting I was made Past Supreme Master Workman.

GOES TO STEELVILLE, MISSOURI.

In March, 1873, I received the appointment from A. L. Crawford, of Newcastle, Pennsylvania, as master mechanic on the St. Louis, Salem & Little Rock Railroad, in Missouri, the road being yet under construction. I ran a locomotive until it was finished. I then took two locomotives to Springfield, Missouri, and had them overhauled, after which I commenced to put up a shop at Steelville, and put in the necessary machinery.

In 1875, trade was very dull on the road. The President wanted me to make a hand in the shop and still retain the position of master mechanic. I told him I did not do two men's work for one man's pay, and resigned.

OPENS A STORE.

I then opened a provision store in Steelville, and ran it for eight or nine months, when the superintendent of the Cuba Planing Mill Company wanted me to take charge of the works as superintendent.

GOES TO CUBA, MISSOURI.

I then sold out my store and went to Cuba. In the fall I saw that the company was not making any money, and as I got a chance to sell my stock in the mill, I did so and resigned.

GOES TO ST. LOUIS.

I then hired to run a locomotive on the Cairo & St. Louis Narrow Gauge Railroad. After seeing the road, I con-

cluded to go to work in the shop. During the summer I
was sent to East St. Louis to take charge of the round-
house. I remained there until the winter. The company
had but two pay-days during the year; they, however,
issued meal checks that we could pay our board with.

SUSPENDED—RE-INSTATED.

When I wanted money for the support of my family, I
had to sell my time at a discount of twenty per cent, consequently I became poor, so much so that I was unable to
pay my dues and assessments in the Order, when I was suspended. Bro. J. M. McNair and W. A. Dungan had my
dues and assessments paid up, when I was re-instated, for
which I am under many obligations. Bro. Samuel B.
Myers, of Franklin Lodge, No. 3, made application for my
withdrawal card; the first I knew of it was the receipt of
a power of attorney for me to sign, authorizing Samuel B.
Myers to sign the Constitution for me. No. 3 then paid
my dues and assessments until I got on my feet again, a
kindness that I shall always appreciate.

The road went into the hands of a receiver, and I was
thrown out of employment.

To explain the foregoing, I have received the following copy
of minutes from Bro. W. A. Dungan, Recorder of Jefferson
Lodge, No. 1, Ancient Order United Workmen, Meadville,
Pennsylvania:—

"I have this day, as you request, found the Minute Book
of Banner Lodge, No. 1.

"This Lodge was organized by the consolidation of Jefferson, No. 1; Keystone, No. 4; and Starr, No. 35. Banner was the only name they could agree upon. In said
Minute Book of Banner Lodge, No. 1, I find all the proceedings of your suspension, re-instatement, withdrawal, and
the depositing of your card in Franklin Lodge, No. 3.

"HALL OF BANNER LODGE, No. 1, A. O. U. W. }
"Meadville, Pa., September 12, 1876. }

"On motion it was resolved that this Lodge transmit to Brother Upchurch a statement of his standing in this Lodge, so that he may visit other Lodges.

CHAS. W. STEWART, *Recorder.*"

"HALL OF BANNER LODGE, No. 1, A. O. U. W., }
"Meadville, Pa., October 24, 1876. }

"The following brothers were suspended from insurance: Thos. Brannan, J. H. Davis, Nathan Hausmicht, E. C. Kipler, J. C. Rupp, Peter Linen, Jas. L. Murray, A. C. Smith, J. H. Sweeney, and J. J. Upchurch.

CHAS. JAMES, *Recorder.*"

"HALL OF BANNER LODGE, No. 1, A. O. U. W., }
"Meadville, Pa., November 7, 1876. }

"On motion of Bro. Wm. A. Dungan, Brother Upchurch was re-instated in the insurance department of this Order.

J. H. WILLIAMS, *Recorder pro tem.*"

"HALL OF BANNER LODGE, No. 1, A. O. U. W., }
"Meadville, Pa., January 6, 1877. }

"A communication received from Brother Upchurch. asking that this Lodge grant him a withdrawal card. Moved that this Lodge cancel his dues and grant the card. Laid over for one week. J. H. WILLIAMS,
Recorder pro tem."

"HALL OF BANNER LODGE, No. 1, A. O. U. W., }
"Meadville, Pa., January 23, 1877. }

"On motion of Bro. W. A. Dungan, an order was drawn for $3.80 for Brother Upchurch's dues, and his withdrawal card was then granted. J. H. WILLIAMS,
Recorder pro tem."

"HALL OF BANNER LODGE, No. 1, A. O. U. W., }
"Meadville, Pa., February 27, 1877. }

"Communication from Franklin Lodge, No. 3, communicating that Brother Upchurch has deposited his card in that Lodge. W. A. DUNGAN, *Recorder.*"

286281

VISITS SUPREME LODGE AT ST. LOUIS.

After leaving the Cairo & St. Louis Road, I could get nothing to do, so I visited the Supreme Lodge while it was in session at St. Louis. They were kind enough to donate to me one hundred dollars.

I placed my claim against the Railroad Company, amounting to two hundred and thirty-five dollars, in the hands of Ex-Governor Thomas C. Fletcher. It was not collected, however, until June, 1882.

RELIEF FROM PENNSYLVANIA.

In the meantime, the Grand Lodge of Pennsylvania called on its members to contribute to my relief, which was responded to nobly in the sum of five hundred dollars, which was indeed a Godsend. It took a mortgage off my home, which otherwise would have been sold.

TRIES FARMING.

Having nothing to do, I rented a piece of land, bought a horse, and tried to do something in farming on a small scale. I worked hard, but owing to the dry season, did not make much.

["It seems that there was a disposition among some of the Lodges about this time to ignore the fraternal obligation, to help the brothers, in extreme cases, outside their own jurisdiction—a disposition which culminated so unhappily some years later, in Iowa. The following letter on the subject was written by Father Upchurch, to the *Propagator.*—ED.]

"We call especial attention to a letter from Brother Upchurch, in another column, which should interest every intelligent member of the Ancient Order of United Workmen,

from the fact that Brother Upchurch is known and acknowledged as the founder of our Order, and he therefore styles
himself with great propriety, our ' Old Father.' As such, his
counsels and advice should not only be listened to, *but followed*, particularly as the matter is one of vital importance to
every member of the Order, whether he lives in Pennsylvania, Ohio, Kentucky, Iowa, or Michigan. We know not what
the future has in store for us; it is therefore wise to heed
the call of distress, lest when we call there may be *no response.*

A GOOD FATHERLY LETTER.

" MARYSVILLE, Mo., August 29, 1879.

" EDITOR *Propagator—Dear Sir and Brother:* I regret
very much that I feel called upon to make known my feelings to the brothers of our beloved Order, on the subject
of separate beneficiary jurisdictions. In the first place, it
was never intended that any Grand Lodge should have the
control of its beneficiary fund, but that it should be collected
by the Grand Lodge officers, and handed over to the Supreme Lodge for disbursement as it is thought best.

" But, at the suggestion of Representatives of the Supreme Lodge, that to allow each Grand Lodge, when they
attained two thousand members, the privilege of a separate
beneficiary jurisdiction, would work to the advantage of the
Order generally, by inducing members to labor more zealously in building up Lodges, thereby reducing the number
and amount of death assessments, which might have resulted
in good had our brothers kept the objects of our noble
Order in their minds; but, unfortunately, it seems that a
portion of our Order have lost sight of these obligations,
and the great object for which our Order was established,
viz.: to assist each other, our wives, widows, and orphans;
to protect, sustain, and elevate them to that position God
in his wisdom created them to fill. Are we fulfilling that
obligation? Are we carrying out those great principles which
are the life and sinews of our beloved Order, when we
refuse or neglect to respond to the call of those who are in
need and have a right to call upon us for assistance in time

of adversity? Let us lose sight of self, and extend the
hand of charity to relieve the wants of the loved ones of
our departed brothers; let us do our duty faithfully and true,
and by so doing we will not only have the blessing of the
living but of the dead. Let, for instance, the situation be
reversed. Should we of Pennsylvania, Ohio, Iowa, or Missouri be in trouble, should we not expect, and of right, too,
that the brothers of other States and jurisdictions would
render assistance? Would we be worthy the name of
brother should we refuse to do so? It seems that jurisdictions are of the opinion that because the Supreme Lodge
in its wisdom has seen fit to grant separate beneficiary jurisdictions, they are independent of the Supreme Lodge,
and are not bound to respect and abide by its orders. Do
you not know that it is the head of the Order? There is
no appeal from its mandates. It can create and destroy;
the power that creates a law also has the power to repeal it.
The Supreme Lodge grants Charters to State Grand Lodges,
and I do not believe that any of us for one moment would
deny the Supreme Lodge the right to revoke that Charter.
That would indeed be the spirit of secession, which I trust
will never be raised in our beloved country and especially
in our noble Order.

"Now, brothers, let me, your old father. call upon you, as
noble sons, to lay aside all bickerings and discontent. Let
us come up to the work of relief manfully; let us contribute
of our means to the wants of those who are in need, and
have a right to expect assistance from us. Not knowing
how soon our dear ones may be placed in the same situation, what a happy thought it is to a dying brother that the
loved ones are watched over by faithful and true friends;
but should we neglect that duty, would they not look down
upon us from that Grand Lodge above, with scorn and contempt?

"I trust that these few thoughts may cause you to reflect,
and discharge your duties faithfully,

"I remain yours most truly, in C., H., and P.,

J. J. UPCHURCH."

PILE DRIVING.

In the spring of 1879, J. W. Blanchard, Superintendent of Construction on the St. Louis & Council Bluffs Railroad, gave me a situation of looking after a number of piledrivers on bridge work. I commenced work west of Marysville, and remained with them until they reached the State line.

["Increasing years, a large family, irregular employment, and ill health combined to keep his financial condition at a pretty low ebb about this time. And it was in the hearts of many good brothers, in consideration of the sacrifices he had made for, and his position as founder of, the Order, to relieve his condition by a ten-cent subscription throughout the Supreme Jurisdiction. The following letters to the *Propagator*, and editorial comment, were written as dated.— ED.]

RECOMMENDS LIBRARIES, ETC.

"SEDALIA, Mo., August 4, 1880.
"EDITOR *Propagator—Dear Sir and Brother:* Your kind letter came duly to hand, also paper, for which accept thanks.

"I promised to write you a few lines, but since my return I have not been able to gather my scattered thoughts for the task until now, being on the sick list for a few days. Am better to-day, but not able to go to work; so I will try to explain to you my views on a few points which are carried on in our beloved Order.

"I have had the pleasure of visiting a number of Lodges both East and West, and invariably found a slim attendance. Now, what is the cause of this? Is it because the work has become less interesting than formerly? or is it because the social advantages are lost sight of in looking after the financial or beneficial advantages?

"It is commendable that all make a preparation for sick-

ness, old age, and death, in laying up something to supply
our wants and those of our families; but this was a second-
ary consideration in the formation of our noble Order,—
the social advantages to be derived by meeting together as
a band of brothers tried and true, to discuss and devise the
best means of advancing our brothers in the highway of intelligence and prosperity. I am sorry to state that but few
Lodges have libraries, which is one of the leading features
of the Order—to induce its members and their offspring to
search for knowledge, and fit them to fill high and honorable stations. I have always contended that the laboring
classes had the requisite amount of brain, but, unfortunately,
they have had no chance to develope and expand it by re-
search. Let it be said that the Ancient Order of United
Workmen has done more in developing the genius of the
country than any other organization that was ever established.

"There is another feature, I am sorry to say, which to
some extent is not carried out as fully as, in my mind, it
should be; that is, the employment feature, or labor bureau.

" All must admit that the Lodges would be far better off
if their members were kept in steady employment. It may
be possible that I am prejudiced in favor of the original
employment plan, but if so. it is from the honest conviction
of my heart that it would be the best plan yet produced,
and would be equally beneficial to both those who labor with
the head as well as the hands.

"I trust that the good work will continue to spread until
its influence may be felt for good all over the Christian
world.

" I tender my warmest regards to my children everywhere.
This I can do, though I may never be able to see them.

" Fraternally yours in C., H., and P.,

J. J. UPCHURCH.

UPROOT THE WEEDS, ETC.

SEDALIA, Mo., August 22, 1880.

" EDITOR *Propagator—Dear Sir and Brother:* You have
certainly placed me under many obligations for the interest

you have taken in my welfare. I do not claim that the
brothers of our noble Order are under any obligation to
me; what I have done was for the benefit of others, not
expecting to reap any pecuniary benefit from it more than
another. I am truly thankful that so much good is being
done through my humble efforts. To know that the tears of
the widow and the orphan have been dried, that they have
been clothed and fed, and placed beyond the reach of the
cold charities of the world, gives me a satisfaction that
money could not purchase. I know that thousands have
been relieved in times of distress, that to-day appreciate my
labor, and thank God that such an Order was instituted. I
shall feel amply repaid for all the labor that I have expended
if the Order continues to grow, and its influence is felt for
good in every State and county. You wish to know what
my financial condition is? It is low. I am at work at
low wages. It takes about all I earn to make both ends
meet; but should I continue to have good health and steady
employment, by the help of God I will try to get along a
few years longer, when my mission will have an end, when
another will take it up and push it forward to a more noble
and successful purpose than I have done. I tried to select
good seed, and sowed them, as I believe, in good ground.
My brothers are the husbandmen that are to dig about
them and uproot the weeds, that in many Lodges are chok-
ing out the life of its true principles. Let us wait and hope
that our members may speedily return to a deep, sober
thought, which will point out their duties plainly, not only
to themselves, but to the whole Order.

"I am sorry to learn that some of the jurisdictions still
refuse to respond to the call in aid of the yellow fever suf-
ferers. Is it possible that a Workman should be so lost to
humanity as to turn his back upon their suffering widows
and orphans after so solemnly obligating ourselves to
aid and support? May the great Supreme Master Workman above direct us aright.

"Fraternally yours in C., H., and P.,

J. J. UPCHURCH."

RAILROADING AGAIN.

I was then put on the Clarinda Branch, where I remained until the work was nearly completed. I received a letter from J. W. Blanchard to go to Marysville; he said that he had applied for the position of foreman in the round-house at Council Bluffs for me, and that Mr. Selby, the general master mechanic, said he would give it to me, but wanted me to go to Moberly, when we could have a talk. I called on him, showed him my letters from the best railroaders in the East, when he said he wanted me to go to work in the shop. He thought after awhile he could give me a shop. I went to work.

VISITS THE GRAND LODGE AT MEADVILLE.

Having been previously invited by the Ancient Order of United Workmen Lodges, of Meadville, Pennsylvania, to visit them during the session of their Grand Lodge to be held the second Tuesday in January, 1880, I accepted the invitation. On my arrival in Meadville, I was met at the depot by Bro. W. A. Dungan, Chairman of the Committee of Reception, and was conducted to rooms in the McHenry House. The next day I visited the Grand Lodge, and was warmly received by my old friends. The meeting of the Lodge was a very interesting one. At the close of the session, a grand banquet was given by the Lodges and citizens of the city in Library Hall. About four hundred members and invited guests sat down to this magnificent repast. A number of fine addresses were delivered on the occasion.

GOES TO FRANKLIN, PENNSYLVANIA.

I remained here until Monday, and then went to Franklin, accompanied by Bro. Albert Hayden. On my arrival I was met by a committee at the depot, and escorted to the hotel. In the evening a grand reception was given me at the Opera House, the hall being packed to its utmost capacity. I was conducted to the stage by Bro. Samuel B. Myers, who delivered the address of welcome in a feeling and enthusiastic strain of eloquence, which was responded to by repeated applause.

I was then introduced and gave them a short talk. When I had finished, Brother McClure arose and addressed me in the most beautiful strain of language and fraternal sentiment one could wish to have, concluding by presenting me with a beautiful gold-headed cane, appropriately engraved on behalf of the members of No. 3.

I replied, accepting the beautiful and useful token of their friendship, as well as the fullness of my heart could permit.

At the conclusion of the exercises, all were invited to the banquet-hall, where a magnificent feast had been prepared by the ladies. About six hundred members and invited guests sat down to enjoy the rare viands that had been placed before us. We had a very good time, and one never to be forgotton by me. Franklin is a beautiful as well as a wealthy little city. My friends tried to procure a situation for me, but there was nothing to be had. They said if I was located there it would not be long before I would find employment. I remained here a few days and then returned to Moberly, Mo. On reaching there, I received a letter from my wife, stating that a gentleman wished to purchase my property.

MOVES TO PENNSYLVANIA.

I immediately went home, sold my place, and went back to Franklin, Pennsylvania, and procured a situation in the shops of the Oil Well Supply Company, Oil City, at two dollars and a half a day. I worked two weeks, when the superintendent stated that the other men had found out that I was getting more than what had been agreed upon by the shops; they demanded that my wages be reduced to two dollars and thirty cents. I refused to accept the reduction and left the shop. I then went down to Franklin, and entered into an agreement with Mr. Emery to run his machine shop on shares. I rented a house and sent for my family, or rather a part of them, my wife and two youngest children.

I thought I would do well, but the price of oil went down to seventy-one cents per barrel. The operators would have nothing done unless they were compelled to do so. I remained here two months and received forty dollars. I became discouraged; there was an excursion party going West over the Chicago, Burlington & Quincy Railroad, on Monday morning. I made up my mind to return West. I had posters struck off; Tuesday afternoon I sold out; and on Wednesday morning, at eight o'clock, I was on the train going West.

RETURNS WEST—SICK, AND OUT OF EMPLOYMENT.

We went to Kansas City; I had received a letter that there was a job for me when I arrived; but when I got there the place was filled. I could not find anything to do in the city, so I decided to send my family to Marysville to see some friends, and I went to Sedalia, Missouri, where I got work in the shop of the Missouri Pacific Railroad. I rented a house and sent for my family. In the fall my health became so poor that I was not able to work more than half the time.

RELIEF FROM THE ORDER.

During the winter of 1880-81, the members of the Order contributed about four thousand dollars to my relief, which was a relief, indeed. While in Franklin, being fearful that the manuscript of the work of the Order might get lost, moving around so much, I left it in charge of Bro. Samuel B. Myers, for safe-keeping. He still retains it, and probably will do so until my death.

MOVES BACK TO STEELVILLE.

In the spring of 1881, we again moved to Steelville, Missouri. I opened an undertaker's office and lumber-yard, but did not do much business.

VISITS THE SUPREME LODGE AT CINCINNATI.

In June, 1882, the members of the Order in Cincinnati invited me to visit them during the session of the Supreme Lodge, at their expense. I accepted the invitation, and on my arrival I was met at the depot by a Committee of Reception and escorted to the Gibson House, where most of the Supreme Lodge representatives were stopping.

On the next morning I was presented to the Supreme Lodge by the Past Supreme Master Workman Frizzell, and Samuel B. Myers, in a speech by the latter, to which I replied in a short talk. We had a fine session, and on the re-election of Brother Baxter to the office of Supreme Master Workman, I was elected to the office of Past Supreme Master Workman.

HONORS EXTENDED TO HIM.

A resolution was introduced and passed, inviting me to visit the Supreme Lodge whenever I felt so disposed, and that I be paid mileage and per diem the same as representatives. I replied with many thanks. With some members of the Supreme Lodge I visited the Subordinate Lodges each night we were in the city. We were escorted to the garden on the heights. On Friday, thirty carriages were procured and filled with members of the Supreme Lodge and invited guests under the efficient leadership of Bro. S. S. Davis, Supreme Receiver, and we were driven through the city, the first stop being at the Exposition Building, which is a magnificent structure. The Music Hall is fitted up in grand style and has the next largest organ in the United States, on which the professor gave us some excellent music. On leaving here, went to Cook's Carriage Factory, where we saw vehicles of all kinds and styles being manufactured in all their various branches. There were seven hundred men employed in these works.

We then proceeded to the city work-house, were conducted through the establishment by the warden, and its operations explained. When we were about ready to depart, we were invited to partake of a repast that had been provided in a magnificent style, to which ample justice was done, after which a number of fine speeches were made.

We again entered carriages and were driven to the cemetery, which contains three thousand acres, and is said to be the finest in the United States. On leaving here, we were taken through the suburbs of the city, which surpass anything I have ever seen for beauty and excellence.

PRESENTATION.

We next stopped at the Zoological Gardens, which contain a fine collection of rare birds and animals from almost every nation and clime. At half past three o'clock dinner was announced, to which about five hundred sat down. Old Father Hennessy, of Washington Lodge, No. 1 (the second Lodge that was ever instituted), took me under his especial care. When we sat down to dinner, I noticed that Father Hennessy and myself were placed at opposite ends of the table from the Supreme Lodge officers. After awhile Father Hennessy said that a brother at the other end of the table wished to see me; so we left our seats and went forward, when Bro. John Frizzell arose and presented me with a magnificent gold badge, anchor and shield, with diamonds set in the anchor. On the reverse side is engraved, "Presented to J. J. Upchurch, P. S. M. W., Father of the A. O. U. W., by the members of the Supreme Lodge, 1882."

The presentation was made in a grand flow of language, which characterizes every speech made by the Honorable Workman.

I was taken so much by surprise that for some moments I was unable to reply; but finally did so with many thanks, pledging myself to wear the offering in honor of the donors and with credit to myself.

Dinner over, we again took carriages and drove through the park to the hotel. The next day we visited the water-works, which is a splendid piece of work. At noon we visited the fire department, when the men and horses went through their drill in fine style. On Monday returned home.

ATTENDS THE SUPREME LODGE AT BUFFALO.

In 1883, I attended the Supreme Lodge at Buffalo, which was a very pleasant session; visited several Subordinate Lodges, took a drive around the old fort, and through the park, stopping at the hotel in the park where a magnificent banquet had been prepared for the hundreds of Workmen, ladies, and invited guests, to which ample justice was done. I was introduced to the Mayor and many brother Workmen. There was some excellent music and dancing.

On the next evening we had a moonlight excursion on the lake, which was very delightful. After landing, on our return, three companies of "Select Knights" escorted us to the hotel.

The following day a special train was engaged to convey

4

us to Niagara Falls; we took dinner at the International Hotel, and when we were through, took carriages and drove on to Goat Island, where we had a fine view of the American and Horse-shoe Falls. We then went up to the upper end of the island and had a good view of the Rapids. We here entered carriages and crossed over to the·Canadian side, where we had a view of the falls from John Bull's territory. We then returned to the American side and entered the park. After spending a couple of hours there, we returned to the hotel and took supper. We again visited the park under the electric lights. The sight was most beautiful, the park being illuminated in a magnificent manner. At ten o'clock, P. M., we took the cars for Buffalo. The next day we started for home and arrived safely.

HIS RIGHT TO BE CONSIDERED FOUNDER OF THE ORDER DISPUTED.

While in Buffalo, Dr. A. B. Robbins, one of the representatives to the Supreme Lodge, published a card in one of the Buffalo papers, to the effect that Brother Lenhart, of No 1, Meadville, and himself were the authors of our beneficiary article. Brother Lenhart immediately arose in the Supreme Lodge and emphatically denied the assertion, soon after which, Bro. Samuel B. Myers, of Franklin, No. 3, offered the following from the *Supreme Lodge Journal:*—

HIS RIGHT SUSTAINED BY THE SUPREME LODGE.

"At the late session of the Supreme Lodge, Ancient Order of United Workmen, held at Buffalo, New York, the following resolution was adopted:—

"*Resolved,* That the Supreme Recorder place upon the minutes the record of our Order, together with the objects of our Order as originally promulgated, as well as the fact as to who prepared and submitted the original Constitution and Ritual.

" In accordance with the above resolution, the following statement is submitted:—

" In the year 1868, Bro. J. J. Upchurch, Past Supreme Master Workman, resided in Meadville, Pennsylvania, and was engaged as a machinist in the railroad shops of the Atlantic & Great Western Railroad.

" He was proposed and elected to membership in the Order known as 'The League of Friendship, Supreme Mechanical Order of the Sun.'

" The conduct of the business of the Order not proving satisfactory to the membership, it was resolved by the League at Meadville to abandon its Charter and organize a new Order.

" To this end a committee of seven members of the Lodge, consisting of J. J. Upchurch as Chairman, W. W. Walker, J. R. Umberger, M. H. McNair, Henry Deross, A. Klock, and J. R. Hulse, were appointed to report at a future meeting.

" Brother Upchurch was, at the date of the dissolution of the League, occupying the position of presiding officer, viz., Honorable Master of the Lodge.

" The committee, on the evening of October 11, 1868, met at the house of Brother Upchurch, who presented the objects and plans of an Order which for years he had been considering. The committee was so favorably impressed with the objects and plans presented by Brother Upchurch, that it was resolved to intrust the entire matter of formulating a Ritual, Constitution, and By-Laws to govern the Order, to him.

" At a meeting of the members of the defunct League, held October 27, 1868, Brother Upchurch, as Chairman of the committee, presented a Ritual* and Constitution for a new Order, which was accepted, and an organization was at once perfected under the provisions thereof.

" The following named persons were present and obligated

---

*The Ritual, presented by Brother Upchurch, was continued in use by the Order until the organization of the **Supreme Lodge of the Order,** in the year 1873.

as members of the Order, each paying a fee of one dollar for membership:—

J. J. Upchurch, A. Oaster, P. Linen, T. F. Upchurch, C. W. Newberry, W. S. White, J. R. Hulse, M. H. McNair, Henry Dcross, J. R. Umberger, S. Rositer, P. Lawson, A. P. Ogden, and J. Tracy.

Officers were elected and installed as follows:—

J. J. Upchurch, Master Workman; J. R. Umberger, Chief Foreman; J. A. Tracy, Overseer; M. H. McNair, Secretary; J. R. Hulse, Treasurer; Henry Dcross, Guide; A. P. Ogden, Chaplain; W. S. White, Outside Watchman; S. Rositer, Inside Watchman; Trustees, W. C. Newberry, T. F. Upchurch, and P. Linen.

VISITS THE SUPREME LODGE AT TORONTO.

In 1884, I visited the Supreme Lodge at Toronto, in the Province of Canada. We were nobly received, and everything was done that could be to make the occasion the most pleasant, and cement the Brothers of the two Governments, if possible, more closely together. We had a grand good time at Floral Hall. There was an immense crowd, a number of fine speeches being delivered on the principles and benefits derived from the Ancient Order of United Workmen. A magnificent banquet was prepared at the hotel, the occasion being well attended by the members of the Supreme Lodge, invited guests, and ladies. There were a number of eloquent speeches by the Mayor of the city, the Lieutenant-Governor of the State, and many others. It was a time long to be remembered by all who participated in it. I visited a number of Subordinate Lodges and addressed the members. We were honored with a steamboat excursion on the lake, went up the mouth of the Niagara, passed Fort Niagara, with the flags of the two Governments at the mast-head. Had a most pleasant session.

GETS ROBBED ON THE TRAIN.

I had been invited to visit a Lodge meeting at Buffalo on my return home, which I consented to do. I took the cars at Toronto for Buffalo, but not being directed which car went over to Erie, I got in the wrong one. When the conductor came around, he said that I must get into the next car in the rear, but that I would have ample time to change at the Falls; and as Bro. E. M. Ford was going over the same line, we concluded to wait until we reached the Falls before making the change. On the stopping of the train there was a perfect rush of men, women, and boys for the car that we were in; the passage-way was blocked for some minutes and I was almost thrown down. Finally our train started, and when the conductor came through, I found that I was unfortunate enough at the Falls to have had my pocket picked of all the money I possessed and a return ticket to St. Louis, amounting in all to about one hundred and twenty-five dollars. It was like a thunder-bolt thrown at me; being hundreds of miles from home, and without a cent to pay my fare, you may imagine my feelings.

Bro. E. M. Ford, Grand Recorder of Kansas, paid my fare to Buffalo. Brother Beach, of the *Fraternal Censor*, was in waiting for me at the depot, when Brother Ford related to him my mishap.

MEETS PAST GRAND MASTER WORKMAN WM. H. BARNES, OF CALIFORNIA.

We entered a hack and went direct to the hall. Here were Grand Master Loomis, of New York, and Past Grand Master Workman, Wm. H. Barnes, of California. I was introduced to the audience, when I addressed them with all the enthusiasm at my command under the circumstances. Brothers Loomis and Barnes having been informed of the robbery, the latter made known to the audience my unfortunate condition, when a contribution of twenty-seven dollars was promptly raised for my relief. In the morning, Brother Beach took me to the office of the Chief of Police. I made known my statement to him, but he thought the chance to discover the thief was slim—which proved to be a fact. He, however, went with us to the railroad office and got me a ticket over the Canadian Southern to Chicago. Brother Beach gave me a letter of introduction to the superintendent of the Mail Service, who procured me a ticket over the Chicago & Alton to St Louis. I feel myself deeply indebted to the Brothers of Buffalo, and to the superintendent of the Mail Service at Chicago, for their kindness.

PROTEST OF W. W. WALKER.

The appendix published by the Supreme Recorder, as directed by the Supreme Lodge, held at Buffalo, brought out a protest from W. W. Walker, the head and front of the secession wing of the Order, stating that he was the founder of the Order of the Ancient Order of United Workmen. His assurances were put in such positive language that the Supreme Lodge felt called upon to investigate the matter, and it was called up and referred to Brother Babst, of Pennsylvania, Chairman of the Committee on Appendix, and the following report was adopted:—

VINDICATION BY THE SUPREME LODGE.

TORONTO, Ontario, June 5, 1884.

" *To the Supreme Lodge Ancient Order of United Workmen:—*

" Your committee appointed to investigate the correctness of the appendix to proceedings of Supreme Lodge session of 1883, and the protest of Bro. W. W. Walker against its adoption, would respectfully report that we have examined the protest, and on comparing it with the records, find that Bro. W. W. Walker is mistaken in the subject matter of his protest. We find, from evidence before us, that Bro. J. J. Upchurch, as early as 1865, had submitted to persons the same principles that were afterwards incorporated in the Ancient Order of United Workmen. We find, from the records of the Order, that Bro. J. J. Upchurch was author of the Ritual in the organization of the Order, was the Chairman of the Committee on Constitution, By-Laws and Insurance Article (as it was called). We find, also, that Bro. W. W. Walker was not a member of the Order until the second meeting after the organization. We find the records so plain and complete in this respect, that, in the judgment of your committee, there is no question as to Bro. J. J. Upchurch being the founder of the Order, and recommend the approval of appendix to the proceedings of 1883.

[*Signed*] CHAS. BABST, ⎫
THEO. A. CASF, ⎬ *Committee.*"
O. R. BARRY, ⎭

FIRST-CONSTITUTION OF THE ANCIENT ORDER OF UNITED WORKMEN.

" The following is a copy of the objects and Constitution entire, as presented by Bro. J. J. Upchurch to Jefferson Lodge, No. 1, Ancient Order of United Workmen,—the first Lodge of the Order, instituted at Meadville, Pennsylvania, October 27, 1868:"—

[We make no apology for inserting this document entire, for the reasons, first, because it was the original law by which the Order was first governed, and, second, because it is entirely the work of the founder himself. He has been called "a simple minded, honest man." A careful perusal of this Constitution, however, will convince the reader that no man could conceive and write it out, whose mind was not at once comprehensive and analytical.—ED.]

PREAMBLE AND CONSTITUTION.

PREAMBLE.—The Mechanics and Workingmen generally have long since seen the necessity of an Order being established on principles liberal enough to embrace all the various branches of the mechanical and scientific arts, believing that by so doing, the interests of its members will receive greater protection; for where there is union there is strength.

CONSTITUTION.

ARTICLE I.

SECTION 1. This Organization shall be known as Jefferson Lodge, No. 1, of the Ancient Order of United Workmen, to be composed of mechanics and mechanics' helpers, artists, and their assistants of all the various branches. Its executive functions shall be vested in the officers hereinafter provided for, according to the powers, privileges, and limitations specified and enumerated.

ARTICLE II.

SECTION 1. Its object shall be, first, to unite all mechanics and mechanics' helpers, and those regularly employed in any branch of the mechanical arts, so that they may form a united body for the defense and protection of their interests against all encroachments, by elevating labor to the standard it is justly entitled to.

SEC. 2. To create and foster a more friendly and co-operative feeling among those who have a common interest, thereby enabling them to act promptly and decidedly in any matter which may affect their interest.

SEC. 3. To examine and discuss those laws and usages, National, State, and Municipal, which may be in contradiction to their interest; to establish and maintain a library for the purpose of inducing its members to acquire that knowledge which will prepare and fit them for any station in society.

SEC. 4. To hold lectures from time to time, as the interest of the Order may require; the reading of essays, and the examination and discussion of the merits and demerits of new improvements, etc.

SEC. 5. To use all legitimate means in their power to adjust all differences which may arise between employers and employés, and to labor for the development of a plan of action that may be beneficial to both parties. based on the eternal truth that the interest of labor and capital are equal and should receive equal protection.

SEC. 6. To discountenance strikes except when they become absolutely necessary for their protection, and then only after all efforts at adjustment have failed.

SEC. 7. To give all moral and material aid in their power to members of this Order who may be afflicted or oppressed, or who may be laboring under great difficulties, to ameliorate their condition.

SEC. 8. To combine and direct all their influence for the elevation of the mechanic and laborer in mental, moral, social, and civil positions.

ARTICLE III.

MEMBERSHIP.

SECTION 1. All mechanics, artisans, engineers, firemen, train conductors, blacksmiths' helpers, and all white male persons in any branch of the mechanical and scientific arts and sciences, twenty-one years of age, of a good moral character, are eligible to membership to this Order.

Balloting.

SEC. 2. In balloting for candidates for membership, if one blackball appears, the candidate shall be declared rejected unless a motion is carried to reconsider the vote, when a new ballot may be had at the next stated meeting. Should one or more blackballs appear at the second ballot, the candidate shall be declared rejected. Should more than one blackball appear at the first ballot, the candidate shall be declared rejected, when another application shall not be entertained for six months.

Propositions.

SEC. 3. All propositions for membership shall be made in writing, stating age, residence, and occupation, to be recommended by a member of this Order. The petition shall be accompanied by one-half the initiation fee, and read in the regular meetings of the Order, and referred to a committee of three members, who shall use every lawful means to ascertain the character and standing of the applicant. This application shall be read at each regular meeting, and lay over two weeks, when a ballot shall be had. Any one knowing the applicant to be of bad character shall make the fact known to said committee.

SEC 4. Should any member blackball an applicant on account of personal, political, or religious differences, or for anything except being unworthy to sit in the Ancient Order of United Workmen, he shall, on conviction, be reprimanded, suspended, or expelled, as the Order may direct by a two-thirds vote.

SEC. 5. The initiation fee shall not be less than two dollars, one-half to accompany the proposition, the balance to be collected by the Secretary. Before the initiation, should the candidate be elected and fail to come forward for initiation for the space of one month, the proposition fee shall be declared forfeited, unless a good and sufficient reason be given. Should he be rejected, the proposition fee shall be returned.

ARTICLE IV.

MEETINGS.

SECTION 1. The regular meetings of this Order shall be held weekly, at such time and place as a majority of the members present may from time to time determine.

SEC. 2. Five members and one officer shall constitute a quorum for the transaction of business.

SEC. 3. A member of the Order who may pass an examination, or be vouched for by a member, shall be entitled to sit in the Lodge, but shall take no part in the business transactions unless invited, but may speak under the rule of the Good of the Order.

ARTICLE V.

OFFICERS.

Section 1. The officers of the Ancient Order of United Workmen, shall be a Master Workman, a Chief Foreman, Overseer, Guide, Outside Watchman, Inside Sentinel, Secretary, Treasurer, Chaplain, and three Trustees, who shall be elected with their own consent at the last regular meeting in September, and be installed the first regular meeting in October, or as soon thereafter as practicable.

Sec. 2. All officers shall be elected by ballot and receive a majority of all the votes cast. When there is more than one candidate running for the same office, the one receiving the lowest number of votes shall be withdrawn.

ARTICLE VI.

DUTIES OF OFFICERS.

Section 1. It is the duty of the Master Workman, as executive officer, to preside at all meetings, maintain order, execute, or cause to be executed, all laws, rules, and established usages of the Order, appoint committees, announce all votes, giving the casting vote in the case of a tie vote, call special meetings, sign all orders, certificates, drafts, and credentials, see that each officer attends strictly to his duties, and have full returns and reports made out to the Grand Lodge, and forward therewith the *per capita* tax before the installation of his successor, giving the number of members in good standing and the number reported suspended and expelled.

Sec. 2. The Secretary shall keep a full and complete record of the transactions of the Order, countersign certificates, drafts, and credentials, collect all moneys, and enter the amounts in the minutes, and pay the amount over to the Treasurer, and take his receipt for same, notify candidates of election, call special meetings when ordered by the Master Workman, and perform such other duties as the Master Workman or the Order may direct; and, at the close of the year, make out a full report of the standing and condition of the Order, and deliver to his successor in office all books, papers, and other property belonging to the Order.

SEC 3. The Treasurer shall receive and hold all money due or belonging to the Order, and have the same ready to meet any demands on the Treasury, and make disbursements when directed, by drafts or checks. He shall keep a correct account of all moneys received from whatever source, and how expended, by drafts, or checks, keeping them on file as vouchers. He shall make out a quarterly report of the financial condition of the Order, and, at the close of the year, make out the annual report, and perform such other duties as the Master Workman or the Order may direct, and deliver to his successor all books, papers, moneys, and other property in his hands, belonging to the Order. He shall give a bond, with approved security, in such sum as the Order may direct, for the faithful performance of his duties.

SEC. 4. It shall be the duty of the Chief Foreman to render the Master Workman such assistance as he or the usages of the Order may require, and in the absence of the Master Workman, he shall take the supervision of the Order and preside in his stead.

SEC. 5. The Overseer shall render such service as the Master Workman or Chief Foreman may require, and in the absence of the Chief Foreman, shall fill his station.

SEC. 6. The Guide shall introduce all candidates, and, with a committee, shall examine all visitors or strangers, and see that members are properly clothed, and collect and take charge of the regalia, etc., and perform such other duties as may be required from time to time.

SEC. 7. The Sentinel shall guard well the inner and outer doors, keep off all intruders, and perform such other duties as the Master Workman or the usages of the Order may require from time to time.

SEC. 8. The Chaplain shall perform the opening and closing ceremonies, and assist in such other duties as the usages of the Order may require.

ARTICLE VII.

THE REGALIA.

SECTION 1. The regalia shall belong to the Order.

ARTICLE VIII.

GRAND LODGE TAX.

SECTION 1. Every Subordinate Lodge shall pay to the Grand Lodge a tax of one dollar per annum for each member in good standing, in quarterly installments, for the support of the Grand Lodge.

ARTICLE IX.

OFFENSES AND PENALTIES.

SECTION 1. Any member violating his obligation shall be dealt with as specified herein.

SEC. 2. On conviction of any other offense against the Constitution, rules, or usages of the Order, neglect of duty, or contempt in the meetings, he shall be reprimanded, fined, suspended, or expelled, as the case may require.

Charges.

SEC. 3. All charges shall be made in writing, stating the offense to the Secretary, who shall, under the call for " New Business," read the same in opening assembly; and if not withdrawn, with proper explanations, the Master Workman shall appoint a time when the party shall be tried in open assembly. He shall be permitted to conduct his own case, or select counsel from the members of the Order. The Master Workman, Chief Foreman, and Overseer, Guide, and Chaplain, shall act as judges in the case. Should the party feel aggrieved, he may take an appeal to the Grand Lodge, which shall be final. He will not, however, be permitted to take part in the proceedings of the Order while his case is pending.

ARTICLE X.

ALTERATIONS.

SECTION 1. This Constitution shall not be altered or

amended except by and with the consent of the Grand
Lodge.

ARTICLE XI.

BY-LAWS.

SECTION 1. Each Subordinate Lodge may enact such by-
laws and rules of order as may be required for its workings,
when not in conflict with the Constitution, subject to the
approval of the Grand Lodge.

ARTICLE XII.

SECTION 1. The Board of Trustees shall hold all property,
real or personal, in trust for the Order, invest all moneys
when directed by the Order, taking bond with approved
security, and, at the close of their term, shall make a full
report to the Lodge.

SEC. 2. All special committees shall report at the next
regular meeting of the Order, unless otherwise directed.
All committees shall be appointed from members present.

SEC. 3. The Secretary and Treasurer shall furnish, when
directed by the Master Workman, or the Order, all information that may be in their possession, in the transaction of
business.

ARTICLE XIII.

SECTION 1. No Subordinate Lodge shall be dissolved as
long as there are five members in good standing who object thereto.

SEC. 2. Should a Lodge be dissolved, or charter forfeited,
all books, papers, money, and property of whatsoever description, shall be delivered to the Deputy Grand Master
Workman, having charge of the district for the benefit of
the Grand Lodge.

ARTICLE XIV.

VACANCIES.

SECTION 1. When a vacancy shall occur in any office, an
election shall be held at a regular meeting as soon thereafter as practicable, to fill the office for the unexpired term.

ARTICLE XV.

SECTION 1. In the absence of the District Deputy Grand Master Workman, the Master Workman, or any Past Master Workman, may install the officers.

SEC. 2. The Master Workman, Chief Foreman, Overseer, Treasurer, Guide, and Chaplain, shall constitute a Relief Committee, under the direction of the Master Workman. Each member shall be subject to his orders in attending to the sick or disabled members, subject, on failure, to a fine of fifty cents.

ARTICLE XVI.

SECTION 1. Each Subordinate Lodge shall elect, at their regular annual election, two representatives to the Grand Lodge to serve for one year.

BUSINESS COMMITTEE.

SEC. 2. The Master Workman shall appoint a Standing Business Committee, whose duty shall be to correspond with the different Lodges and members out of employment, and those with situations to be filled, and report immediately the fact to the proper persons, at the intelligence office at headquarters. They shall also report weekly to the Lodge they are subject to.

ARTICLE XVII.

INSURANCE.

SECTION 1. There shall be established, when the Order numbers one thousand members, an insurance office; and policies issued, securing at the death of the member insured, not less than $500, to be paid to his lawful heirs.

ARTICLE XVIII.

SECTION 1. When there are six Subordinate Lodges established in any State, they shall call a meeting of two representatives from each Subordinate Lodge, and establish a State Grand Lodge, subject only to the National or Supreme Lodge.

ARTICLE XIX.

ALTERATION.

SECTION 1. The words "white male person" in Article III. Section 1, of this Constitution shall not be altered, amended, or expunged, but shall remain unalterably fixed as specified.

"Jefferson Lodge, No. 1, organized under the foregoing Constitution, constituted itself the Provisional Grand Lodge of the United States, vesting in an Executive Committee, consisting of J. J. Upchurch, R. Grieves, and P. Linen, full power to act as Provisional Grand Lodge officers.

ORGANIZING GRAND LODGE OF PENNSYLVANIA.

"On the sixth day of October, 1869, the Grand Lodge of the Ancient Order of United Workmen of Pennsylvania was organized at Meadville, Pennsylvania, and the following Grand Officers duly elected and installed: J. J. Upchurch, Grand Master Workman; O. M. Barnes, Grand General Foreman; A. Klock, Grand Overseer; R. Grieves, Grand Secretary; P. Linen, Grand Treasurer; D. Kuling, Grand Chaplain; D. H. Bush, Grand Guide; J. Carronay, Grand Sentinel; P. Oaster and A. Oaster, Grand Trustees.

"At this meeting, Bro. J. J. Upchurch presented the following amendment to Article XVII (Insurance Article), which was adopted and became a part of the Constitution."

INSURANCE ARTICLE.

SECTION 1. Each and every candidate for initiation shall pay to the Financier the sum of one dollar for insurance, and the sum of all such payments, to be known as the Insurance Fund, shall be placed by each individual Subordinate Lodge, in bank or other secure place, from which it can be drawn at sight, when called for by the Grand Lodge, or the immediate necessity of the Subordinate Lodge, as hereinafter provided.

SEC. 2. The highest policy of insurance guaranteed by this Constitution shall not exceed $2,000, and until such time as the above sum shall have been subscribed to, at the rate specified in Section 1, the issue of the insurance policy shall be equal in amount, in dollars, to the actual number of members in the Order.

SEC. 3. On the death of a brother, the Relief Committee, through the Trustees, shall draw the amount of insurance held by the Subordinate Lodge of which the deceased has been a member, and after having defrayed all funeral expenses, deliver the balance to his family, or heirs; provided, however, that the Lodge shall be assured and satisfied that the money thus placed at their disposal shall be judiciously used by and for the maintenance of the family of the deceased; otherwise, it shall be held in trust by the Lodge, and delivered in such sums and at such times as the circumstances of the family may demand. Should it so happen that the death of two or more brothers occur at the same time, the amount of insurance fund on hand shall be equally divided between the families or heirs of each, and as soon thereafter as provided in Section 5 of this Article, when the insurance assessment shall be collected, the balance to which the heirs are entitled shall immediately be forwarded to the respective claimants.

SEC. 4. The Recorder of the Subordinate Lodge in which a death may happen, shall immediately notify the Grand Recorder of the fact, when the Grand Lodge shall collect the several sums of Insurance Fund held by each and all the other Subordinate Lodges, and forward the amount to the Recorder of the Subordinate Lodge of which the deceased brother was a member, and said Lodge shall see that the entire sum thus placed in its hands shall be properly and judiciously applied for the benefit of the family or heirs of the deceased.

SEC. 5. To replace the Insurance Fund drawn on the occasion of the death of a brother, each member shall pay to the Financier of his respective Lodge the sum of one dollar; provided, however, that the number of members in the Order does not exceed two thousand, but if over two thousand, the Grand Lodge, at its regular stated session, shall designate the *pro rata* assessment, which shall be paid to furnish the maximum amount of insurance, which shall be placed as provided in Section 1.

5

SEC. 6. Any member refusing or failing to pay the insurance assessment within thirty days a.ter having been duly notified by the Financier, shall forfeit his membership in the Order; and any Subordinate Lodge failing to forward the amount of insurance held by it for the term of twenty days, after being duly notified by the Recorder of the Grand Lodge, shall forfeit its Charter; and all books, papers, and other property, shall be placed in the possession of the District Deputy Grand Master Workman.

SEC. 7. The Financier of each Subordinate Lodge shall keep a record of all business relating to insurance, in a book set apart for that purpose alone.

DISABILITY.

SEC. 8. A member fifty years of age or upwards, feeling incapable of further pursuing daily manual labor, and who can exhibit an honorable record in the Order for ten successive preceding years, desiring to enter upon a trade or business more suitable to his declining health or strength, may, upon application to the Lodge of which he is a member, obtain half the amount of insurance to which in case of death his family or heirs would be entitled.

SEC. 9. When the insurance contribution shall have reached the sum of not less than $1,000, any member whose record is of good standing for one next preceding year, and clear of all charges on the books, rendered, by disease or accident, permanently incapable of supporting himself or family by manual labor, and wishing to enter upon business suitable to his physical condition, may receive insurance in the sum of one-fourth the amount then on hand; and to a brother afflicted with total disability, the above sum of one-fourth the amount on hand, shall be issued by installments, at such time and in such sums as the Lodge may determine.

SEC. 10. A brother entitled to the provisions set forth in Sections 8 and 9, shall not be permitted to enter upon a business that may have a tendency to bring disrepute or dishonor on himself or the Order, or which may lead directly to favor intemperance, immorality, or vice. And no member shall be entitled to the privileges set forth in Section 9, who may, by disreputable means, reduce himself to a condition of distress.

SEC. 11. When an aged or disabled brother shall make application for insurance, as per Sections 8 and 9, the Master Workman shall appoint a committee of five who shall thoroughly, rigidly, and impartially, investigate the character and record of the applicant, the kind of business he contemplates entering upon, and his qualifications and ability to conduct the same successfully; and in rendering a report to the Lodge thereon, at each of three successive or stated meetings, a decision shall be rendered, subject, however, to the approval of the Grand Lodge at its annual or semi-annual session. A majority of the above committee shall be chosen from the list of elective officers of the Lodge.

SEC. 12. Any member of the committee failing to promptly comply with the requirements of Section 11, or who may by fraudulent representations tend to deceive the Lodge, thereby producing a partial or unjust decision, shall be suspended or expelled, as the Lodge may determine.

SEC. 13. When it is definitely decided to extend to any brother the privileges set forth in Sections 8 and 9, it shall be the duty of the Supreme Lodge, before paying any money to said brother, to demand and receive from him his bond, duly and legally drawn up, and indorsed by two responsible parties, for an amount equal to that which he receives from the Insurance Fund, as security for his observance of compliance with, and maintenance of, all and every requirement of this Constitution at all times and under any and all circumstances during life.

SEC. 14. A brother may designate and have recorded in the insurance book, the person or persons whom he may choose to recognize as his legal heir or heirs, and have the same changed at any time he may desire.

SEC. 15. Should no such designation and record be made by a brother, the Supreme Lodge shall, at its discretion, select one or more, or divide in equal shares, among the following relatives of the deceased: wife, children, father, mother, sister, and brother.

SEC. 16. When no heir shall have been designated, according to Section 14, or the Lodge knows of no legal heir of the deceased brother, the amount of insurance in the hands of each Subordinate Lodge shall thereafter be known as the Relief Fund, to be used in affording relief to brothers out of employment, or traveling in search of the same, or other assistance to a brother in distress, in which event the Insurance Fund shall again be replenished as provided in Section 5.

SEC. 17. A member who has not received the degree of "Master Workman," shall not be entitled to the benefits of insurance as set forth in Sections 8 and 9.

CREDIT FOR PLAN OF ORGANIZATION.

"The foregoing establishes, beyond a question, the fact that to Bro. J. J. Upchurch, Past Supreme Master Workman, is due the credit of first conceiving the plan or organization of the A. O. U. W.; and also formulating a Ritual, Constitution, and Laws for its use and government.

M. W. SACKETT, *Supreme Recorder.*"

I here wish to return my heart-felt gratitude to Samuel B. Myers, of No. 3; W. A. Dungan, and J. M. McNair, of No 1; and others, for their kind interest taken in my behalf in this controversy.

ORIGINAL WORKING TOOLS AND THEIR SIGNIFICANCE.

The original working tools of the Order were, in the second degree, the square and compass, and explained thus:—

"This beautiful instrument is called a square, two of its sides being at right angles, which is emblematic of our integrity, and teaches us to walk uprightly before God and square our actions with all mankind, especially with a brother Workman.

"These, my brother, are compasses. They teach us this lesson: that we should never overreach the bounds of propriety, and live within the circle of brotherly kindness."

These tools formed the badge of the Master Workman.

SECOND DEGREE—ORIGINAL REGALIA. (See Page 68.)

The working tools of the third degree were the plumb and trowel. •

The plumb was used in the erection of perpendicular walls, and was worn as a badge by the Overseer, and reminded us that we should plumb our actions with all mankind.

The trowel was used to spread cement in the erection of the walls, but we used it for the more noble purpose of spreading the cement of brotherly kindness. It was worn as a badge by the Chief Foreman.

In the fourth degree, the protractor and triangles were used as the working tools, and were explained thus:—

" The working tools of this degree are the protractor and triangles. The former represents the earth's circumference, it being divided into three hundred and sixty equal parts, called degrees, and again subdivided into a like number of parts, called minutes and seconds. It also alludes to the human family having been dispersed over the whole face of the earth, for the purpose of extracting the principles of science from the great arcana of nature and giving them practical form of art.

" The triangle of sixty degrees is the one-sixth of the earth's circumference, and may be used to divide the circle into six, twelve, twenty-four, or forty-eight equal parts, without the aid of any other instruments. The triangle of twenty-five degrees is the one-eighth of the earth's circumference, and may be used separately, or in connection with other triangles to divide the circle into four, eight, sixteen, or thirty-two equal parts.

" These being the most useful instruments known to the scientific mechanic, with them he is enabled to reduce to form any mechanical idea, machine, or architectural design, without the aid of any other instrument."

ADVANCED IDEAS.

I will here insert the report of a special committee, to show that my ideas were rather in advance of the times:—

"CHICAGO, Illinois, March 9, 1875

"Report of Committee on Ritual, which was received and placed on file.

"*To the Supreme Lodge, Ancient Order of United Workmen* —

"Your committee, to whom was referred the offer of Past Grand Master Workman J. J. Upchurch, to furnish this Supreme Lodge with a draft of a Ritual of three degrees, would respectfully report: That after mature deliberation we have come to the firm conclusion that we are neither ready nor able to institute and put into operation a new or higher class of degrees. While your committee venerates and loves good Brother Upchurch, and would speak well of the higher degrees (having had them conferred upon them), still we are compelled to recommend that this Supreme Lodge, for the present, do not burthen herself with this extra expense, as we have a new Ritual to be translated into the German language, and the whole printed in both the German and English languages.

J. M. McNAIR, *Committee.*"

RETURNS HOME—HIS FAMILY.

On reaching home, I went to work with renewed energy to try and regain position. My wife is still living. We have had born to us fifteen children, eleven boys and four girls; the youngest is fifteen years of age. Six of them are now living, being all boys, and four of them are still with us. In 1883, I bought of A. W. Johnson, of this place, a half interest in store building and stock of general merchandise, which cost me two thousand eight hundred dollars; the other interest was owned by W. H. Davis, of this place. We carried on the business for eighteen months, when money matters became tight and I sold out my interest in the stock of goods to J. H. Hamel, holding onto the building. Owing to the credit system, many bad debts were made, which will in all probability never be collected.

FOURTH DEGREE—ORIGINAL REGALIA. (See Page 71.)

Through this erroneous business system, nothing was made. I concluded to become a retired merchant. Not having business to keep myself and boys employed, I added agricultural implements to my business, but owing to the stringency of the times, failure of crops, etc., I have made nothing yet above a bare living.

ENGAGES IN BUSINESS.

In 1885 I bought a patent right for six counties, on a new harrow, and undertook to manufacture them. Thus far I have not got my money out of them, but I have fourteen years longer to try my luck.

VISITS AND PRESENTATION.

In April, 1885, I was invited to visit a Lodge in Potosi, Missouri, which I did, and addressed a fine audience in the Masonic Temple. There was great interest taken in the proceedings, and I am of the opinion that much good will result from it.

In May, I was surprised, on visiting Founders Lodge, No. 257, of this place, whose name was given it in honor of myself, who got up the Lodge, by the presentation of a magnificent shaving mug and razor, with the emblems of the Order artistically arranged upon them. This presentation was made by Dr. J. T. Coffee in a splendid address on behalf of the members of the Lodge, to which I replied, thanking them earnestly for this token of their appreciation of my labors in the interest of my fellow-men. The second meeting night after the above, I presented to the Founders Lodge my photograph of a suitable size to hang in the Lodge room.

INVITATION TO VISIT CALIFORNIA.

THE following telegram was received at Cuba, Missouri, April 10, 1885:—

"OAKLAND, Cal., April 9, 1885.
"To J. J. Upchurch, P. S. M. W., Steelville, Mo.:—

"The Grand Lodge of California has by resolution authorized our Representative to invite you to come to California at our expense. Pack your trunk now and get ready, as we propose to bring you back with us from Des Moines next June.   WILLIAM H. JORDAN."

This telegram was so unexpected I did not know how to answer it. I, however, wrote to Brother Jordan that I did not see how I could leave my business, but should I be able to do so, I would accept the invitation and try to comply with their wishes. My family were opposed to my going for several reasons:—

First, I was not a public speaker, and in all probability the members in California would be sadly disappointed, and I would create an unfavorable impression upon their minds.

Secondly, That to go would be to neglect my business, which was yielding but a mere living with all my attention. About ten days later, my son agreed to take charge of my business and do the best he could. Then it was decided that I should accept the invitation, and visit the Pacific Coast.

ACCEPTS THE INVITATION.

I then wrote Brother Jordan that I would be ready to return with him from the Supreme Lodge Session.

The following letter was received:—

OAKLAND, Cal., May 23, 1885.

"MY DEAR BROTHER UPCHURCH: The brethren here are making extensive preparations for your coming, and propose to give you such a reception as has seldom been accorded any citizen. A change has been thought advisable in the date of your arrival here, placing it on the 26th instead of the 17th, as was first proposed. So we shall not be able to leave the East until about the eighth or tenth day after the Supreme Lodge adjourns. I mention this to you so that if you wish to return home after the adjournment you can do so, and we will meet you at any point on the line of the Chicago and Rock Island Road you may prefer, or at the Missouri River. The exact date, however, we can arrange when we meet at Des Moines. The only important thing is to arrange that we can come on together, and yet not arrive here before the 26th of June. All the details we will talk over when we meet at Des Moines at the Supreme Lodge.

"All loyal Workmen in California (and we have none other) are anxiously looking forward to your coming. With sincere assurances of affection and esteem for you,

"I am yours in the bands of C., H., and P.,

WILLIAM H. JORDAN.

VISITS THE SUPREME LODGE AT DES MOINES, AND MEETS PAST GRAND MASTER WORKMAN WM. H. JORDAN.

June 9 I started for Des Moines to attend the session of the Supreme Lodge. Here I met Bro. W. H. Jordan, who informed me that our reception in San Francisco had been postponed from the 17th to the 26th, and that we should not reach there before the time appointed, and that I could remain in Des Moines or return home. I chose the latter. On the 17th I started for Council Bluffs, Iowa, and was joined by Brother Jordan from New York on the 18th.

STARTS FOR CALIFORNIA.

At twelve o'clock noon we took the Union Pacific Railroad for San Francisco; saw some fine country, very productive, in Nebraska. At five o'clock took dinner at Grand Island. On the morning of the 19th we reached La Salle, in Colorado, five hundred twenty-two and one-half miles from Omaha. I arose early and went out on the platform

of our car, but a young man was there before me. I asked
what it was so white on the mountain. He laughed, and
replied that it was snow. I did not anticipate seeing snow
until I had passed Denver. I stated that I would like to
take a walk to it. He asked me how far I supposed it was.
I replied, About three miles. He then informed me that it
was eighteen or twenty miles off, which astonished me more
than ever.

ARRIVES AT DENVER.

We reached Denver at five minutes past seven o'clock,
A. M., and were met at the depot by a committee, and taken
to the Windsor House. In the afternoon we took a carriage
and were driven over the city. It is a splendid city, many
very expensive buildings, lovely drives, and from the high
ground in the west you have a view of the city. There is
an immense business transacted here. We drove out to the
water-works, which are first-class in every particular. We
then drove out to the trout hatchery establishment; there
we saw millions of young fish, and some that would weigh
from three to four pounds, all so gentle that the keeper
could raise them out of the water with his hands. Then we
visited the Court House, which is a splendid building,
everything arranged in magnificent order. From its dome
we had a fine view of the city and the surrounding country.
Pike's Peak was pointed out to us, seventy-five miles away.
I supposed it nearly twenty miles off. We descended from
the Court House, and drove to the Capitol Square, which is
a lovely spot, and I have no doubt but the building to be
erected on it will be in keeping with the balance of the
city.

HONORS EXTENDED TO THEM.

In the evening, the Select Knights of No. 7, in full uniform, assembled at the Windsor House, and escorted us to

the First Congregational Church, where a hearty welcome was extended to me as the father and founder of the Order, and to the Supreme Overseer W. H. Jordan, Past Grand Master Workman of California. A large audience had assembled at the church before the procession arrived, and when the officers of the Order and their escorts marched into the church it was nearly filled with people, there being just about seats enough to accommodate the Select Knights. Grand Master Louis Aufinger called the great assemblage to order, and invited all present to join in singing the opening ode. Prayer was offered by Rev. C. J. Adams, of All Saints' Church, North Denver. A fine quartette was then sung.

Grand Master Louis Aufinger then delivered the address of welcome as follows:—

WELCOME BY GRAND MASTER WORKMAN LOUIS AUFINGER.

"FATHER UPCHURCH, BROTHER JORDAN, BROTHERS OF THE ORDER, LADIES AND GENTLEMEN: In every family there are events which are celebrated by festivities, where joy and happiness are supreme. Is there anything more joyful than where children meet their father, especially if that father is advanced in years, and has been for a long time separated from them? Is it not, then, an occasion of great joy, this occasion of our having the privilege of welcoming our venerable father who sixteen years ago brought into existence our beloved Order, which has grown to such proportions, and has accomplished so much for the cause of humanity? And I deem it no less a privilege to welcome our distinguished guest from California, who has done so much for the growth and prosperity of the Order. He has always proved a friend to our jurisdiction. And now, my dear brother, in behalf of the jurisdiction of Colorado, New Mexico, and Arizona, and in behalf of the Denver Lodges and Legions, I welcome you to our beautiful city. Our good wishes and prayers are for you, that prosperity, health, and happiness will follow you wherever you may go. I now have the honor and pleasure of introducing the founder of our Order, Father J. J. Upchurch."

I then stepped forward and addressed the audience. I assured them that I could not do justice to this occasion or express to them my gratitude 'and surprise at that great gathering, and that magnificent reception. I replied:—

"I have been pleased and surprised at what I have seen in your beautiful mountain city. I have been very much surprised to see such a beautiful city, and am gratified at the good fortune that has brought me here. I never anticipated meeting you here, and it is doubtful whether I could ever have had this pleasure had it not been for our good Brother Jordan, here, and the members of his Jurisdiction, who took it into their heads that I should visit California. But I am very glad to be here, and I bid you Godspeed in your grand and noble work. You have five Lodges here. Look at their faces—you can see intelligence and uprightness. It does my heart good to know that the work of our Order has been of such permanent advantage in this Jurisdiction. I find that the Jurisdiction of Colorado, New Mexico, and Arizona pay fewer assessments than any other Jurisdiction. I can say of a truth, that there is not another Order in existence that is doing the amount of good that the Workmen are doing. I am glad that you are doing so much here for the relief of the people, and I trust that you will go on in the good work with renewed energy. When I look at the present and let my mind run back seventeen years, my heart is filled with gratitude that I should have been chosen to present those glorious truths to the world. I believe that our Order will continue to grow and expand until every good man and woman will be brought under its beneficial influence. I am pleased to see so many ladies here. This Order was gotten up for their benefit and that of their children; so I trust that you will become more deeply interested in our noble work. I will retire, after thanking you for your patient attention."

PAST GRAND MASTER WORKMAN WM. H. JORDAN'S AD-
DRESS.

After music, Bro. William H. Jordan was introduced.
He gave a very pleasing and logical address, which at times
caused an outburst of merriment; at other times the audience relapsed into deep thought, showing that the list-
eners were entirely carried away with his eloquence. He
further said:—

"We come here to-night with two objects: first, to pay
our respects to that old hero, Father Upchurch, out of
whose brain has come the aid which gave life to our Order.
There is some satisfaction in looking into his face, and to
know that we have the man with us who has done so much
for us and for humanity generally. Furthermore, we are
not only here to honor the man who founded the Order of
United Workmen, but the man who called into life those
principles from which other great Orders have arisen. The
Knights of Honor, the American Legion of Honor, and
many other benevolent organizations, all sprang into existence out of the Order of United Workmen.

"Father Upchurch may well be called a hero. Not one
who has come to us stained with the blood of battle-fields;
not one who has brought privation, sorrow, and suffering to his
fellow-man, but one whose name will be honored and valued
as one who has assuaged sorrow and suffering, and brought
joy and peace to thousands of his fellow-beings. Secondly,
We honor the institution of which he became the founder.
We know how he founded them in that little town of Meadville, Pennsylvania, in 1868, where for nine long months the
organization only numbered twenty souls. From that small
beginning has suddenly sprung into existence an organization which is rapidly spreading itself all over the continent,
and which now numbers more than one hundred and fifty-
two thousand souls.

"Brethren, we love and honor that institution which was
thus founded, and has grown to such proportions, and we
may well honor it when we think that under this beneficiary
6

system, since the Order was founded, there has been paid out in benefits the sum of thirteen million five hundred thousand dollars, and when we find that this year more than two hundred and seventy-three thousand dollars will be paid out to other beneficiaries. Brethren, this is a wonderful work, and it has cost us individually so little, it is now a dollar and then a dollar, yet look at the enormous sum paid out. Why, in California, where we use gold and silver money as a rule, this amount of thirteen million five hundred thousand dollars, represents as much gold and silver as would take twenty-one teams to haul through the streets of Denver. I say it is a wonderful thing to be done by an institution of this character, and yet no man feels the burden. [*Great applause.*] And where has the money gone? Not into the rum-shops, nor out on the race-courses, to be squandered, but it is constantly going into the laps of weeping widows and sorrowing orphans."

Brother Jordan then described the wonderful Bartholdi Statue, as it was soon to stand in the New York harbor with its electric light held three hundred feet in mid-air, and compared it with gas-lights and light-houses in other parts of New York Harbor. So the Ancient Order of United Workmen, like the electric light of the nineteenth century, held aloft at a proud elevation, towered above all other benevolent organizations. He continued:—

"This institution not only visits the sick, but it throws two thousand dollars into the laps of every widow and orphan. It is the electric light of the nineteenth century, and we love the man out of whose brain this Order has come. But why, someone may ask, call this the Ancient Order of United Workmen? Why call it 'ncient? Our founder is advanced in years, but we don't call him 'ancient.' There were many men born before him who are not ancient, and yet this child of the nineteenth century is called 'ancient' because the principles that it has taken hold of and has made practicable, are as old as the hills of God."

The speaker compared the Order with the great trees of California:—

" They were there at the present size, nearly, when Washington crossed the Delaware ; they were standing there when Joan of Arc was giving up her life for others at the fagots and the stake ; they were standing there when Abraham watched his flocks and herds on the hill-sides ; they have been there since the earliest records we have of the world's being ; there they stand, but they are not as old as the mountain-side on which they stand, or the solid earth out of which they grow. And they are young indeed compared with the principles which underlie the present Order of United Workmen." [*Great applause.*]

The speaker then related the story of a Yankee, who visited Europe:—

" The Yankee was very patriotic and was always exclaiming, ' Hurrah for America!' They showed him the lochs of Scotland, small, smooth, and beautiful sheets of water ; he exclaimed: 'Why! they are not half equal to Lake Champlain. Hurrah for America!' They showed him the great water-fall of Ireland, and he said: 'That is nothing; look at the great Niagara. Hurrah for America!' They showed him the wonders of Rome, and mentioned their great age. They showed him Pompey's Statue and the ampitheater, and he said: ' Look at the mounds of the Mississippi Valley. Hurrah for America!' Finally they touched upon a weakness common to too many of our countrymen, and gave him too much rum, and he went to sleep in the Catacombs of Rome. He awoke amid bones and skulls and asked where he was, and they replied, ' You are dead.' ' No,' said he, ' I ain't. This is the resurrection and I am the first man on deck. Hurrah for America!' [*Great applause.*] So will the Ancient Order of United Workmen be on deck at the resurrection."

Appropriate remarks were then made by T. J. Malt and others, after which the exercises closed. Brother Jordan, myself, and other members and their ladies, repaired to the residence of Grand Master Workman Louis Aufinger, where a bounteous repast was spread, which was partaken of with pleasure, and was enjoyed by all present. At a late hour we returned to the Windsor.

INVITATION TO VISIT VALLEY LODGE, SALT LAKE.

Before leaving home I received the following communication:—

"VALLEY LODGE, No. 12, A. O. U. W. }
"Salt Lake City, May 21, 1885.   }

"J. J. UPCHURCH, ESQ.—*Dear Sir and Brother:* In reading the *Pacific States Watchman*, published in San Francisco, that you have concluded to visit the Pacific States, calling at Salt Lake on the way, we hereby cordially invite you to stay in our little town and honor us with a visit. We shall feel it a pleasure to welcome the founder of our noble Order to the city of the Saints; and if you can notify us of the time, we will call a special meeting of the brethren in this Lodge and vicinity.

"Yours very truly, in C., H., and P.,

S. B. PHILLIPS, *M. W.*,
S. W. DARK, *Recorder.*"

HIS REPLY.

I replied that, if it was possible, I would call on their city, going out or on my return home. I handed this letter to Brother Jordan at Omaha. He stated that we had only two days to spare, and that one of them had been promised to Denver, and that Brother Kinsley requested that the other be given to Ogden. But before leaving Denver, it was found that there was a part of a day (Sunday) to be disposed of. A telegram was forwarded to the effect that we would stop at Salt Lake City on Sunday, requesting that an informal meeting be called for Sunday night.

The following communication had been received by Bro. Louis Aufinger, and handed to Bro. W. H. Jordan, before leaving Denver:—

INVITATION TO VISIT CANYON CITY, COLORADO.

" *Select Knights, A. O. U. W.,* }
" Headquarters Colorado Legion, No. 1. }
"Canyon City, Col., June 16, 1885. }

" Louis Aufinger—*Dear Sir and Comrade:* Colorado Legion, No. 1, extends to Comrade Father Upchurch, a hearty invitation to stop over and visit our Legion, providing he comes this way, trusting you will do what you can to induce him to stay.

"I am yours in C., H. and P., and E., I., and U.,
James Remington, *Recorder."*

" Royal Gorge Lodge, No. 7, A. O. U. W. }
" Canyon City, Col., June 17, 1885. }

" Louis Aufinger, Grand Master Workman—*Dear Sir and Brother:* By request of our Lodge and Master Workman, I write you, asking information in regard to the route that Father Upchurch and Brother Jordan will take on leaving Denver for California; also when they will leave. It is the wish of No. 7 that they stop off here for one night, if not longer, and deliver a lecture on ' Our Order' and its benefits. We are all very anxious to see them and have them speak; if it is possible for them to stop over, it will give us great pleasure, and I think it will be a great benefit to our Lodge and the members. If you succeed in gaining their consent to stay over, wire me at my expense. If they cannot stop, wire me when they will leave Denver, if they go *via* the Denver and Rio Grande, as we wish to meet them at the depot, anyway.

" Hoping they will give us the pleasure of their presence for a day or so, I will close, hoping to hear from you soon.
"Yours in C., H., and P.,
Ed. Miner, *Recorder."*

"SELECT KNIGHTS, A. O. U. W.
" HDADQUARTERS OF COLORADO LEGION, No. 1.
"Canyon City, Col., June 18, 1885.

"L. AUFINGER, ESQ., Grand Master—*Dear Sir and Brother:* At our last meeting of the Lodge, we appointed a committee to make all the necessary arrangements for the entertainment of Father Upchurch and Brother Jordan, and to extend to them, through you, a hearty invitation to visit our city and our Brothers and Comrades here; and by request of said committee I write you to know if they will accept the same, and have Brother Jordan deliver an address here. We have made all the necessary arrangements for their entertainment, and it is our wish and desire that they visit us. Please answer by wire as soon as possible if they will be here, and if they will take the Denver & Rio Grande route to California, and not stop here, we will meet them at the depot. I hope you can prevail on them to visit us, as I think it will be a great benefit to our Order here if they will come, and if they do not, it will be a sad disappointment to us all. Hoping to hear from you soon, and that we may all have a chance to grasp the hand of our noble benefactor and father of our Order,

"I am respectfully yours,

J. E. EDILER,
Lodge Deputy Royal Gorge, No. 7.

"And in behalf of committee as follows:—

"E. Shiston, S. S. Nichols, Past Master Workman; D. D. Lewis, Past Master Workman; George Wilkens, H. L. Smith, Past Master Workman; Thos Hunter.

Per J. E. EDILER,
Recorder Colorado Legion, No. 1.

ON THE WAY.

June 20, we left Denver, *via* the Denver & Rio Grande route, for Salt Lake City, at forty minutes after seven o'clock, A. M. I saw some fine country, very romantic; passed a beautiful little lake with many skiffs riding upon its blue waters, to invite the pleasure-seekers to avail themselves of an opportunity that would probably never present itself again. Passed Colorado Springs. It has some fine buildings, and its very picturesque lakes, like the Deity, had an eye to the wants of pleasure combined with romance. Six miles distant, Pike's Peak showed its lofty summit, towering high above its sister mountains.

South Pueblo is quite a city, and several iron works are located here, which manufacture a great deal, of various kinds and shapes. It is said to be the hottest place in all that section of country, lying, as it does, in a deep valley. Here quite a number of Workmen had assembled to bid us welcome, and, if possible, persuade us to remain overnight with them, which we could not do, owing to our limited time. Here dinner was prepared for us, and we were conducted to the dining-room in the midst of a goodly number of Workmen, who did ample justice in putting away the many good things prepared for the occasion.

We again boarded the train, and at Canyon City a large number of Select Knights and Workmen were in waiting to receive us, having been misinformed by a blundering operator that we would stop overnight with them. When they were informed as to the mistake they seemed to be much disappointed, for they had everything already arranged to give us a grand reception, including a banquet; and I must say that I never disappointed any people that I regretted so much as I did on this occasion; but it had to be done. At Hot Springs we were met by twenty-five Brothers, anxious to have us stop over. The scenery all the way up the mountain was indeed sublime. On this route we pass through the Grand Cañon of the Arkansas. The most noteworthy picture is the Royal Gorge, situated six or seven miles west of Canyon City. Through this pass run torrents of water, the rocks towering up to twelve or fifteen hundred feet high, and almost vertical, the walls being so close together that the Railroad Company had to make a bridge for their road by cutting a rest in the solid rock on either side of the stream. In this rest strong iron girders were placed, standing at an angle of about forty-five degrees. Secured at the top under this, the bridge is swung with heavy bolts, which serves for passing all trains over the road. In passing up the mountain it required three locomotives. The first took the mail and baggage cars, the other two were coupled to the passenger coaches. The run up the mountain was grand beyond expression. The train would wind around the mountains so that at one point I saw the track in four places where our train had passed over only a few minutes before. At times I looked far below into almost unfathomable depths, and again, far above, at the ponderous rocks, as if ready to crush all beneath to powder. We passed many long snow-sheds, and at last reached the summit, ten thousand eight hundred and fifty-eight feet above the sea. The train stopped here about twenty minutes, to give passengers a chance, I suppose, to try their lungs. I availed myself of the opportunity, and got out and walked about thirty yards, when I became excessively tired and returned to the car as soon as possible. We soon began to descend the mountain on the Pacific side, and the further we went the better I could breathe. About sunset we reached a hotel at the foot of the mountain, where we got supper. That night we passed Black Cañon. I had taken my berth with the promise that I would be called when we arrived at this place, but it was thought best to let me remain undisturbed.

ARRIVAL AT SALT LAKE.

June 21 we reached Salt Lake City, and were met at the depot by a committee of Workmen. We entered a carriage and were driven to the hotel. At the depot an old man stepped up to me and asked if I knew anyone that left Pennsylvania for Salt Lake City. I replied that I knew Henry Rudy, the Postmaster of our town. He said he was the man, and I was indeed glad to see him after so many years. After remaining at the hotel a short time, two brother Workmen, who also belong to the church of Latter Day Saints, called for us in carriages, and showed us the city, which I must say is the most beautiful little city that I ever saw. Its broad streets are lined with fine shade trees, with an abundance of pure, limpid water from the mountains, flowing continually through them. We were shown the Temple, which is a magnificent structure of granite, or so called "Utah marble." The Tabernacle is large and with an arched roof, but we could not induce our brothers to take us into the Temple or Tabernacle. They said no one was permitted to enter there on Sunday unless service was being carried on. At this hour service was over, and we had to content ourselves with looking upon the outside. We were shown the residence of Brigham Young, which was simply beautiful, and I suppose very comfortable. The Endowment House was also shown us. This is where Brigham kept his many wives. We had many fine buildings shown us as the residences of the officers of the church.

We were taken up to Prospect Point, which gave us a magnificent view of the city and valley. Above was a splendid fresh-water lake, a mile wide and three miles long, abounding with splendid fish of all the choice varieties. Below lies the Great Salt Lake, extending for forty miles. Upon its banks large piles of fine salt are gathered and taken to market. In this valley, wheat, oats, and many other crops grow luxuriantly. From this point we were driven to Fort Douglas. This fort stands upon elevated ground overlooking the city. A great many soldiers are located here, and this being Sunday, they were having a good time in the form of a military concert. After remaining for half an hour, we returned to the hotel. After supper quite a number of the brothers called on us at our hotel; they stated that they could not procure a hall, but we had an informal meeting in our room, and had a good social time. We encouraged them to continue in the good work. At eleven o'clock, P. M., we retired for the night.

The following communication was received at Denver, Colorado:—

INVITATION TO VISIT OGDEN.

"OGDEN, Utah, June 11, 1885.

"W. H. JORDAN, care L. Aufinger, 383 Chambers Street Denver, Colorado—-*Dear Sir:* Father Upchurch and yourself are cordially and earnestly invited to stop over at Ogden, Utah, one day when *en route* to the Pacific Coast, and become the guests of Fidelity Lodge, No. 3, A. O. U. W. It is intended to have a special meeting of the Lodge, and a reception with refreshments. Please telegraph your acceptance with the date of arrival at Junction City, so that timely arrangements can be made. Brother Grand Recorder Thorburn, of our Grand Jurisdiction, will be with us in our entertainment of Brother Upchurch and yourself.

"Yours in C., H., and P.,   E. W. PIPER,
*Recorder Fidelity Lodge, No. 3. and
Member of Com. of Invitation.*"

ARRIVAL AT OGDEN.

June 22, in the morning, we took the train on the Central Pacific, for Ogden. The Committee of Reception was in waiting when we arrived. We were placed in one of the carriages and taken to the hotel. The members of the Order were soon provided with gum coats and then re-entered carriages and started for Ogden Cañon. The scenery was grand—the cañon narrow, barely wide enough for the road, and the beautiful torrent of pure mountain water to pass, the mountain looming up a thousand feet high on either side. We finally reached a neat little cottage, built in the narrow gorge, where we stopped. Rod and line being furnished us, we tried our luck at catching fish. Brother Jordan took the first, a beautiful brook trout. Dinner was soon announced; then we sat down to a magnificent repast of sparkling trout and luscious strawberries, with everything nice accompanying them. To this we did ample justice. About two o'clock we re-entered the carriages for the city, where a special meeting of the Order had been called. The meeting was called to order by the Master Workman, when an address of welcome was delivered, to which I replied, followed by Brother Jordan, Supreme Overseer, which was responded to by several members.

Ogden is a lively city, and the members of the Order left nothing undone that would make our stay pleasant. After supper we again took the train for San Francisco.

June 23 we took breakfast at Elko, five hundred and sixty-eight miles from San Francisco. The scenery passed that day was grand. The rocks were formed in almost every conceivable shape, but the most noted wonder was Castle Gate. The opening is narrow, the walls on either side rise

perpendicularly, hundreds of feet high, carved by the hand
of time into many curious shapes to please the eye and ex-
cite the admiration of the mind.

We took supper at Reno, Nevada. Here we were met
by a committee from Virginia City, expecting us to stop off
and visit them, but, owing to limited time, we had to decline
the invitation, with the promise that I would do so before
my return East.

CALIFORNIA.

We again entered the cars and started on our way. Immediately after crossing the California line, Brother Jordan
handed me the following dispatch:—

"SACRAMENTO, Cal., June 23, 1885.

"WILLIAM H. JORDAN, Supreme Overseer, on west-
bound overland: Father Upchurch, thrice welcome. Breakfast with us in the morning at Sacramento.

GEO. B. KATZENSTEIN."

AT THE CAPITAL CITY.

[From the *Pacific States Watchman*.]

"AT SACRAMENTO.—The first formal reception in California was had at Sacramento. Grand Master McPherson
and Grand Lecturer Reading, who had left San Francisco
the day before, with a large delegation from Union Lodge,
No. 21, Sacramento Lodge, No. 80, and the Degree of
Honor Lodge, were at the depot, and as the train stopped,
at seven o'clock, A. M., Past Grand Master William H.
Jordan emerged from the sleeper, having upon his arm the
aged guest of the California Jurisdiction of the Ancient
Order of United Workmen. Father Upchurch was formally
introduced to the Grand Master of California, who bade
him a cordial welcome to the State. Under the leadership
of Brothers Katzenstein and Young, the party was ushered
into the Crystal Palace dining-room, where a special table
had been ordered by the committee, and which had been

profusely decorated with flowers and evergreens by the ladies belonging to the Degree of Honor. A hasty but excellent breakfast was had, numerous introductions were made, hundreds had shaken hands with the ' Father,' the conductor gave the signal, the train started, and cheers filled the air, as the founder of the Ancient Order of United Workmen passed from the capital of the State to receive the grand reception awaiting him at San Francisco.

"AT PORT COSTA.—According to arrangements, a committee of the members of the Ancient Order of United Workmen went to Port Costa on Wednesday morning, to meet Father Upchurch and escort him to Oakland. The committee consisted of Brothers Peter Abrahamson. Dr. R. E. Williams, Dr. Irwin, J. F. Wilby, Emanuel Lewis, J. C. Hoag, W. W. Hanscom, E. F. Loud, W. Broderick, Geo. T. Shaw, A. F. Bell, P. Vesey, F. S. Poland, J. A. Guisti, H. G. Pratt, J. G. Severance, G. A. Bordwell, J. O. Moore, H. Wolfson, J. M. Camp, J. H. Macdonald, F. Blight, W. T. Thompson, J. Davis, L. Livingston, T. W. Bethel, A. K. Kipps, E. Rodecker, George Jordan, Thomas Murray, S. F. Purdy, G. W. Lemont, C. W. Daniels, C. H. M. Curry, D. Sewell, and E. Danforth. When Port Costa was reached the special car was switched off, and afterward coupled to the car bringing the distinguished Workman. Father Upchurch then entered the special car, escorted by Supreme Overseer W. H. Jordan, Grand Master Duncan McPherson, and E. M. Reading, Grand Lecturer. The two last-named had met the guest at Sacramento. Mr. Jordan introduced Mr. Upchurch to Grand Foreman Danforth, saying that his pleasant duties were now at an end, having escorted the father of their Order across the continent, and he now gave him into the hands of the San Francisco committee. Mr. Danforth welcomed the veteran brother in behalf of the fraternity in California, and the members of the committee were then individually introduced.

AT OAKLAND.

"On the arrival of the special car at the Sixteenth Street Station, Oakland, Brethren T. H. Corder, W. H. Wilkinson,

E. H. Lake, J. W. Watson, C. H. Eitel, W. Winnie, David
S. Hirshberg, and Charles E. Alden, of Oakland Lodge,
met the party, and escorted Mr. Upchurch and a few of the
San Francisco committee to carriages, which were driven to
Mr. Jordan's residence. There the host's wife had a lunch
prepared for the guests. A number of toasts were proposed, and responded to informally, Mr. Jordan proposing
the first: ' A Health in California Wine to Father Upchurch.' This was followed by toasts to the host and host-
ess, 'California,' responded to by Mr. McPherson, and
' California and the Ancient Order of United Workmen,'
responded to by Mr. Pratt. Later in the afternoon he drove
out to the Asylum for the Deaf, Dumb, and Blind, and returned to the Jordan residence for dinner. At six o'clock
Oakland Legion, No. 3, Select Knights, Ancient Order of
United Workmen, in uniform, commanded by C. E. Alden,
called for Mr. Upchurch, and escorted him to the station.
There he was met by California Lodge, No. 1; Oakland
Lodge, No. 2; Brooklyn Lodge, No. 3; Occidental Lodge,
No. 6; Pacific Lodge, No. 7; Oak Leaf Lodge, No. 35;
Keystone Lodge, No. 64, together with the Alameda and
Berkeley Lodges, and a large number of citizens, and a
band of music. The train ran down to the ferry, crowded
to the doors, and the ferry-boat itself was crowded. On
the boat Mr. Jordan introduced a number of officers of
the Order to Mr. Upchurch, and the Lodges formed on the
lower deck, from which they marched, escorting Mr. Upchurch to the waiting carriage.

ARRIVAL IN SAN FRANCISCO.

" AT SAN FRANCISCO.—In the vicinity of the ferry landing, on this side of the bay, an immense crowd had gathered,
mainly made up of San Francisco Lodges. The San Francisco Legion of Select Knights, in uniform, also turned out.
    " An elegant open barouche, drawn by four white horses,
had been prepared for the distinguished guest, and when
the large party arrived and the line of march was formed,
Father Upchurch entered the carriage with Messrs. Jordan
and Barnes.

THE PROCESSION.

" The following was the order of the procession:—

"A platoon of police, headed by Sergeant Fitzpatrick, Grand Marshal Frank B. May and aids, Henry J. Lask and Henry E. Plate.

" FIRST DIVISION.—J. W. Scott, Marshal; Second Artillery Regiment Band, N. G. C.; Select Knights of San Francisco Legion; San Francisco Lodge, No. 4; Golden Gate Lodge, No. 8; Harmony Lodge, No. 9; Yerba Buena Lodge, No. 14; Bernal Lodge, No. 19; Unity Lodge, No. 27.

"SECOND DIVISION.—J. T. Dufan, Marshal; First Regiment Band; Valley Lodge, No. 30; Spartan Lodge, No. 36; Magnolia Lodge, No. 41; Myrtle Lodge, No. 42; Franklin Lodge, No 44.

" THIRD DIVISION.—A. Rollins, Marshal; Phœnix Band; Hercules Lodge, No. 53; Washington Lodge, No. 60; Burns Lodge, No. 68; St. John Lodge, No. 73; Excelsior Lodge, No. 126; Olympic Lodge, No. 127.

" FOURTH DIVISION.—Capt. C. C. Keene, Marshal; Walcott's Band; Fidelity Lodge, No. 136; Bay View Lodge, No. 159; Memorial Lodge, No. 174; Friendship Lodge, No. 179; Triumph Lodge, No. 180; Noe Valley Lodge, No. 185.

" FIFTH DIVISION.—(Composed of delegates from Lodges in Oakland) D. S. Hirshberg, Marshal; California Lodge, No. 1; Oakland Lodge, No. 2; Brooklyn Lodge, No. 3; Occidental Lodge, No. 6; Pacific Lodge, No. 7; Berkeley Lodge, No. 10; Temple Lodge, No. 11; Oak Leaf Lodge, No. 35; Hearts of Oak Lodge, No. 61; Keystone Lodge, No. 64; University Lodge, No. 88; Ashler Lodge, No 165; West End Lodge, No. 175; Escort of Honor, Oakland Legion of Select Knights, under command of Charles E. Alden; a barouche containing Father Upchurch, and President of the Day, William H. Barnes; ten barouches containing officers of the Grand Lodge.

"The procession moved up Market Street to California, to Kearny, to Market, and halted on reaching Larkin Street. There the column was drawn up in line, and Father Upchurch passed in review, preceded by the Oakland Legion of Select Knights, after which the procession filed into the Pavilion, the Oakland Lodges entering first, and the San Francisco Lodges following. It is estimated that there were from two thousand five hundred to three thousand men in line.

"Throughout the whole line of march great enthusiasm was displayed on the part of the street spectators, and Father Upchurch was kept busy bowing in response to the cheers which were bestowed upon him. The Workmen expressed great satisfaction at the manner in which their Order and its founder were honored by the great mass of people.

RECEPTION IN THE PAVILION.

"Around the Larkin Street entrance of the Pavilion so large a crowd had gathered by half-past eight o'clock that it resembled a mob more than a host of invited members who had come there to be present at the reception of the founder of their Order. Old and young, men and women, boys and girls, jostled each other rudely in their frantic endeavors to pass the great entrance. The doorway on either side was lined by officers, and at the entrance were stationed several of the Order to inspect the tickets of those seeking admittance.

"The interior of the enormous parallelogram presented an animated scene. The seating accommodations on either side of the great parade ground were full to overflowing. The huge wings were crowded with idle promenaders. At the northern end of the right wing were set four long tables, upon whose hospitable boards was placed an ample collation. The immense stage was densely packed with benches, soon to be filled with the selected guests. Behind the drop scene were hundreds of people awaiting anxiously the order for them to take their places upon the unoccupied benches. The great middle space was clear. From the dome of the building to the balconies were stretched a multitude of various colored streamers, and upon the balcony supports were suspended numerous banners bearing the quaint insignia of the Order and the mystic letters, A. O. U. W., in different colors.

"ENTRANCE OF THE PROCESSION.—In hushed silence the enormous gathering awaited the entrance of that procession, which was to tell them that the principal ceremonies of the evening had begun. It was nearly ten o'clock before the gong of the Pavilion gave forth its warning note, and ere the echo had died away among the high rafters, the order was given to clear the entrance, and the huge doors were flung open. Then flowed in the sound of martial music. It was that of the Oakland Civic Band. In close array, with military bearing, with uniforms of black, and white accouterments, and helmets with long red feathers, in marched the Select Knights. Before each division marched the standard-bearer, carrying a banner of bright red silk, upon the broad face of which, in letters of gold, were inscribed the words of the division.

"Following the Knights came Father Upchurch, a quiet-looking old man, with gray hair, a gray goatee, and upon his dress all the stains of long travel. He wore a rough, plum-colored great coat. In one hand he carried a fresh-cut bouquet, and in the other his hat. As he marched down the hall-way his glances fell curiously upon the thick-lined sides. Anon the spectators would break into simultaneous applause, and the clap of hands sounded like the roar of breakers dashing against a bold face of rock. Then the people on the stage caught the infection, and brother after brother jumped from his chair and proposed for Father Upchurch many a rousing cheer. When the stage was gained, Past Grand Master Workman Wm. II. Barnes delivered the introductory address of welcome, which was as follows:—

WELCOME ADDRESS BY PAST GRAND MASTER WORKMAN
BARNES.

"'OFFICERS, BRETHREN, AND FRIENDS: Often have mighty processions been seen in our streets; often have triumphal arches been erected on the public thoroughfares of San Francisco, and banners swinging to the breeze in token of joyous celebration. Time and again, statesmen, sages, and warriors have found, in this city on the western

7

slope of the continent, ovations and hearty w.lcome unparalleled; and yet I say that to none who thus far have
visited our land of the setting sun, is a mighty recognition
of gratitude more due than to the grand old man who is
now the guest of the Workmen of California—this man,
who in his life-work has said, like Abou Ben Adhem to the
angel,—

" Write me as one who loves his fellow-men,"—

This nobleman of nature, who, with the magic rod of
humanity, has smitten a world's petrified selfishness, and
caused the flinty mass to open and pour forth a living and
continuous stream of practical benevolence to gladden and
make green what otherwise would have been waste and
desert places.

" ' It is meet and proper that here in California he should
receive the grandest ovation of his life, for California is not
only the land of metals, grains, fruits, and flowers, but it
also stands first and foremost as the land of fraternity, and
in the name of that universal fraternity, which here is part
and parcel of our every-day life; in the name of the widows
and orphans comforted, relieved, and blessed by fraternal
aid; in the name of the seventeen thousand gallant sons of our
Order in this State, and of their wives and children, I bid
a welcome, to our hearts and homes, to him who, Franklin-
like, caught the living spark from the dark clouds surrounding humanity, brought it into subjection, and sent it forth,
an electric light, under the title of Fraternal Co-operation,
to shed abroad its brilliant beams until—

"Misfortune has no want to relieve;
Sorrow no tear to dry. "

" 'Once more, thrice welcome to our Father, Brother,
Friend, Past Supreme Master John J. Upchurch, founder
of the Ancient Order of United Workmen.'

" With modesty Father Upchurch rose to make answer.
His voice was hardly audible, so overcome was he with
emotion.

HIS RESPONSE.

" 'My heart is too full for utterance. This great audience so overpowers me that it is impossible for me to say all that I would wish. I was never called to speak, nor am I known as a speaker. I have been more of a working man than an orator. I appreciate, from the bottom of my heart, this great demonstration. It will remain engraven through all years in my heart far greater than any event in my life. I only wish that I could do it justice, but I cannot, and so I sincerely thank you for your kindness.'

ORATION OF PAST GRAND MASTER WORKMAN WM. H. JORDAN.

"After the applause had subsided, Wm. H. Jordan, Supreme Overseer, gave the oration, of which the following is a synopsis:—

" 'MR. CHAIRMAN, BROTHER WORKMEN, LADIES AND GENTLEMEN: This grand outpouring of the people of San Francisco evinces the tendency of the human race to honor those who have achieved much in the battle of life. From time immemorial it has been the custom of mankind to throng the streets and shout at the sight of those who return from the field of battle laden with the honors of war. Napoleon and Wellington, Garibaldi and Von Moltke, are names that rouse the blood of patriots throughout the earth, and to-day the eyes of all the world are strained towards the little cottage on the summit of Mount McGregor, and the pulse comes quick and fast as the click of the telegraph tells the story of each day's suffering, as the silent hero of Shiloh, Vicksburg, and Appomattox fights alone the battle of life and death. These grand heroes of the battle-field are honored because of the sacrifices and dangers they have encountered in the face of shot and shell of battle. But sometimes—thank God for it—sometimes it happens that the people have an opportunity to honor a man who has achieved fame, not upon the field of battle, not through the sorrows he has brought to the human heart, but through the joy he has caused to spring up in the lives of his fellowmerf. Such a man is our honored brother, the guest of this immense outpouring to-night, J. J. Upchurch. [*Applause.*] Seventeen years ago Father Upchurch, in the quiet village of Meadville, Pennsylvania, gathered together a little band of thirteen, and laid the foundation of the Ancient Order of United Workmen. Thirteen true and noble men! The very number was an omen of good. Christ and his twelve apostles constituted a band of thirteen, who undertook the work of Christianizing the world. In 1775 thirteen States banded together to form the American Union, and to-day there are thirteen stripes in that grand old flag that floats over land and sea, the emblem of human liberty. [*Applause.*] We honor this grand old man, and to-night bid him welcome to our golden shores. We honor him for the good he has done; and not we alone. Toward us are turned the eyes of one hundred and fifty-two thousand men, and they all shout aloud a grand anthem of praise to the honored man who is to-night the guest of California Workmen. [*Applause.*]

"'Seventeen years ago Father Upchurch planted the seed that has to-day sprung up to such grand proportions. The plan which he then devised to relieve the distress of humanity has worked more marvels than the magician's wand. Eleven million five hundred thousand dollars have been scattered among the grief-stricken families of our fraternity, and God above can tell what wounds have been healed, what sorrows assuaged. Last week I stood in New York Harbor, upon the pedestal that soon is to receive the great Statue of Liberty,—that colossal wonder of the nineteenth century. Soon the electric rays from its uplifted torch will stream far out to sea, welcoming the storm-tossed mariner as he approaches the haven of political and religious freedom. With its face turned toward the east, it will be the first to greet the rising sun and announce the approach of day. But we are to-day erecting upon these Western shores a greater wonder than that of the great Bartholdi. It is a colossal statue of fraternity, upon the base of which is engraven, in characters of gold, the letters A. O. U. W. [*Great Applause.*]

" ' In its outstretched hand it holds the electric torch of brotherly love. Its face is turned not toward the East, but toward the West. Its eyes do not greet the rising sun, but they follow it as it sets among the billows of life's tempestuous sea; and when the dark gloom of life's night falls upon the sullen waters, the rays, glittering and gleaming from its mighty torch, sweep over the waves, carrying comfort and hope where'er they are seen. [*Applause.*]

" ' Father Upchurch is welcomed to-night by his children of the West; and as a token of your enthusiasm I ask you, in conclusion, to join with us in three hearty cheers for the founder of the Ancient Order of United Workmen.' "

After the conclusion of the exercises at the Pavilion, I shook the hand of hundreds of Workmen and their families. A beautiful little girl, Nelly Cattran, the six-year-old daughter of the Recorder of Triumph Lodge, No. 180, approached me with such confidence that I could not forego kissing her. At a late hour I was conveyed to the Baldwin Hotel. Here I must confess that I was taken entirely by surprise, never anticipating anything that would compare with this grand demonstration.

[From the *Watchman.*]

THE PICNIC AT FAIRFAX.

" Over five thousand people attended the Seventeenth Anniversary Picnic of the Ancient Order of United Workmen, at Fairfax, on Thursday, June 25, and a most enjoyable day was passed. No accident of any kind happened, and the programme was carried out successfully. The facilities of transportation were taxed to the utmost to take the crowds from the city, and hundreds came also from the surrounding towns. Father Upchurch came over on the eleven o'clock boat; and not only did the people who had come over with him wait at the station to see him alight and escort him to the grounds, but an assemblage of over five hundred, made up of those who had come over on the early boats, was awaiting him. No games or amusements had been indulged in; they had felt that the picnic had not begun until the Father had arrived. Duncan McPherson, Grand Master, welcomed the veteran guest in a few well-chosen remarks. Amid cheers and acclamations, Father Upchurch was escorted up the winding path to the pavilion. Here, on the music stand, the old gentleman, with a beam of pleasure lighting up his countenance, made a brief address in which he thanked his "children" for their universal expressions of love toward himself. It was such an overwhelming ovation that he could not control his feelings. He could feel what he could not express. His remarks were loudly applauded, and the glen echoed with the cheers which were given.

ORATION OF PAST GRAND MASTER WORKMAN WILLIAM H. BARNES.

" The orator of the day, William H. Barnes, Past Grand Master of California, was then introduced. He briefly sketched the growth of the Order which Father Upchurch had founded, and outlined the grand work which the founder had accomplished. His speech closed with a brilliant peroration eulogistic of the Order and Father Upchurch. The pavilion was then cleared for dancing, and the remainder of the day was given up to enjoyment. Lunch baskets were unpacked and groups formed all over the ground, each individual enjoying himself heartily. The Second Regiment Band was in attendance for the benefit of those who desired to dance.

" The following 'Acrostic' was composed, and read at

the dinner table at Fairfax Park on the day of the grand picnic:—

ACROSTIC.

BY WM. II. BARNES.

" A mechanic stands in his Eastern home,

Thinking of days gone by ;
Rich are his thoughts as on they roam,
In blessing and harmony.
Bright glows his eye as he thinks of his toil
Under the guidance of Heaven,
That has bro't into light from Fraternity's soil,
Endless joys, and protection has given

To widows and orphans, and many of those
Of whom the dear Saviour has said:

' Find the wayworn and weary; the naked ones clothe;
And unto the hungry give bread.'
The good old man stands and communes with his heart:
' How gracious hath God been to me,
Each hour hath he given the efforts I've made
Rich fruitage of prosperity.'

Unto him, as he muses, a messenger comes,
Placing into his sinewy hand
California's kind bidding to visit our home,
Here, by the Pacific's bright strand.
Unspeakable joys enkindle his eyes;
Rapture fills, in each pulse, every part.
' California has called,' he exclaims in surprise,
' Heaven bless her benevolent heart!'
Peace scoreth her victories oft and again
As well as war's carnage and whirl;
Sweet is the song and thrilling the strain
That Fraternity sings to the world.

Swiftly the journey is made from the East,
Unto where the Sierra's great dome
Proclaims to our brother, 'Soon you will rest,
Rest sweet in Fraternity's home.'
Each city and town now a welcome extend,
Most hearty the shouts and the cheers;
Every brother his presence doth willingly lend

When good 'Father' Upchurch appears.
Orders open their arms, and hundreds of men
Round him gather in love day by day;
Kings might envy this one, who, though humble and plain,
Men delight a true homage to pay;
And the reason, so plain that none can efface,—
Nobly he hath worked for the good of his race."

THE "WATCHMAN'S" WELCOME.

On my arrival in Oakland, Brother Jordan handed me
the following letter, which explains itself:—

"A NOBLE RESPONSE.—Wishing to add our mite toward
making Father Upchurch's visit pleasant to himself and
friends, we entered his name as an honorary subscriber for
life on our mail list, and addressed him the following letter, which is self-explanatory. For his generous-hearted
response and noble words of acknowledgment to our whole
brotherhood, we are exceedingly grateful and appreciative:—

"'OFFICE OF "PACIFIC STATES WATCHMAN," }
"'San Francisco, June 24, 1885. }

"'*To Father Upchurch*—

"''DEAR FATHER UPCHURCH: Allow us to extend to you
the congratulations of the *Pacific States Watchman* upon
safely arriving in our "Golden State." We are thankful
that you were kind enough to visit our Jurisdiction. We
are most happy to voice to you the sentiments of a great
and thoroughly united brotherhood, and say welcome, a
thousand times welcome, to our fraternal altars and to our
firesides.

" 'Allow us to further extend to you the support of your old friend, the *Watchman,* and ask you to accept as a memento from us one hundred complimentary copies of your engraved portrait, which we have had prepared by one of our best artists, with as much care and truthfulness as possible.

" 'We do this with the thought that you may possibly be pleased to make use of some of them, perhaps indorsed with your autograph to some of our brotherhood as a *souvenir* of your visit to us.

" ' May we not hope that you will pay the *Watchman* Publishing House a visit, where we will make you, at all times, as welcome as our humble abilities will permit ?

" ' We also invite you to say a good word now and then to your loving and faithful " children of the Order " on this Coast, through our columns.

" ' Yours fraternally,

" Watchman " Publishing Co.,

*A. T. Dewey, Past Master Workman, Manager.' "

MY RESPONSE.

" San Francisco, June 26, 1885.

" A. T. Dewey, Past Master Workman, Manager *Watchman* Publishing Company—*Dear Sir and Brother:* Your kind favor of the 24th inst., accompanying a roll of one hundred copies of my portrait, beautifully engraved, was handed me by Brother Jordan, yesterday morning. Your generous congratulations and flattering expression of fraternal love, as well as the handsome gift by which they are accompanied, are to me most dear. No words can express my appreciation, nor measure the debt of gratitude which I feel constrained to acknowledge for all that the *Watchman* and my ' children ' of California have done. The grandeur and hearty spontaneity of my reception here, far surpasses anything that had ever entered into my mind to conceive. Truly, the spirit of fraternity glows in the hearts of the Workmen of California, with a brilliancy that I have never beheld elsewhere. I thank you and them for all. God bless you to the end of life.

" Your brother, always, J. J. Upchurch."

VISITING THE SAN FRANCISCO LODGES.

June 26, I visited Yerba Buena, No. 14; Spartan Lodge, No. 36; and Hercules, No. 53. I acted as Past Master Workman, and administered the obligation to three Master Workmen. Also delivered a short address to the Lodge. We had a good turn-out, and a great deal of interest was manifested.

June 27 I was conducted through the California market by Brother Jordan, which surpassed anything of the kind that I have ever seen for its great variety. We then took lunch with Brother Guisti.

VISITING OAKLAND LODGES.

In the evening I was escorted to the Hamilton Church, Oakland, where a grand reception was given me. At half-past seven o'clock, P. M., Grand Master Workman McPherson introduced me to the audience in his happy style. Then I delivered a short address, followed by Past Supreme Master Workman Fish, Supreme Overseer Jordan, and others, with fine music, both instrumental and vocal. The number of Workmen, and the Select Knights in uniform, had a grand time. A beautiful floral offering was presented me by the Degree of Honor ladies. June 28, I attended the Episcopal Church with Brother Jordan and his estimable lady. In the afternoon I returned to San Francisco   In the evening a grand reception was given me by Brother E. Lewis at his residence. About fifty guests were present. We had a magnificent time. I was presented by Brother Lewis with a beautiful floral offering with the device, "Long Live Upchurch."

SELECT KNIGHTS' ENTERTAINMENT.

At night I visited Select Knights, No. 1, and acted as Chaplain; took in six members, one of whom was Grand Master Workman Duncan McPherson. We had an interesting meeting and a social time. At the close, the members repaired to the banquet hall, where a fine spread was in waiting, of which we partook with relish.

INVITATION OF THE KNIGHTS OF HONOR.

"OFFICE OF GRAND DICTATOR
K. of H., of Cal., June 29, 1885.

To Father Upchurch, and Grand Master Workman Mc-Pherson, Ancient Order of United Workmen—

"GREETING: A fraternal invitation is hereby extended to each of you to attend our Twelfth Anniversary Picnic at Stephen's Park, East Oakland, Tuesday, June 30, 1885, at fifteen minutes past twelve o'clock, P. M. Committee will receive you at Central Pacific ferry on boat leaving San Francisco at half past eleven o'clock, A. M., and at the ferry at fifteen minutes past eleven, A. M. In the name of the Knights of Honor,   Fraternally,

WM. H. BARNES, *Grand Dictator of Cal.*"

At the appointed time I was escorted to the boat, on the Oakland side, took the train, and after a short run was put off at the Park, which is a magnificent place tastefully arranged to please the most fastidious. A goodly number were ushered into a spacious dining-room, where lunch was already prepared, and was partaken of greatly to the joy of the inner man.

I was then introduced to the audience, and addressed them on the origin and progress of the Ancient Order of United Workmen, the opposition we had to overcome, also the benefits that are to be derived by the families of its members. Brother W. H. Jordan was then introduced, and addressed them in that happy manner that commands the attention of everyone within the sound of his voice. He dwelt at length upon the relationship of the two Orders, and the amount of suffering and distress that had been alleviated. He also spoke in glowing terms of the future of the two Orders. He took his seat amid roars of applause. Several other brothers were called upon, who spoke with interest and enthusiasm on the many virtues of the Order.

Before leaving the stand, a committee requested that I should permit them to elect me as an honorary member of the Knights of Honor, to which I readily consented, but I regret to say I could not make it convenient to take the degree. At the close of the exercises in the pavilion, all went out to see the sports, which consisted of foot-races, of both sexes, old and young, which added greatly to the amusement of the occasion. At four o'clock we again took the train for San Francisco.

In the evening I visited Unity Lodge, No. 27. The members turned out well. I gave them a short talk and had a pleasant time. They seem all alive to their work.

VISITS CHINATOWN.

July 1, in the afternoon, Grand Master Workman Mc-Pherson, W. H. Barnes, F. S. Poland and myself, accompanied by Sergeant Bethel, visited "Chinatown." I do not wonder that Californians are opposed to the Chinese, for they are certainly the most degraded beings that I ever saw. They occupy quarters that a decent rat would scorn to live in. In several places there would be five or six in a room not more than seven feet square, piled in like sardines, on shelves with nothing to lie on but a piece of mat, and a block of wood for a pillow. Here they smoke opium until they "keel over," drunk. We called on their Medicine Man; and also saw their god. They worship the devil as well as other gods. To prevent him from punishing them, they keep a cup of whisky and a cup of tea sitting before him continually. They said he sometimes drinks tea and sometimes whisky. When one is sick, a bundle of sticks is handed him, and he draws out one, which indicates the kind of medicine that is required to reach his case. He takes this stick to the drug store and gets what it calls for—it may be a dried locust shell or a lizard skin, or something else equally as noxious. At another place they were packed under the sidewalk. In the theater, down underground, we found a Chinese woman—an actress—and three children, living in a room about seven feet square. My head touched the ceiling. All the work, including cooking, was done in this room. The smoke had to escape through a window about two feet square, out under the sidewalk. It is said there are forty thousand of them occupying twelve squares of the city. Language cannot express the degradation that I beheld in this locality.

VISITS VALLEY, EXCELSIOR, AND OTHER LODGES.

In the evening I visited Valley Lodge, No. 30 This is the second largest Lodge in the Order. There was a fine turnout, it being installation night. I gave them a short address, which was followed by a number of other speakers. Upon the whole, we had a grand time, which wound up with a banquet.

July 2 I visited Excelsior Lodge and three others, which had been called together as a district. I gave them a short talk on the rise and progress of the Order, its mission, duties, etc., which was followed by Brother Jordan and others, whose discourses were deeply interesting. At eleven o'clock P. M., we visited Silver Star Lodge, Degree of Honor, but being detained at Excelsior longer than we expected, Silver Star Lodge had closed, but a large number of ladies and gentlemen were still in the hall. They reopened the Lodge, when I gave them a short address on the fraternal relations existing between the Degree of Honor and the Workmen. We had a very social time, and all went away benefited.

VISITS GOLDEN GATE PARK.

July 3 Brother Poland, two Degree of Honor ladies, and myself took a carriage and visited the park, in which stands President Garfield's statue. It is a magnificent park, large, and laid out with the finest collection of flowers and shrubbery that I ever saw. The conservatory is beyond description in loveliness. After spending a couple of hours here, we again entered our carriage. The next place we visited was the Life-saving Station. Here we were shown the *modus operandi* of shooting a line to a ship and its return. The whole operation was, to me, very interesting. The next place of interest was the Cliff House, built upon the rocks overhanging the ocean. From this popular place of resort could be seen upon the rocks extending above the surface of the ocean, dozens of sea-lions and seals, who created a perfect Babel with their continuous howlings. Some of them were as large as an ox. After spending an hour here, we returned to the city.

Grand Lecturer Reading and myself visited Bay View Lodge. The hall was well filled on our arrival. After an address of welcome, I was introduced and addressed the Lodge on the principles of the Order, showing the duties that we owe our families by joining the Order and providing for them when we are called away. Brother Reading followed in

his happy, logical, and convincing manner, which always demands strict attention. The business of the Lodge being
through with, all were requested to repair to the banquet-
room, where a fine spread was prepared for the enjoyment
of all.

VISIT TO GRAND RECORDER PRATT.

July 4 on invitation of Bro. H. G. Pratt, Grand Recorder,
Bro. E. Lewis and myself paid him a visit in the country,
four miles from Oakland. We mistook the station that we
were to get off at and had to walk two miles, but I enjoyed
it, as we passed through the finest rural district I ever beheld. We remained with Brother Pratt until the 6th, and
had a splendid time. On the morning of the 6th we returned to San Francisco. Brother Lewis would have me
stop at his business office. He presented me with a pair of
Congress gaiters and slippers. In the evening we visited
Magnolia and one other Lodge, which was very interesting,
and I believe all were benefited by coming together.

July 7 we visited California Lodge, No. 1, of Oakland,
and addressed the meeting, and encouraged them to continue the good work with renewed energy until every good
man and woman should be brought under its beneficial influences. At nine o'clock we returned to San Francisco
and visited Unity Lodge. I talked to them a few minutes,
when several others followed, giving new interest to the
meeting.

VISITS THE OFFICE OF THE "WATCHMAN."

July 8 I called at the office of the *Pacific States Watchman*, and was introduced to the employés, who had been
called together, and I gave them some of the incidents of
our early history, trials, etc. I stated some of the many

8

blessings that had been dispensed to suffering humanity. A pot of earth was then brought in, and I planted a black walnut and the seed of the large pine or redwood of California, for Master Alfred H. Dewey, which I trust may spring up and do well. I then went to the office of Brother Jordan, and got letters from home, which I had been expecting. In the evening I went with Brother Jordan to Oakland. We instituted Upchurch Legion, No 9, with seventeen members. There is a deep interest taken in the work of the Select Knights, and it will be the means of adding many good men to the roll of the Ancient Order of United Workmen. I remained overnight at the residence of Brother Jordan.

July 9 we returned to San Francisco, and I visited the office of Brother Jordan; took lunch at the restaurant of Bro. J. A. Guisti, at California Market. After lunch, Brother Guisti conducted me to the macaroni factory, which was something I had not seen; it was quite a novelty. On leaving here, I was taken to the champagne factory, where, I suppose, millions of gallons of wine were stored. The basement occupied the whole of one square, including the streets, which had been excavated and arched for the purpose. I thought that it would be many years hence before California would adopt prohibition. We then visited Telegraph Hill. It is a high point overlooking both bay and city. Here, in early times, a watch was set to signal ships coming in when news from loved ones in the East was expected. To reach this elevated point we had to ascend an inclined plane at an elevation of about twenty feet to the one hundred, or a total elevation of two hundred and ninety-six feet in the length of a cable railroad of one thousand five hundred and fifty feet. There is a fine hall erected on this point, and refreshments kept for those in want of them.

In the evening we visited Union Lodge, No. 29, Degree of Honor. The hall was well filled with both male and female members. There was a great deal of interest manifested by all. A number of speeches were delivered, which were entertaining and instructive, and all present seemed to enjoy the exercises to the utmost. At the conclusion of the exercises, the Lodge adjourned to the banquet hall, where a collation was served.

VISIT TO STOCKTON.

July 10 Bro. E. M. Reading, Grand Master Workman McPherson, and myself, visited Stockton, and were met at the depot by a Committee of Reception, and taken in carriages to a hotel. In the afternoon we took in the town by visiting the large manufacturing establishments and the insane asylum for males, which contains about seven hundred patients. The buildings are fine, convenient, and, no doubt, managed to the best advantage. In the evening I was tendered a warm reception by the Order, at the Masonic Temple. Master Workman Pritchard occupied the chair, and the address of welcome was delivered by Brother Clement, to which I replied, thanking them for their marked reception and cordial greeting on this occasion, and was followed by Grand Master Workman Duncan McPherson, who gave a fine oratorical address on the Aims and Objects of the Order in its dissemination of bounties to the needy. Brother Reading then addressed the audience in his usual style, followed by music by the band. Following this came the public installation of the officers of Stockton Lodge, No. 23, the ceremony being conducted by District Deputy E. Lehi, assisted by the Grand Officers. After the ceremony in the hall, myself and Grand Officers, with a goodly number of brothers and their ladies, were sumptuously entertained, which closed the evening's exercises.

On the 11th we were driven to the female asylum, which contains eight hundred inmates—some quiet, others boisterous. The buildings are spacious, everything being kept as neat as a pin, and seems to be managed in the best possible manner.

VISITS SACRAMENTO.

At noon we took the train for Sacramento. A committee was in waiting at the depot, who placed us in carriages and took us to the hotel. In the evening the reception took place in the commodious hall of Union Lodge, No. 21, which was filled with brethren of the Order and their families. The introductory speech was made by Bro. P. M. Henry, to which I replied, creating a favorable impression upon all. I was followed by Grand Master McPherson and Grand Lecturer Reading, whose addresses were received with unmistakable satisfaction. The officers of both Union, No. 21, and Sacramento, No 80, were installed; and then followed recitations and music, Miss Annie Ash, Mrs. Sam Katzenstein, Mrs. Al. Pritchard, and Mrs. Maggie Moore, being the principal performers. A magnificent banquet was partaken of at the close of the exercises. While in the city I received the following letter, which will explain itself:—

REQUESTING HIS AUTOGRAPH.

" 1894 BROADWAY, SAN FRANCISCO, Cal.

" J. J. UPCHURCH—*Dear Sir:* I am a little girl, and have, for the past two years, been confined to the house, under medical treatment for spinal and hip disease. I pass most of my time collecting the autographs of celebrated people, and if you will be so very kind as to send me your autograph, it would give me great pleasure. I inclose a card for you to write it upon, and I hope you will pardon me for the liberty I have taken.

"Believe me, very respectfully,

MARIA GENEVIEVE MEE."

The interest of this dear little girl touched my heart deeply, and I complied with her request with pleasure, hoping that she would speedily and permanently recover from her affliction.

[From the *Watchman* of June 9.]

PRIZE POEM.

"UPCHURCH PRIZE POEM OFFER.—In view of the interest aroused by the near approaching visit of Father Upchurch, the *Watchman* wishes to encourage the ambition of our local poets having a fraternal tendency, to produce something in the way of literature that will be intrinsically valuable and worthily commemorate the visit among us of the founder of the Order.

"Accordingly, we make the following offer: To anyone who will send us, by July 4, the best poem on Father Upchurch, not to exceed sixty lines, we will give an order on the well-known and extensive book-selling establishment of A. L. Bancroft & Co., of this city, for twenty dollars, payable in books or similar articles from their choice and well-selected literary stock. Poems may be either in rhyme or blank verse. An intelligent and impartial committee will decide on the merits of the poems.

"Those competing will please sign a *nom de plume*, and inclose real name and address in a separate envelope, to be opened after the award. We trust that the returns will be as satisfactory for this offer as they were for our prize poems on 'Fraternity,' published last year.

"An admiring friend adds a five-dollar cash donation to the above. We will extend the time for receipt of the poem to the 8th of July, which will be in time to publish it for our next issue, on the 11th."

" The following poem has been adjudged to be entitled to the prize offered by the *Watchman* for the best poetical production on Father Upchurch. The prize consists of an order on A. L. Bancroft & Co., for twenty dollars, payable in books, and five dollars in cash, payable at this office on behalf of a friend who donated the amount additional."

"FATHER" UPCHURCH.

A. O. U. W. PRIZE POEM.

BY SAM BOOTH.

The minstrel bards of ancient days,
To arms and war attuned their lays.
They sang their heroes' glorious deeds—
The clash of arms, the rush of steeds,
The clang of steel, the cannon's roar,
And fair fields dyed with human gore;
They sang of kings, whose palace stood
An island in a sea of blood,
Whose wild ambition led them on
To "wade through slaughter to a throne;"
Of warriors, who to greatness rose
Over a hecatomb of foes,
Who, that they might be great and free,
Ground nations down to slavery.
But wounds and death and all the wrack
Of desolation in the track
Of horrid war, no pen or tongue
Gilds with the glamour of a song.
The smiling fields that bloomed so fair,
The cheerful homes burnt black and bare,
The widow's tear, the orphan's cry,
Alas! are passed unnoted by.
Be mine the privilege to rehearse
(Albeit in the humblest verse)

The praises of a crownless king,—
The blessings peace and love can bring.
No warrior he, with lance and shield,
Thirsting for fame on tented field;
But one whose aim it was to bind
In bonds fraternal all mankind.
While England boasts of Howard's fame,
And France still sings her Hugo's name,
Americans in UPCHURCH see
The " Father " of Fraternity,
Who shunned the wrathful ways of strife,
And walked the peaceful paths of life;
Brother and Sire, whose virtues lend
New luster to the name of Friend.
No portents heralded his birth,
His only heritage, honest worth;
Nor did the smiles of Fortune shed
A golden aureole round his head;
To learning he makes no pretense,
His genius is just common sense.
In youth and manhood simply bred
To daily toil for daily bread.
But over all the ills that wait
On lowly birth or adverse fate,
His regal soul superior rose
In sympathy with all life's woes.
His grand ambition was to be
Of service to humanity;
His great life problem: how he could
Unite mankind in brotherhood.
How grandly he hath wrought and well,
Let Knights and Friends and Workmen tell—
A hundred thousand men who greet
In each a Brother when they meet;
A thousand widows' thankful tears,
Ten thousand orphans' daily prayers,
All these attest the grateful sense
Of his benign beneficence.
Hail! then, dear " Father," Brother, Friend,

To you our hearts in homage bend.
No monument of sculptor's dream
Could raise you in our high esteem.
And far above all praise or blame
Is he, beneath whose honored name
The Recording Angel's pen shall trace:
" The Benefactor of the race."

"Our offer has fortunately proved opportune. Other creditable poems have been received, some of which we shall give hereafter, by consent of the authors, who are worthy of commendation by all for their noble efforts."

VIEWING SACRAMENTO.

July 12 we were driven around the city and shown the most interesting places. First the capitol, which is a magnificent building. In the rotunda is the statue of Queen Isabella, of Spain, with Columbus and his son kneeling before her. This building stands on an eminence in the center of the large and cultivated park. Near by is the Mechanical Pavilion, which will accommodate nine thousand persons. It is used for the exhibition of the arts and sciences, and other like purposes. The next place of interest was the Art Gallery, a splendid structure, containing a rare collection of the finest paintings, which was donated to the city by Mrs. Judge Crocker, a widow lady of the city.

We were next driven through the Public Park and Fair Grounds, which are in keeping with the public spirit and energy of Californians.

In the evening I visited Pat. Connor, formerly of Meadville, Pennsylvania, who was hurt on the Central Pacific Railroad. He has been somewhat out of his mind ever since he was hurt, but he recognized me as soon as he saw me. He belonged to Jefferson Lodge, No. 1, of Pennsylvania.

July 13 I took the train for San Francisco, at half past seven o'clock A. M. At Port Costa the Central Pacific Company runs and operates the largest ferry-boat I have ever seen. It is capable of taking, at one load, a locomotive and twenty-eight long passenger cars, or forty-eight freight cars. The cylinders are five by eleven feet, and it is said to be the largest boat in the world.

VISITING A MASONIC LODGE.

Reached San Francisco at eleven o'clock A. M., and in the evening visited King Solomon Lodge of Masons, with Bro. E. Lewis. The Lodge was well attended, and after examination by committee, was admitted to a seat in the Lodge. Raised one member to the sublime degree of a Master Mason.

July 14, in the evening, Brother Poland and myself visited Triumph Lodge of Workmen. The Lodge was well attended, and the members were very much interested in the work of the Order. I spoke a short time, and my remarks seemed to be appreciated.

July 15 the Grand Foreman and myself took dinner at the residence of Brother Poland, whose hospitality was very much enjoyed by myself. In the evening I visited District No. 5, with No. 136. The meeting was largely attended, and, after an address of welcome, I was introduced, and spoke to them on the rise and progress of our Order, and the opposition and difficulties we had to overcome to get the work before the people. I was followed by W. H. Jordan, Supreme Overseer, Past Grand Master Workman Wm. H. Barnes, and Past Grand Master Workman Brewer, who addressed the audience in a grand and convincing strain of eloquence, so much so that they were frequently interrupted by a deafening roar of applause.

GOES TO NAPA.

July 16 with Brothers Barnes, Severance, and Poland, I left San Francisco at three o'clock P. M. for Napa; arrived at Vallejo Junction, took the boat and crossed the Straits of Carquinez; again boarded the train and reached Napa at half past six o'clock, where a committee was in waiting at the depot who escorted us to the Palace Hotel. After supper, members of the Order formed and marched to the hotel and escorted us to the Grand Opera House, which was well filled. After music, the address of welcome by Bro. H. C. Cesford was delivered, to which I replied in my usual common, plain way. Brethren Severance and Barnes addressed the audience, and were received with rounds of applause, Brother Barnes being called out the second time. Sam Booth's " Prize Poem " was read by Henry Hogan, and the whole was a grand success, as had been my receptions throughout the entire Jurisdiction. At the close of the exercises, a fine collation was served at the Palace Hotel, which wound up the evening's festivities. A year before my visit here, I was elected to membership in the Past Master Workman's Association, and on my arrival the badge of the association was presented to me.

July 17 Brother Smith gave Brother Poland and myself a carriage ride through Napa Valley. Our first stop was at the water-works. They have fine pumping machinery. The engineer said that in digging for water they struck an underground river. On going up the side of the mountain, on our way to the Napa Soda Springs, a large jack rabbit bounced into the road, and I thought it was a gray wolf until better informed. The Springs are fourteen miles from the city, and it is a charming summer resort; a fine hotel of stone, and a number of neat cottages for visitors are here;

also numerous fine walks, with the many fragrant, as well as beautiful, flowers for which California is noted. There are several kinds of mineral waters here, and in a room there are several men employed bottling soda water, with natural gas, as it comes from the mountain, and it is shipped to all parts of the country. On leaving the Springs, we made for the main valley, and took lunch with a Mr. Gray, seven miles from St. Helena, and fourteen miles from Napa. Mr. Gray said that the yield of grapes this year would be about three tons per acre, the best yield being ten tons per acre. They sell for twenty-five to thirty-five dollars per ton. Fifteen dollars per ton pays better than raising wheat. He last year sold fifteen hundred dollar's worth of grapes that cost him only seventy-five dollars to tend and market. On leaving Mr. Gray's, we started down the Napa Valley. I saw large orchards of English walnuts and almonds, and about thirty thousand acres of grapes. This is the finest valley that I ever saw, and it occurred to me that this must have been the Garden of Eden, at least had I an opportunity, I think it would satisfy my desire to wander in it. We returned to Napa at four o'clock P. M., just in time to take the train for Vallejo, where we were met at the depot by a committee and conducted to the hotel. In the evening we were escorted to the Grand Opera House, which was well filled with members of the Order, their families and friends. The audience was entertained with fine music, both vocal and instrumental. On being introduced, I addressed them, pointing out some of the beauties of our Order, and the many blessings that had been conferred upon the widow and orphan. Brother Poland followed, giving some excellent advice to the members in building up the Order. This city has about fifteen hundred inhabitants, and lies on the north side of the Straits of Carquinez. The United States Government has its navy yard here.

GOES TO SANTA CRUZ.

July 18 we left Vallejo at eight o'clock A. M., and arrived at San Francisco at ten o'clock A. M. Visited the offices of Brothers Danforth and Jordan, and at two o'clock P. M. Brother Poland and myself took train for Santa Cruz. We passed through several little towns; at Big Tree Station saw some large redwood trees, but did not stop.

[From the *Watchman* of July 25.]

FATHER UPCHURCH AT SANTA CRUZ.

"Last Saturday night, the 18th, the Workmen of Santa Cruz and vicinity had an opportunity to testify their admiration and respect for Father Upchurch, which they did in a royal manner and in a style that did credit to the home of the Grand Master Workman of the State. The venerable veteran was met at the depot of the South Pacific Coast Railroad by the Reception Committee, and with a team of four white horses, driven to the residence of Grand Master Workman Duncan McPherson, and then to the Opera House, where a large concourse of citizens had assembled. An address of welcome was delivered by Dr. O. L. Gordon, who referred in eulogistic terms to the guest of the evening. Grand Master McPherson followed in an introductory speech that was full of good things for the laws of the Order, closing by presenting Father Upchurch to the audience in the following glowing sentence: 'Mr. President, to you and through you to the Brothers here assembled, and this audience, I have the pleasure of introducing the Workman's Abou Ben Adhem, the founder of the " Poor Man's Insurance," the widow's support, and the orphan's help, and whose name in letters of Fraternal light will be written by the angel of charity high above all other human benefactors.' The response of the founder was brief, but full of feeling. He sketched the rise of the Order, and added that he should always remember California and his warm-hearted brother Workman with the deepest gratitude.

"The principal address of the evening was delivered by Bro. Adam Bane, of San Jose, and it is described as the finest effort ever heard in Santa Cruz. After music, the programme was closed by a repast at Aonian Hall, provided by the ladies of Workman families. The whole affair did the brethren of the little city by the sea great credit."

July 19 Grand Master McPherson and myself walked down to the beach, which is a magnificent resort for those seeking health as well as pleasure. There are a great many cottages and tents for the accommodation of visitors. In the afternoon I was driven around the city and out to old ocean; then out in the country. The whole scene was one of beauty. My sojourn here was attended with a great deal of pleasure, which I shall ever remember with gratitude, especially toward the Grand Master Workman and his estimable family.

VISITS WATSONVILLE.

July 20 Grand Master Workman McPherson and myself took the train for Watsonville, where Lodge No. 45 gave us an appropriate and most cordial reception. A delegation met us at the depot, and escorted us to the Mansion House. At seven o'clock about sixty members, visiting brethren, Grand Master McPherson, and myself, met in the Lodge-room, and after the business of the Lodge had been transacted, a short time was taken up with congratulatory speeches, after which a procession was formed, and marched to the rink, where a large audience was anxiously waiting our coming. After an overture by the band, Deputy Friermuth introduced Doctor Bigsley, who delivered a finely-worded address of welcome, to which I replied, followed by Grand

Master McPherson, who spoke with earnestness and enthusiasm, and was listened to with satisfaction by a large
audience of members, their families, and invited guests.
The exercises being through, all then repaired to the
hall, where a fine spread was in waiting, which was partaken
of with pleasure. After a social time of two hours we returned to the hotel.

July 21, in the morning, the committee, in carriages, took
us to the beach. After viewing the cottages, etc., we drove
to the strawberry ranches, which are immense in size both of
territory and berries. A gentleman told me that he had
gathered berries eight inches in circumference. In the
afternoon we took the train for San Jose, and were met by
a committee before reaching the city.

[From the *Pacific States Watchman* of July 25.]

GRAND OVATION TO THE FATHER OF THE ANCIENT ORDER
OF UNITED WORKMEN AT SAN JOSE.

"No finer public demonstration in honor of any man
was ever witnessed in the Garden City, than the welcome
extended to Father Upchurch there last Tuesday evening,
the 21st inst. The enterprising home Lodges, Mt. Hamilton, No. 43, and Enterprise, No. 17, earnestly seconded by
Magnolia, No. 6, Degree of Honor, had long been preparing for the event, and none of the Lodges of the county
had been behind in furthering the work. The welcome
amounted to an ovation that did honor to the noble Workmen of Santa Clara County, and was one that Father Upchurch can never recall without feelings of warm gratitude
and pleasure. Following the grand tribute paid him by his
brethren of San Francisco and Alameda Counties, as well
as by those of other points in the State since visited, the
San Jose reception must have conclusively proven to the
founder of the Order, if that were needed, that the Workmen of California appreciated to the fullest extent their
obligations to him.

"Father Upchurch was met at the depot by a large number of members of the Santa Clara County Lodges. He was accompanied by an escort of Select Knights from San Francisco Legion, No. 2, and Upchurch Legion, No. 9, of Oakland, who, with members of their families and lady friends, had gone down to participate in the ceremonies. A procession was formed to conduct the distinguished visitor to his hotel, which was composed of brethren from a dozen different Lodges, besides Grand Officers McPherson, Jordan, Murgotten, Danforth, and Loud, in carriages, Select Knights and members. The founder was drawn in a four-in-hand carriage. The cavalcade presented a fine appearance, the knights forming a striking feature thereof.

"The reception in the evening took place at the California Theater, the interior of which had been decorated in a very beautiful manner with flowers in all manner of devices, the work of the ladies of Magnolia Lodge, Degree of Honor. The address of welcome was delivered by Brother Adam Bane, of Mt. Hamilton, and at its conclusion the entire audience arose and gave, six times, three cheers for the honored guest of the evening.

"As he arose to acknowledge the ovation, a string was pulled that loosed upon his head, from a beam, a perfect shower of flowers, while more than two hundred bouquets were thrown and placed on the stage in the way of floral offerings, and nothing could have been finer. After Father Upchurch's response, which was in his usual quiet vein, eloquent speeches were made by Past Grand Master Workman William H. Jordan, of Oakland, Rev. J. H. Ingram, of San Jose, Grand Master McPherson, and M. T. Brewer. There were also recitations, musical selections, etc., and the exercises concluded with a splendid banquet and dance."

I must confess that I was completely surprised, not anticipating anything like such a demonstration. I felt like one born out of season, not being able to express my gratitude and appreciation for the marked respect that was paid to me. It shows conclusively that the people here, as well as in other parts of the Jurisdiction, appreciate my labors in the interests of humanity. Fraternity seems to predominate.

They are alive to the best interest of the Order, rendering relief to the widows and orphans, and assisting the members to assist themselves. The banquet hall had been prepared to seat four hundred guests, the tables being supplied with all the good things that this favored land affords. One thousand and six hundred partook of refreshments, and many baskets were left untouched.

July 22 a committee took Brother McPherson and myself to drive around the city. We went out to Mineral Springs, a fine drive through a magnificent country, looming up in all its romantic beauty. In the afternoon we drove out to the silk factory; saw them at work manufacturing the fabric in its various forms. From here we drove over the city, and had a fine view from the dome of the Court House. The view is grand, and well may it be called the Garden City. It might very appropriately be termed the garden of the world.

In the evening we visited the hall of Hamilton Lodge, No. 43, and Enterprise, No. 17, and after going through with the business of the evening, several very instructive speeches were made. Upon the whole we had a grand time.

[From the *Pacific States Watchman* of July 25, 1885.]

PRESENTATION.

" On Wednesday evening, the 22d inst, during the progress of a Lodge meeting, in the hall of Mt. Hamilton Lodge, San Jose, Wm. Vintner, Past Master Workman, in an eloquent and pleasing speech, presented Father Upchurch, in behalf of Enterprise, No. 17, and Mt. Hamilton,

No. 43, with an elegant, gold-headed cane, the staff being a rare orange limb, and the handle inlaid with quartz, and engraved as follows:—

"Presented to Father J. J. Upchurch by Enterprise Lodge, No. 17, and Mount Hamilton Lodge, No. 43, A. O. U. W., San Jose, California, July 22, 1885.

"This magnificent cane was manufactured by Bro. Edward B. Lewis, one of the leading jewelers of San Jose, and its chaste, unique, and artistic design reflects great credit on the designer and manufacturer. Brother Vintner, in his speech, pointed with good effect the triumphs of peace as compared with those secured by the warrior. In an impassioned manner he pointed with pride to Father Upchurch as one of the great organizers in the interests of humanity of the nineteenth century. Father Upchurch received the testimonial with evident satisfaction, and in a fervid and emotional manner, thanked them for it."

This beautiful present I cherish very highly, and it will be retained by me in remembrance of the noble-hearted Brothers who presented it. I trust that happiness and prosperity may attend them through life.

GOES TO LIVERMORE.

July 23 arrived at Livermore at ten A. M., and stopped at the Livermore House. After dinner took a carriage and drove into the country; saw many fine vineyards; visited a winery under construction, that was being made of concrete. In the evening, the members of the Order formed in line and marched to the Rink, where Grand Master McPherson, W. H. Jordan, Brother Smith and myself delivered addresses. We had a large audience of both ladies and gentlemen, and great interest was taken in the work of the Order. I trust that much good may result from their meetings.

BACK TO SAN FRANCISCO.

July 24 reached San Francisco at nine o'clock, A. M., and called at the office of Brother Jordan for mail. In the evening I attended District meeting, No. 4, with Yerba Buena, No. 36, and four other Lodges in attendance. Past Grand Master Workman Wm. H. Barnes, myself, and several other Brothers addressed the meeting, I think with profit to those present. We had a very pleasant meeting, and after the close of the exercises, I returned to the hotel at half-past eleven o'clock, P. M.

VISITS THE PIONEER WOOLEN MILLS.

July 25, having been invited to visit the Pioneer Woolen Mills, I did so in the morning, accompanied by Grand Foreman Danforth and Brother Hoag, a representative of the *Pacific States Watchman.* On entering the office I was introduced to Brother Platt, the superintendent of the mill; was in the office about half an hour, when the employés of the mill—members of the Order—came in to the number of twenty. I was introduced to each of them; and the superintendent, in behalf of the Workmen of the mill, presented me with a splendid pair of blankets, with "Upchurch" woven across the center. He stated that they were of the best material and workmanship that could be had, and cost fifty dollars, and that the Queen of England could not get any better. He also stated that each of the Workmen contributed his part of the labor in producing them. I replied, accepting the present with many thanks, assuring them that they would be kept in remembrance of the generous-hearted Workmen from whom they were received. Brother Danforth then made a few appropriate remarks. After the business of the office was over, we

were conducted through the mill by the gentlemanly superintendent, who took a great deal of pains in explaining the
different processes of manufacture. When through at the
mill, we repaired to the residence of Brother Platt, and
after an introduction to his amiable wife and daughter, partook of a bountiful repast. In the afternoon I accompanied
young Mr. Poland to Woodward's Zoological Gardens. In
the museum were many fine specimens of birds, beasts,
reptiles, fish, etc.

VISITS GOLDEN DAWN, DEGREE OF HONOR.

In the evening, Golden Dawn Lodge, Degree of Honor,
invited me to be present at their regular semi-monthly meet-
ing, with the Grand Officers of this Jurisdiction, Past Grand
Master Workman William H. Barnes, Grand Foreman
Danforth, Grand Lecturer Reading, Deputy Grand Master
Poland, District Deputy Grand Master Payson, the install-
ing officers, and District Deputy Grand Master McDonald.
During the installation ceremony the chairs were occupied
as follows: Past Grand Master Upchurch, Grand Master
Payson, Grand Foreman Barnes, Grand Overseer Danforth,
Grand Guide McDonald. After installation, a musical
selection for two violins, two cornets, and piano was rendered by Golden Dawn Band, and a piano solo by Miss
Danforth. Bro. S. F. Poland officiated as Master of Ceremonies. Then Bro. Sam. Booth was called upon to extend
the welcome and hospitalities of Golden Dawn Lodge to
their honored guest, which he did in his usual happy manner. By universal request, Brother Barnes, in his inimita-
ble style, sang a couple of humorous songs. The guest
and Lodge members were then invited to the supper-room,
where a bountiful collation had been duly laid, and when

ample justice had been done to this part of the entertainment, Brothers Barnes, Danforth, McDonald, and myself were called upon for remarks, all responding in brief speeches. Brother Booth put his response in the shape of the following song:—

GOLDEN DAWN'S GREETING TO FATHER UPCHURCH.

I'll sing to you a modern song, made by a modern pate,
Of an antiquated Workman with a very small estate;
Who earned a modest livelihood in Pennsylvania State,
And comes to see his children, living by the Golden Gate—

　This fine American gentleman all of the modern time.

When he was born no songs were sung, no flattering things
　　were said;
Nor did kind fortune on his path her bounteous blessings
　　shed;
Nor was the realm of knowledge to his youthful vision
　　spread,
But every day he had to say he'd earned his daily bread—

　Like a fine American gentleman, etc.

As one by one the years rolled on, he grew to man's estate,
And then, no doubt, he cast about until he found his mate.
Then, like a loyal citizen, he began to populate
The State of Pennsylvania at a very rapid rate—

　Like a fine American gentleman, etc.

To keep his numerous family well clothed, and housed,
　　and fed,
And make provision for them 'gainst the time when he was
　　dead,

A mutual protection plan kept running through his head,
And lo ! our "Ancient Order" on its glorious mission sped.

From this fine American gentleman, etc.

From State to State the Order spread among the great and
small,
And Lodges organized in every city and town hall;
And thousands of good citizens to join them got a call,
And look on 'Father Upchurch' as the Daddy of them
all—

This fine American gentleman, etc.

But not alone the Brethern come their filial love to pay,
The Sisters of the Order too, would like a word to-say;
And Golden Dawn extends to-night her hospitality
And loving greeting to the Father of Fraternity—

This fine American gentleman all of the modern time.

At a late hour the festivities were concluded, and the
ladies of Golden Dawn, Degree of Honor, No. 10, did
themselves great honor, and afforded their guest great
pleasure, by their cordial reception and pleasant entertainment.

July 26 attended meeting of Picnic Committee, and took
dinner with Brother Whitten.

July 27 called at the office of Brother Jordan for mail, and
wrote home, notifying them of the shipment of blankets.
In the afternoon, visited, with Brother Reading, the pano-
rama of the Battle of Waterloo. The sight filled me with
sadness, everything was gotten up so very natural. It is a
grand painting. In the evening, went to California Theater
with Brothers Loud and Danforth.

VISIT TO WOODLAND.

" The reception of Father Upchurch at this place, July
28, by the various Lodges of the Ancient Order of United

Workmen of this county, was a grand success, notwithstanding the fact that many of the members are at present out of town. The distinguished guest arrived on the quarter to three o'clock, P. M., train, with Brother Danforth, and was met at the depot by the Reception Committee, and taken to the Byrnes Hotel, where rooms had been engaged. Soon many of the prominent citizens, members of the Order, and those who were not, called to pay their respects to the pioneer Workman, and welcome him to the Sylvan City. After introduction and hand-shaking, our carriages were ordered, and the party spent a pleasant hour driving about the city. Father Upchurch expressed himself much pleased at the indications of thrift and prosperity visible on every hand.

"The grand event, however, was the reception at the Masonic Hall, in the evening. The hall, which in itself is a model of beauty and would do credit to a city many times larger than Woodland, was beautifully decorated for the occasion by a committee of ladies, consisting of Mrs. J. Westlake, Mrs. G M. Bently, and Mrs. H. Ervin. The artistic manner in which the hall was decorated was sufficient evidence of those ladies' taste. Conspicuous among the decorations was a fine picture of the honorable founder of our beloved Order, encircled with evergreens, and crowned with flowers. Before eight o'clock the hall was crowded to its utmost capacity, standing room being at a premium.

" Professor McCormell called the assembly to order, and introduced Brother E. Danforth, of San Francisco, Grand Foreman, who delivered a brief address, explaining the beneficial features of the Order, and showing that it costs less than five cents per day to each member, to insure their families the sum of two thousand dollars in case of death.

After Brother Danforth concluded, Professor McCormell introduced Father Upchurch, whose appearance on the stage was the signal for prolonged applause.

" When silence was restored, the speaker, after thanking the audience for their cordial reception, spoke briefly on the inception and progress of the Order. He stated the difficulties and discouragements that had to be met and overcome in the beginning, but that now it had grown to be the most powerful Fraternal and Beneficiary institution among men; its influence for good was felt throughout the length and breadth of the land.

" Father Upchurch was listened to with profound attention. Though, as he says, he makes no pretense to being a public speaker, his ideas are clear and his words well chosen.

" The next on the programme was the recitation of the ' Prize Poem,' by Sam Booth, published in the *Watchman* of July 11, by a little Miss May Powers. The little lady acquitted herself most charmingly, and was applauded most heartily.

" After the literary exercises were concluded, the banquet hall was thrown open, and refreshments, such as fruit, ice-cream, cake, etc., were served. The chairs were removed from the center of the main hall, and a pleasant hour was spent in music and dancing.

" The reception of Father Upchurch was an event that will long be remembered by the people of Woodland."— *Correspondent Pacific States Watchman, August 8.*

This is one of the most pleasant, as well as beautiful little cities that I have had the pleasure of visiting while on the coast. The people are generous to a fault. They left nothing undone that would tend to make my visit an enjoyable one.

July 29 I visited the vineyard and raisin factory of Mr. R. B. Blair, three-fourths of a mile from town. Here is the finest grapery I have seen, though not the largest. It produces from five to seventeen tons per acre, with twenty-five acres of the finest peaches, plums, prunes, and apricots I have ever seen. I was shown through his evaporating-house, where tons of dried fruits are made annually.

GOES TO COLUSA.

At thirty-five minutes past eleven o'clock we bade farewell to our friend and took the train for Colusa, where I met

Brother Jordan. We alighted at the town of Williams, about ten miles from Colusa. Here the Committee of Reception was waiting, and we were placed in carriages and driven across a lovely country to Colusa, a pretty little town on the banks of the Sacramento River, in Colusa County, and put down at the Colusa House.

At four o'clock, P. M., Supreme Foreman Wm. H. Jordan, assisted by Bro. E. Danforth and myself, instituted Colusa Legion, No. 11, Select Knights, in Workman's Hall, with twenty-two charter members. In the evening, the Workmen formed in front of the hotel and escorted Brothers Jordan, Danforth, and myself to the theater, which was packed to its fullest capacity. Judge Bridgeford delivered the address of welcome, when he introduced me to the audience. I was received with enthusiasm. I addressed them, after which Brothers Jordan, Danforth, and Black delivered fine addresses in the interests of the Order, showing the advantage to be gained by becoming members thereof.

FROM THE "PACIFIC STATES WATCHMAN."

" The reception tendered Father Upchurch by the Workmen of Colusa County, took place at Colusa on Wednesday evening, July 29, and it was in every respect a splendid ovation. The theater was packed full, and all could not get in, while the enthusiasm was unbounded. People came to the reception from all parts of the country; five carriages filled with members came thirty miles, and one brother came seventy miles. Many came from Marysville and other points outside the county.

" The exercises in the theater comprised a vocal quartette by Mrs. Chas. Whitney, Mrs. Kate Sherman, and Misses Graves and Pryor; an introductory speech by Judge Bridgeford; addresses by Father Upchurch and Past Master W. H. Jordan, of San Francisco—which the Colusa *Sun* characterized as a very fine oration—an address by J. S. Black, of Butte City, and two songs by the Ancient Order of United Workmen Glee Club.

" The exercises were followed by a general hand-shaking with Father Upchurch, and then came dancing and a fine supper at the Colusa House, to which nearly four hundred persons sat down.

"Grand Foreman Danforth and Past Grand Master Jordan were the only Grand Officers present, and they are both of the opinion that the Colusa reception was ahead of anything that has yet taken place in the State."

July 30 Judge Bridgeford took Brothers Danforth, Jordan, and myself in a carriage and drove into the country, which is the finest wheat-growing district in the State. Last year the county produced more than eleven million bushels, or one-fourth of all the wheat grown in the State. We drove to Judge Bridgeford's ranch and had some fine melons. On our return to the hotel, some brother had sent in to me a fine melon that weighed fifty pounds, and named it "Pea Nut," which we cut, and it proved to be a splendid one indeed. On leaving this place, Bro. W. G. Puig presented me with a beautiful finger ring, which I will cherish as a memento of my trip to this lovely little town and country. At eleven o'clock, A. M., Judge Bridgeford took us in his carriage to Williams, where we took the train, Brothers Jordan and Danforth for San Francisco, and I for Sacramento. Williams is a station on the California & Oregon Railroad. It has a Lodge of twenty-two members. On the next evening after the meeting at Colusa, they received fifteen applications for membership, which was a grand accession to that Lodge.

GOES TO VIRGINIA CITY.

I stopped over a few hours at Sacramento to wait for Grand Lecturer E. M. Reading, who was to accompany me to Virginia City, Nevada. At half past seven o'clock, A. M., on the morning of the 31st, we reached Reno. Here a Committee of Reception, Brothers Dunne, Holman, Cowan, and Gladding, were in waiting from Gold Hill and Virginia City. After breakfast, a coach and four was driven up, and we started for the Great Bonanza. I was much surprised at the beauty of this valley, its fine residences, fragrant flower gardens, well-cultivated farms, and all watered from the snow-clad mountains that loom up on either side. There is a splendid mountain road the whole distance of twenty miles. We stopped at Steamboat Springs, celebrated for its medicinal properties. The water and steam gushes forth from a rent in the rock of the mountain hot enough to boil an egg in three minutes. The shock of an earthquake a few years ago opened the rock six inches wide. There are splendid accommodations for visiting invalids. I thought of what the Dutchman said, that "hell was not a mile from this spot." Only a few rods away is a cold water spring. We again entered the carriage, and started up Geiger's grade; passed Robber's Turn, and Dead Man's Point, which derived their names from the many robberies and murders that had been committed at these points in early days.

AT VIRGINIA CITY.

Arrived at Virginia City at half past twelve o'clock, P. M., and stopped at the International Hotel, where rooms had been engaged for us. In the evening the Select Knights, in full uniform, formed in front of the hotel, and escorted us to the Piper Opera House, which was packed to its utmost capacity with the most orderly audience I ever saw. Men stood in the aisles for two hours, and not a dozen left the hall. The proceedings are better described by the *Inter-Mountain Workman*, as follows:—

" The brethren of our Order at Gold Hill and Virginia City, Nevada, had Father Upchurch with them on July 31. It was a royal occasion, and one that will long be remembered by all who had the privilege of participating therein."

The Virginia City *Enterprise* had the following glowing account in a recent issue:—

" J. J. Upchurch, the famous founder of the Ancient Order of United Workmen, arrived in this city, from San Francisco, shortly after noon yesterday. Capt. P. J. Dennis and Heber Holman, of Storey Lodge, No. 3, and J. F. Gladding and A. G. Cowan, members of Gold Hill Lodge, No. 2, who went to Reno to meet him, brought him up from Storey in a four-in-hand carriage. He found plenty of members of the Order to receive him and shake hands with him, and during the afternoon he took a look about town. In the evening the grand reception tendered him by the members of the Order in this section, took place at Piper's Opera House. The doors were opened at seven o'clock, and people poured in from all quarters. At eight o'clock the spacious theater was crowded full, and no more could get in. The gallery was closely packed, and all the standing room down below fully occupied, as also were the stage boxes and wings. It is estimated that fully fifteen hundred persons were present. The audience was largely composed of ladies, and on the stage were seated prominent members of the Order beside Father Upchurch, and in the rear, next to the scenery, were arranged a double row of Select Knights, in uniform. These are of a higher degree of the Order, and presented a very handsome appearance.

" Father Upchurch is a fatherly-looking gentleman of sixty-five years of age, with gray hair, white goatee, and no moustache. He is unpretentious in his manner and speech, and looks more like a plain farmer or a third-class Postmaster than the famous founder of one of the very best and most popular Orders or fraternal organizations in the United States. Naturally caring for and fraternally regarding his fellow-man, all feel naturally attracted toward him. Few men in this world have more true and earnest friends than good Father Upchurch.

"After a fine overture by the Virginia Orchestra Band—-
Professor Zimmer, leader—J. C. Harlow, Grand Foreman of
the Ancient Order of United Workman in this State, called
the assemblage to order, and made a well-delivered introductory address, speaking of the occasion of this grand meeting
to do honor to the distinguished founder of the Ancient
Order of United Workmen. It was a Workmen's welcome
to a Workman. He introduced Bro. J. A. Stephens, who
delivered the address of welcome.

"Mr. Stephens is a natural orator, and he threw his whole
soul into the spirit of the occasion. He referred to Father
Upchurch in eloquent terms, as the founder of the Order.
He saw the needs of his fellow Workmen, and devoted the
energies of his mind to the perfection of a plan to ameliorate and improve their condition. Labor, to be respected,
must respect itself among mankind as well as at home. It
must command the respect of the rich, and thus influence,
and induce a willingness to divide the accumulations of
wealth. He recapitulated the history and career of Father
Upchurch, and related what he had done. The Order in
the United States already numbered over one hundred and
forty-five thousand, and he predicted that before the end of
the present century the Order would number over one million of fearless Workmen. He closed with a cordial greeting to Father Upchurch, 'Such as we have we give unto
you.'

"'The founder of the Order of United Workmen came
forward, and was introduced amid universal applause. He
disclaimed being a gifted orator, but would give a little plain
talk. He spoke easily and without much effort, yet not in
a loud voice. He expressed his gratification at the way he
was received on the occasion, and could say with an earnest
heart that he appreciated the honor conferred. He was one
of those who had followed railroading for thirty-eight years,
as a working mechanic in the shops. He saw the disadvantage under which his fellow-laborers, as well as himself, were
suffering, most of which was brought about by their own
imprudence, and felt impelled to study out some plan by
which their condition might be bettered. There were

Trades Unions, but he found them all selfish, and their aims and ends were detrimental to the interest of the employers as well as those of the workingman. He thought he would try and bring them into an Order that would obviate and harmonize all their difficulties, make them united in their plans for mutual improvement and benefit, and make provision for the future; and he was happy to see that his object was accomplished. He gave a brief history of the earliest formation of the Order. Jefferson Lodge, No. 1, was instituted at Meadville, Pennsylvania, October 27, 1868, with only fourteen members. He showed them the work he had conceived, and the next morning a number of them demanded that the word 'white,' should be stricken from the Constitution. This he squarely refused to do, and the Recorder refunded to every man his entrance fee. On the 3d of November, the second meeting night, he was more than gratified at having six of the members come in and pay their initiation fee the second time. One by one new members joined, 'and we began to feel in a flourishing condition.' Why he gave it the name 'Ancient,' was because he wanted to give the origin and progress of the arts and sciences, and to do this, he had to refer to ancient history, which showed him that Tubal Cain was the founder and instructor of all who worked in brass, iron, and other metals. He then referred to the building of the city of Babylon and Solomon's temple, so well described in holy writ. The Order had opposition from the very first, from other Orders, as well as from Workmen themselves; but in spite of all opposition, thank God, the Order has flourished until to-day we number more than one hundred and fifty-two thousand Workmen, whose families repose to-night secure from the contingencies of adversity and death. Multiply one hundred and fifty-two thousand by five, the estimated number of each family, and we have seven hundred and sixty thousand souls directly interested in the growth and prosperity of our beloved Order. He congratulated the members of the Jurisdiction on their success, with a membership of three thousand already, and rapidly increasing in members and prosperity. He was proud to see so many ladies pres-

ent, as it shows the interest they take in the Order, which
was formed for the benefit not only of their fathers, brothers, and husbands, but for themselves and their children.
He addressed a few pertinent remarks to the Select Knights
on the stage, reminding them of their obligations to stand
by each other, and to draw their swords in defense of inno
cence and virtue, and, thanking his audience for the earnest
attention shown to his remarks, he sat down, amid great
applause.

" Grand Foreman Harlow now read telegrams from James
Sullivan, Grand Master Workman, and J. W. Kinsley, Supreme Representative Ancient Order of United Workmen,
Helena, Montana, congratulating Father Upchurch on his
very gratifying reception in this city.

MESSAGES FROM ABSENT WORKMEN.

" ' HELENA, Mont., July 30, 1885.

" ' J. J. UPCHURCH, care of J. F. Gladding: Accept my
compliments and the assurance that the brotherhood about
you fairly represents the Order of this Jurisdiction.

JAMES SULLIVAN, *Grand Master Workman.*'

" ' HELENA, Mont., July 30, 1885.

" ' J. F. GLADDING: I congratulate the brethren of Storey
County, the first to extend a public reception to Father
Upchurch within our borders. The honor of our Jurisdic-
tion is confidently intrusted to worthy hands. .

JAMES SULLIVAN, *Grand Master Workman.*'

" ' HELENA, Mont., July 30, 1885.

" ' J. F. GLADDING: I join with you in welcoming within
our borders Father Upchurch, the Abou Ben Adhem of
the nineteenth century.

J. W. KINSLEY, *Supreme Representative.*'

" A double quartette of four ladies and five gentlemen,
principally from Gold Hill, now appeared on the stage, and
sang, in beautiful style, 'The Fisherman and His Child,'
which was very deservedly encored.

"The following letter was received from Grand Recorder Thornburn, of Ogden, Utah:—

"'Ogden, Utah, July 28, 1885.
"'J. F. Gladding, Secretary of Committee —*Dear Sir and Brother:* Time and distance alone prevent me from following my very strong desire to be present with you at the reception of Father Upchurch. The reverence of one for his parents is sure evidence of his early training. The respect of the members of a fraternal society for the originator of their system of government is also a sure indication of their standard of membership. Therefore, I know that Past Supreme Master Workman J. J. Upchurch, the founder of the Ancient Order of United Workmen, will fare well at your hands. At this place I had the pleasure of becoming personally acquainted with him, and am sure that every member of the Order will esteem it an honored privilege to cordially grasp the hand of this great benefactor of the widows and orphans of our brotherhood. I trust the occasion will redound to the advantage of our Order, be creditable to the brethren, and acceptable to the grand old man. Fraternally yours,
D. Thornburn, *Grand Recorder.*'

"An original poem, by W. G. Hyde, Recorder of Gold Hill Lodge, Ancient Order of United Workmen, was a feature of the evening. It was read in a fine voice and style by the gentleman himself, and received with applause. It was a very well-written and creditable effort, and was followed by another fine overture by the band.

PRESENTED WITH A SILVER BRICK.

"The presentation of a silver brick was made by Past Master A. G. Cowan, in a very neat, well-delivered address, in the name of the Order. It is a very handsome little brick, appropriately engraved, and inclosed in a neat box or casket, and when the well-pleased recipient took it into his hands, rounds of applause resounded throughout the theater. He expressed his hearty approval of this beautiful and valuable offering in a very appropriate little speech of thanks, and said he should remember the brethren of the Order and the beautiful city of Virginia as long as he remained on the top of the earth.

" E. M. Reading, Grand Lecturer of the Ancient Order of United Workmen, of California, was introduced and made a very pleasing address, full of amusing recitals, which drew forth frequent applause. He represented the beautiful character of the Order in an effective style.

" The double quartette now sung, ' Come Where the Lilies Bloom,' with fine effect and great applause, and this concluding the regular exercises, the floor was cleared for dancing. While this was being done, the audience was given an opportunity to visit Father Upchurch, and shake his good old hand, which all proceeded to do. At a late, or early, hour this morning the theater was still densely crowded with merry dancers."

VISITING THE MINES.

August 1 Bro. Jerome Caldwell presented me with some fine specimens of silver ore from the Comstock Lode from the one thousand six hundred and fifty foot level, worth eighteen thousand dollars per ton. In the last twenty years four hundred million dollars were taken out of these mountains. At this mine there is a pump one hundred inches in diameter, and a fly-wheel thirty-four feet in diameter, which weighs one hundred and five tons. We also visited the Combination Shaft. The largest pump I ever saw is at this place—high-pressure steam cylinder, thirty-five inches in diameter, with ten-foot stroke; low-pressure cylinder, seventy inches in diameter, with ten-foot stroke, and pumps one hundred inches in diameter, which lift one hundred thousand gallons of water per day. This shaft is three thousand one hundred and fifty feet deep. The water is emptied into the Sutro Tunnel, sixteen hundred feet below the surface. At this shaft the valves of the pump are worked by a separate engine; they also have a pump that gets up a pressure of one thousand pounds per inch. This machinery was built and set up by a firm in San Francisco. There are sixty thousand tons of iron under the surface at this shaft. We also visited the Hale & Norcross shaft. I fully intended to go down this shaft, but when I got there the steam was coming out of it so fast that I changed my mind. Here I got some very fine specimens of ore. We then visited the Yellow Jacket Mine, of Gold Hill. Brother Estep, Superintendent, presented me with fine specimens of gold and silver ore combined. After showing us through the building, we returned to our hotel. In the evening, attended Lodge meeting at Gold Hill and had a grand time. There were several addresses, and after the business of the Lodge was transacted, the doors of the banquet hall were thrown open, when all sat down to a magnificent supper prepared by the ladies. At a late hour all retired to their several places of abode, highly elated at the success of the evening.

AT CARSON.

August 2 District Deputy Grand Master Workman Gladding and Grand Foreman Harlow, took us in carriages to Carson City; went through Gold Hill, Silver City, and Gold Canyon. Not much gold is being taken out at the present time, on account of there being no water for washing. We stopped at the Mexican Quartz Mills, four miles from Carson City. I think there are about eighty stamps which crush the quartz into powder. The quicksilver holds the precious metal and then carries off the refuse. It is a grand operation, so much so that with my limited knowledge of it I am unable to describe it. After being shown through the mill, we proceeded on to Carson City.

10

The brothers of Carson met us at the hotel, when the parlors were thrown open to us and we held an informal meeting, with many introductions and hand-shakings. Brother Reading and myself gave them a short talk. After dinner we visited the railroad shops with the master mechanic. They are admirably arranged for the work of the road. We then visited the State House, which is a magnificent building, well arranged; were in the office of the State Zoologist, and were shown a great number of fine specimens that had just been returned from the New Orleans Exposition. We then visited the library and State Treasurer's office. Here I was introduced to the holder of the public funds of the State, who, I think, is the right man in the right place, as his size would deter anyone from assault, for fear there would be nothing left of them. After a social chat, we were driven to the State Prison, where we were introduced to Warden Bell, who is a courteous gentleman. He took every pains to show us everything of interest about the place. The floor of the prison yard is solid rock, there having been forty-five feet of rock taken off for the building of the Capitol, prison, and other buildings. Here are tracks of horses, and elephants whose track measures twelve inches across, birds of many varieties, plain and large tracks of the sand-hill crane, eighteen inches apart; there are also tracks of human beings about three feet apart, supposed to be of the present stature. There are tracks of the wolf with the ball of the foot about two and a half inches across; in one place there are tracks of three persons— we judge from their size to be the old man leading a child and the old lady bringing up the rear. Here the impression of the carcass of an elephant is to be seen imbedded in the rock. When the top rock was taken off two tusks were found, one where the animal lay, the other about twenty feet away. They were eight feet long and in a good state of preservation, and it took four men to carry them. Having seen all that was interesting, we returned to the city. Carson is a beautiful place, situated in a valley with fine shade trees and some magnificent residences. The brothers of Carson, as well as Virginia, seemed to be very much interested in the work of the Order. After supper we took a carriage for Virginia City, arriving there at half past eight o'clock, P. M.

THE SUTRO TUNNEL.

August 3 Brothers Dunne and Brown called for us at nine o'clock, A. M., with a carriage, and took us to the mouth of the Sutro Tunnel, seven miles distant. Here a car was placed at our disposal, and we went into the Tunnel about five thousand feet. It was extremely warm. This tunnel takes the water from the mines, one thousand and six hundred feet below the surface. Six hundred thousand gallons of water pass through here every twenty-four hours, and are discharged into the Carson Valley. It is so hot that you can hardly leave your hand in it. We then went to Dayton and took lunch. This is a little town of five hundred inhabitants, with a Lodge of eighty members, which shows for itself what interest is taken in the Order there. We then took a carriage through Gold Canyon for Virginia City. At Gold Hill I had a fine lot of gold and silver quartz presented to me by Bro. Adam Bay.

AT RENO.

At half past five o'clock took the train for Reno, accompanied by Brother Estep. In the evening we attended Lodge meeting. There was a good turn-out of members, and especially of the ladies. Had some excellent music, both vocal and instrumental, and addresses by Brother Reading, several members, and myself, and after business was through with we partook of a fine collation in the banquet hall adjoining the Lodge hall, and had an enjoyable time generally.

August 4 was driven around town, which has some very fine buildings, among them the school buildings. There are about two thousand inhabitants in this pretty litttle city. We then visited the insane asylum, which has one hundred and fifty inmates. One of the patients presented me with a "bill of sale," as he called it, for the whole establishment. Another of the inmates called me by name, and handed me a petition signed by twenty-eight patients, requesting me to hand it to the District Attorney, who would let them out.

RETURNS TO SAN FRANCISCO.

At half past eight o'clock, P. M., we took the train for San Francisco. Took breakfast on the 5th at Sacramento, and arrived at San Francisco at half past ten o'clock, P. M. I went direct to the office of Brother Jordan, and got letters from home, stating that my wife and grandchild were sick. At half past four o'clock I took dinner at the residence of Grand Foreman E. Danforth, with Brothers Barnes, Poland, and a number of ladies. Had an excellent time, and all seemed to enjoy it hugely.

August 6 a man calling himself Thomas Francis, a brother of Edward Francis, who at one time worked at the railroad shop in Steelville, Missouri, stated that he had lost all his money at mining, and could not get work in the city, but had been offered a job on a farm at Stockton at twenty-five dollars per month and board, but had no money to get there with. I loaned him one dollar and fifty cents, and he promised to write me at home. In the evening I went with Brother Jordan to Oakland, and visited Pacific Lodge, No. 7; the hall being well filled, Brother Barnes and myself addressed the audience. The members of this Jurisdiction are full of fraternity, consequently take a great interest in the growth and prosperity of the Order. Had a find collation of fruits and melons, and remained with Brother Jordan over night.

August 7 returned to San Francisco, and in the evening visited Occidental Lodge, No. 6, of Oakland. A number of speeches were made, one of which was by Bro. W. H. Jordan, and one by myself. We had a very good meeting, and I believe much good will result from it. At the close we had a fine collation, which was enjoyed by all present. After adjournment we returned to San Francisco.

August 8 I was in my room nearly all day, watching the procession in honor of U. S. Grant. In the evening I visited, with Grand Master McPherson and Grand Lecturer Reading, Harmony Lodge, No. 9; had a very pleasant time, and, I trust, a profitable meeting. This Lodge has three hundred and forty members, pays ten dollars a week sick benefit, and has over one thousand dollars in bank. They are alive to the interest of the Order.

GOES TO LOS ANGELES.

August 9 Grand Master McPherson and myself left San Francisco at half past three o'clock, P. M., for Los Angeles, on the Central Pacific; going up the Tehachepi Mountain, saw what is called the Loop. It was a new idea to me, how to get to the top of a mountain. Took breakfast at Mohave, three hundred and eighty-one miles from San Francisco. This station is on the edge of Mohave Desert, and is the

terminus of the Tulare and San Joaquin Valley. All provisions must be transported over the mountains, and the water
is carried in pipes from a spring ten miles away. There are
several stores and residences here, and the railroad company has a round-house for fifteen engines, a machine shop,
and a large freight warehouse. Freight wagons are always
on hand to unload bullion and other freight, and carry them
to different parts of the country and Mexico. From this
point there is a line of stages running to all the principal
towns, the fare being about twenty cents per mile. The
Atlantic & Pacific Railroad forms a junction at this place.

This district produces nothing but a species of sage
brush and cactus, which grows from ten to twenty feet high.
Its wood is used for making paper, which is said to be equal
to the best bank-note paper.

Between Sand Creek and Lancaster, off to the left, I saw
what appeared to be a fine lake. The waves seemed to roll
naturally; but on inquiry I learned it was what is known as
the mirage of the desert, formed of sand and alkali. Lancaster is a station with half a dozen buildings, just south of
the desert. Here is a flouring mill, and it is said that the
soil produces well when watered. There were some fruit
trees and about one hundred grape-vines that looked thrifty.
At Newhall Station, a town of half a dozen houses, were
piles of two-inch gas pipe, to be sent to the oil wells. At
this point there is a good hotel, and a short distance from
here is the San Fernando Tunnel, six thousand nine hundred feet long, with a grade of one hundred sixteen feet
to the mile.

SAN FERNANDO.

"At San Fernando Father Upchurch and Grand Master
McPherson were met by a Committe of Welcome, consisting
of the following members: James Booth, J. F. C. Johnson,

J. S. Mills of Pasadena, Al. Cobler, Walter Deveraux, W. F. Poor, Robert Sharp, F. A. Haskell, W. Myers, Dr. E. T. Shoemaker, E. C. Glidden, J. L. Livingstone of the *Express*, and Robert Farrell. The committee from Los Angeles boarded the down train for San Fernando, and were introduced to Father Upchurch and Duncan McPherson, Grand Master Workman, by Deputy Supreme Commander of the Select Knights, Ancient Order of United Workmen, Al. Cobler; after which H. C. Hubbard, Master Workman of San Fernando Lodge, No. 214, introduced the several members of his Lodge, who were presented to Father Upchurch. In an interview, our distinguished visitor, on his way to the city, expressed himself more than delighted with his reception in Nevada and California. This being his first visit to the Pacific Coast, he had been surprised at the growth and wonderful development of the country which he passed through. His visit had been a continued ovation, not only from members of the Order, but by representative men of the coast, who had done all in their power to make his journey a pleasant one, and to afford him a vast amount of information. He had looked forward with pleasure to his visit to Southern California, where the Order had made such wonderful strides in a short time, and whose world-wide reputation for hospitality had no equal.

AT LOS ANGELES.

"Immediately after the arrival of the train in this city the party took carriages to the St. Elmo, where an elegant dinner was prepared for the reception of the distinguished guests and the Reception Committee. Father Upchurch and Grand Master Workman Duncan McPherson occupied the head of the table, while Deputy Supreme Commander Al. Cobler occupied the opposite end.

"After dinner the distinguished visitors made friendly visits, and then awaited the grand procession, which formed on Los Angeles and Commercial Streets in two divisions and marched under command of Al. Cobler, Marshal, with Asa Green, John Hughes, and J. D. Campbell as aids.

"The first division was composed of Los Angeles Lodge,

No. 55; Santa Ana, No. 82; Silver Star, No. 84; Anaheim, No. 85; Compton, No. 120; Wilmington, No. 130; Pasadena, No. 152; El Monte, No. 188; Southern California, No. 191; San Fernando, No. 214; Newhall, No. 218; Pomona, No. 225; East Los Angeles, No. 230; Azusa, No. 232; Alhambra, No. 233, escorted by the City Band. The second division was escorted by the Eagle Corps Band, and consisted of California Lodge, No. 1; Pomona, No. 4; San Bernardino, No. 5; Los Angeles, No. 6; and Wilmington, No. 8—Select Knights. In an opening of this division was a carriage drawn by six bright bay horses, containing Father J. J. Upchurch, Grand Master Workman Duncan McPherson, Past Master Workman Walter Lindley, President of the Day, Past Master Workman William D. Morton, Orator; second carriage, Deputy Grand Master Workman James Booth, Deputy Grand Master Workman John F. C. Johnson, Deputy Grand Master Workman John S. Mills. Following the second came the Knights, bringing up the rear of the column. The procession marched down Main Street to Fourth, to Fort, to Temple, to Spring, to Turn Verein Hall, where the parade was dismissed; and the immense throng moved into the hall to witness the reception and literary exercises.

"Following were the exercises at the hall: Overture by Eagle Corps Band; Brother Walter Lindley, Chairman, then addressed the audience in a very appropriate and instructive manner, and, of course, giving the rise and progress of the Order in Southern California, also the advantages to be derived by the families of those who associate themselves with the Order, etc. Then followed a fine quartette, after which the address of welcome by Past Master Workman W. D. Morton was delivered in a very glowing and feeling manner, to which Father Upchurch replied, giving the circumstances that caused an impression on his mind which led to the organization of the Order, its progress and benefits. He was followed by Grand Master Workman Duncan McPherson, who spoke in his pleasing and entertaining manner, giving many interesting, as well as amusing, incidents. At the close of the exercises, all partook of a sumptuous banquet, and wound up with a dance."

' VIEWING THE COUNTRY.

August 11 the Grand Master Workman and myself, accompanied by Brothers James Booth, Al. Cobler, Robert Sharp, E. C. Gladdin, and A. C. Hall, made a tour of a few of the most beautiful and noted places about Los Angeles. The San Gabriel Valley was visited, taking in Pasadena, a little town, and the surrounding country, which is lovely beyond description. There are some fine country residences and magnificent lawns, fine orange groves, and fruits of all descriptions. We went forward until we reached Sierra Madra Villa, which is a magnificent summer resort, surrounded by fine groves of orange, lemon, lime, and many others, with fountains of pure water rushing down from the mountain. After lunch we again took carriages and started for the city, passing through "Lucky" Baldwin's ranch, which consists of a whole township of the fruit land in the valley, with fine buildings, fountains, lakes, etc., also fine orange, lemon, and walnut orchards. On leaving here we called at the winery of J. L. Rose. He has fifteen hundred acres in grapes and three hundred in oranges and English walnuts. Some of the trees are fifteen inches through. The gentleman informed me that he would make two hundred and fifty thousand gallons of wine, and fifty thousand gallons of brandy from his own crops. They had just begun to gather their grapes. On leaving here we called at the San Gabriel Mission. The old mission house still stands, an adobe or sun-dried brick structure one hundred and four years old. It is in a rather bad condition; there are a number of buildings, but very few in good condition. There are quite a number of Mexicans still living here, and they also have a Lodge here.

In the evening we attended a meeting of three Lodges

at the Odd Fellows' Hall.   Ten new members were initiated
into the Ancient Order of United Workmen.   I find that
the brothers here, as well as in other parts of California, are
full of fraternity and good-fellowship.   It would give me
the greatest satisfaction if all the Jurisdictions were as much
interested in the growth and prosperity of our beloved
Order, as is the case in California.   August 12 we visited
East Los Angeles Lodge.   The hall was densely packed.
There was speaking by Grand Master McPherson, myself,
and several of the members, and we had a very social and
instructive meeting.

This Lodge is called the Baby Lodge, but if it continues
to grow in the future as it has in the past, it will become
larger than the Mother, which is of good size.   Los Angeles
is a lovely city and is making some fine improvements.
The business of the city is also increasing remarkably fast.
One great improvement could be made by removing the old
Spanish adobe houses.

GOES TO SANTA MONICA.

August 13, at half past nine o'clock, A. M., took the train
for Santa Monica, a summer resort, on the beach of old
ocean.   This place has about four hundred inhabitants.
The beach is fine, and many enjoy bathing in the surf.
Along the beach are about forty tents for the use of bath-
ers, and quite a number of our party availed themselves of
the pleasure of a plunge.

At half past three o'clock, P. M., we again took the train
for Los Angeles.   In the evening we attended the Legion of
Select Knights.   I acted as chaplain, and we took in two
comrades, conferred all the Degrees, and gave them a short
talk on our duties to the Order and each other.   Brother

Dexter, of No. 6, presented me with a fine meerschaum pipe, here.

RETURNS TO SAN FRANCISCO.

August 14, at half past twelve o'clock, P. M., took the train for San Francisco. Nothing of note occurring, we arrived at half past ten o'clock, A. M., on the 15th, and went to the Baldwin Hotel. In the evening was called upon by Past Grand Master Workmen W. H. Barnes and W. H. Jordan. I accompanied them to Alameda Lodge, No. 165, which gave a theatrical entertainment entitled the " Mistletoe." Returned to the city at half past twelve, A. M., on the 16th. As the time drew near for me to leave the brothers of California, and especially those of San Francisco and Oakland, my heart grew sad. I felt that I was parting with dear friends, whom, in all probability, I should never meet again—friends who had done all that any people could do to make my visit the most pleasant and enjoyable, every pains being taken to show me everything of interest in and around the city. I had been escorted either by the Grand Master Workmen or some of the Grand Officers throughout the State of California and Nevada. But this is not all; they had paid every expense and supplied every want since I left my home in the East, and contributed about five hundred and fifty dollars to meet my liabilities on my return home. .

On the morning of the 16th, Grand Master McPherson, Grand Foreman Danforth, and Grand Lecturer Reading took breakfast with me, when we took a carriage for the steamer. On our arrival on the wharf where passage had been secured on the steamer *Columbia*, for Portland, Oregon, having accepted an invitation to do so from the Grand Lodge of that Jurisdiction, Brothers Grand Master McPherson, Grand

Foreman Danforth, Grand Lecturer Reading, Past Grand
Master Barnes, Past Master Lewis, F. H. McDonald, A. T.
Dewey, Ex-Governor Perkins, and many others, attended me
to the steamer and placed me in charge of the officers, the
captain and a number of the officers being members of the
Order.

FAREWELL TO CALIFORNIA.

I bade adieu to my California sons with great reluctance,
feeling a deep sense of my obligations, not only to the
officers of the Grand Lodge, but to the members generally,
trusting that the spirit of fraternity might attend them
throughout all time to come. Among my fellow-passengers
were Brother John McIntosh, of San Francisco, and several others, who tried to make my trip as pleasant as possible. At half past ten o'clock, A. M., we steamed out, with
clear weather—Captain Bolles; as first officer, Augustine
Maynard; chief engineer, Van Deusen; first assistant,
Brinkerhoff. The weather continued fair until after we
passed the Golden Gate, and toward night it got very foggy
and the sea ran high; had to sound fog-horn every half
minute. Came very near running into a schooner. Was
a little sick that evening. August 17 sea was still rough;
saw a few whales; passed a number of vessels. At three
o'clock, P. M., saw land and a number of rocks standing
high out of the water.

August 18 fog was thick enough to cut; could not see
more than fifty yards from steamer; automatic fog-horn
sounded every minute. We drifted off and on from six o'clock,
A. M., to twelve. We crossed the bar at half-past twelve,
and passed the wreck of the *Great Republic*, which went
down a few years ago. It lay about two hundred yards from
the course of our steamer. There are establishments for

canning fish all along the shores of Oregon on the right, and Washington Territory on the left. Passed New Fort, under construction. A revenue cutter was lying off the fort.

ARRIVAL IN OREGON.

Arrived at Astoria, Oregon, at half past one o'clock, P. M., and was met at the wharf by a Committee of Reception and escorted to the Occidental Hotel. After dinner, Dr. Tuttle took me in a buggy around the town, which has about five thousand inhabitants, some good buildings, a Custom House, opera house, Odd Fellows, Knights of Pythias, Ancient Order of United Workmen, Masonic halls, and a number of saw-mills, that cut from fifty thousand to one hundred and fifty thousand feet of pine lumber per day, and twenty-four canning establishments for salmon. We also visited the cemetery. One headstone reads as follows:—

IN

MEMORY OF

D. McTAVISH, ESQ.,

AGED 42 YEARS,

DROWNED CROSSING THIS RIVER, MAY 22, 1814.

ASTORIA.

We then went on top of Cockscomb Mountain, and could see the bar and several bays. A fine view of the city can be had from this point. In the evening we visited Seaside Lodge, No. 12, Ancient Order of United Workmen, and had a very good attendance. Grand Master George B. Dorris was to have met me there, but failed. I addressed the members for about half an hour, and was followed by several members. This Lodge has a membership of one hundred and fourteen, and they are alive to the interest of the

Order. At the close of the exercises the Lodge closed, when I was conducted to the steamer *Telegraph*, which started for Portland at six, A. M., on the 19th. The Columbia River is a beautiful stream. The boat touched on either side.

AT PORTLAND.

We landed at Portland at two o'clock, P. M., and was met at the boat by Dr. J. A. Child, with a Committee of Reception. Entered carriage and was taken to the Gilman House. Committee of Arrangements held consultation, and decided to reduce the length of time that I was to remain in this Jurisdiction to the 6th of September.

August 20 I visited, with Doctor Child, the High School building, in course of erection. It will cost, when completed, one hundred and fifty-three thousand dollars, and is an honor to the city and the Board of Directors. It was to be completed the beginning of September. This city has about thirty-five thousand inhabitants, and is a very substantial city, with many fine and costly edifices. In the afternoon, Dr. J. H. Kessler and lady, old acquaintances from my home place, called on me at the hotel, and we had quite a pleasant chat on old times. In the evening I visited, with Doctor Child and a few others, East Portland Lodge, Ancient Order of United Workmen. The attendance was very slim, only forty members present. After an introduction, I addressed the audience, followed by several other brothers. There seemed to be a good feeling existing among the members present. On adjournment, we returned to the hotel.

August 21 I visited Brother F. Abel's photographic gallery, and sat for a picture. None of the brothers called on me that day but Brothers Child and Jefferas, of No 2, Oakland, California. I felt quite unwell all day. In the evening took boat for Fort Vancouver; only ten persons on board, which was a disappointment to the committee and commander of the boat. Was met at the landing by a committee and escorted to the hall, where a public meeting was held, about one hundred persons being present. After the address of welcome, I was introduced and addressed the audience. A good feeling existed among the members of the Order there. Returned at half past twelve o'clock, A. M.

McMINNVILLE.

August 22 did not get up till half past nine o'clock, consequently got no breakfast. Went with Doctor Stephenson to see the car being prepared for the exhibition at New Orleans. It contained fine grain, grapes, and fruits. It was to start on its journey the next day, and be in St. Louis from the 4th to the 10th of October. This car was gotten up by the Emigrant Aid Association, and put under the direction of E. W. Allen, Commissioner appointed by the Governor. Visited the wholesale house of Murphy, Grant & Co., the largest firm in the West. This house is managed by Captain White, who showed us through the building. The Captain gives a bad lookout for the future business of this city. At five o'clock, P. M., took the train for McMinnville, arriving at eight o'clock. Was met at the depot by a number of the members. They stated that there would be no meeting, as it was impossible to get a hall. I was introduced to about two dozen brothers and their ladies, after which we were all called to the dining-room, where a fine supper was in waiting, to which we did ample justice. I then gave them a short talk on the duty they owed to their families and the Order.

August 23, in the morning, I took a stroll through the

town; called on Doctor Moore and talked to him, he agreeing to send in his application to join the Order. The town
has about one thousand five hundred inhabitants, four
churches, and two banks. The Lodge numbers forty-three
members. I saw only two members of the Order that day,
but found a good many young and middle-aged men who
did not belong to the Order. Fraternity, here, seems to be
as scarce as angels' visits. Took dinner with Brother
Harver; in the afternoon visited Sabbath-school in the
Christian Church, about twenty children attending. In the
evening I attended the same church, and listened to a
temperance lecture, by Mr. Anderson, of Chicago.

August 24 left for Portland on the quarter to six train.
In the evening a public reception was given me at the
Masonic Hall, about five hundred persons being present.
Address of welcome by J. F. Capus, when I was introduced
to the audience by Dr. J. A. Child. I replied, giving them
the origin and progress of the Order, the many blessings
that had been conferred through its influence, and the
duty we owe to our families and the community by living
up to its principles, and using our means to induce others
to unite with us in pushing the good work forward. I was
followed by Bro. J. A. Stephens, in a fine address, which
was convincing and instructive, calculated to arouse enthusiasm in the interest of the Order, and plant fraternity
deep in the hearts of his hearers. Everybody seemed to
enjoy it, and after the exercises of the meeting were over,
the floor was cleared for the merry dancers. On adjournment, about half a dozen brothers and their ladies went to
a restaurant and partook of cream and cake.

August 25 Doctors Stephens and Coader took me in a
carriage around the city. Saw some fine residences, and

beautiful streets, well set with shade trees; crossed the river to East Portland, thence to Milwaukee, where we recrossed the river to White House, which is a place of summer resort. From here we visited the water-works. In the evening visited Hope Lodge; only fourteen persons were present, and only five of them members of Hope Lodge. There was a fearful state of affairs in this Jurisdiction, especially in and around Portland.

I talked to them and tried to show them their duty, and induce them to arouse from their lethargy and do something to build up the Order. Duty to themselves demanded that they go to work with renewed energy for the interest of the Order. They told me that a former Grand Master Workman told them it was not a fraternal organization, that its beneficiary feature was its only consideration. It will take more than I am able to give to enthuse them.

GOES TO VICTORIA, B. C.

August 26, at half past eleven o'clock, took the train, with Dr. J. A. Child, for Victoria, British Columbia. A perfect wilderness nearly the whole distance through Washington Territory, excepting at Chehalis, which has one church, one bank, and about three hundred inhabitants. The next town is Centralia, which has two churches, a bank, and about three hundred inhabitants. There are some pretty good farms. A few miles below this town the country is nothing but a bed of gravel for thirty or forty miles, extending to the Sound. At Tacoma we took the steamer *Olympia*, for Victoria. Reached Seattle about eight o'clock, P. M.; went up-town while freight was being unloaded. Left Seattle at twelve, and reached Port Townsend at six o'clock, A. M., on the 27th. Discharged some freight and left at half past seven o'clock. This was a very good boat, but had quite poor accommodations. Landed at Victoria at half past ten o'clock, and was met by a Committee of Reception, a part of whom were Custom House officers, who passed us through without detention. We were placed in carriages and driven to the Occidental Hotel. Here I met three brothers from Meadville, Pennsylvania; one of them was Brother Wright, who said he knew me there, and that he belonged to Jefferson Lodge, No. 1. Was introduced to Hon. J. McKinney, Governor of Alaska. In the afternoon a committee, consisting of Brothers W. S. Wright, H. Short, A. R. Nielan, and others, called at my hotel with three carriages, and took Dr. J. A. Child and lady, Dr. Funda, and myself, with other brothers, out to Esquimalt, where we dismounted, and were taken in boats out to the British man-of-war, *Triumph*, a ten-gun ship, besides about a dozen small guns, where we were shown through the ship, and everything pointed out to us and explained, for which our conductors were well paid. After leaving the ship we were conducted to the new dry dock that is being constructed. It is six hundred feet long, and built of granite. We then re-entered the carriages and returned to the city, which is beautifully laid out, and has many fine buildings, including residences, churches, and public buildings. In the evening we visited the Lodge room, where, after an introduction to the members, a procession was formed, and, headed by the band, we marched to the Olympic Theater, about five hundred persons having assembled. The meeting being called to order, the address of welcome was delivered by Bro. A. R. Nielan, after which I addressed the audience, followed by Doctor Child. Here there was a good deal of enthusiasm; the people all seem to be interested in the growth of the Order. The exercises being over, all repaired to the Oriental, where a fine spread was in waiting, and was partaken of with satisfaction, a good feeling existing. We had a nice time generally.

IN WASHINGTON TERRITORY.

August 28, at one o'clock, P. M., took steamer, *Geo. E. Law*, for Seattle. Landed at Port Townsend, and went ashore for about twenty minutes. Reached Seattle at a quarter past one o'clock, on Saturday, the 29th, and was taken by committee in carriages around the city, which has a population of twelve thousand, with some splendid buildings, both public and private. This is a very rough and broken country. A public reception was given in the evening, at Yester's Hall, which was largely attended by members of the Order and citizens of both sexes. The meeting being called to order, an address of welcome, by Bro. James F. McNaught, was delivered, and was replied to by myself, Dr. J. A. Child, and others. After adjournment, a banquet was had at the Oriental Hotel, to which one hundred and fifty persons sat down, and seemed to enjoy themselves to the utmost. One brother arose and thanked me for the part of my address that applied to himself. He stated that he belonged to the Order, but it had been so long since he attended the Lodge meetings that he did not know which one he belonged to. He confessed that he had not attended to his duties, but if I would forgive him, he would attend more punctually in the future. The members here are more enthusiastic, and take more interest in the Order, than any place I have been since my arrival in this Jurisdiction. At a late hour the meeting adjourned, well satisfied with everything. We were up nearly all night, waiting for the boat, but, owing to the fog, it could not get in.

TACOMA.

August 30, in the morning, took the boat for Tacoma (the Indian meaning for this being "breast milk"). In the afternoon Bro. A. S. Howell, an engineer on the North Pacific Railroad, escorted me through the machine shops, and round-house. In the evening I visited the Lodge room, and met a number of the brothers there; held an informal meeting, but had a very pleasant time in social conversation. I spoke to them of the importance of going to work with energy and determination to build up the Order. Stopped at the Tacoma House, said to be the largest and best hotel north of San Francisco, being able to accommodate three hundred guests, and all take seats at the table at the same time. Tacoma Mountain lies off to the east, but the fog was so dense that we could not see beyond fifty yards.

OLYMPIA.

August 31 took the train for Olympia, arriving there at half past ten o'clock, A. M. Was met at the depot by a committee and conveyed to the Carleton House. After dinner, the committee called in carriages, and took us to the water-falls, which are very fine, though small. We then drove around the city, which contains some good buildings, three or four churches, with good schools. Called at the wood water-pipe factory; they were making some necessary repairs, and we did not see them in operation; two grist-mills and one door and sash factory. The water here descends one hundred and fifty feet in three hundred yards. That forenoon I had an introduction to Governor Squires, and invited him to attend the meeting, which he promised to do if he could get away from his office. In the evening I visited the Lodge room, and was introduced to many members, and had a good time generally. On adjournment, a procession was formed, and, headed by the band, moved through the principal streets of the city, halting at the City Hall, which was well filled with people of both sexes. Meeting being called to order by the chairman, an overture was played by the band; an address of welcome was delivered by Past Master Workman Brown, to which I responded, being followed by both instrumental and vocal selections of music; after which Dr. J. A. Child, and others, addressed the audience. The meeting was both entertaining and instructive, everybody being delighted. On adjournment, all repaired to the Carleton House, where a fine banquet was in readiness, which we partook of enjoyingly. Many toasts were read. Among the most prominent persons present were Governor Squires and lady, with whom I held quite a lengthy conversation on the principles of the Order. In response to a toast, the Governor said that he had made some inquiries as to the principles and aims of the Order, and from what he had learned to-night, he would be glad to become a member of such a noble institution, and requested the Recorder to call on him with an application, and he would sign it. There were many fine speeches, and all present enjoyed themselves to the fullest extent. At the proper time all dispersed, highly elated over the enjoyments. Here the brothers are full of fraternity, and are doing all that is in their power for the upbuilding of the Order.

GOES TO ALBANY, OREGON.

September 1 left Olympia for Albany, Oregon, passing through Portland, and reaching there at nine o'clock, P. M. Was met at the depot by Committee of Reception, composed of Brother Allen and others. We were taken in a carriage direct to the Lodge room, there being assembled about twenty-five members and half a dozen ladies. They said it was so late their members would not stop. There was an address of welcome by one of the brothers (whose name I have forgotten), to which I replied, being followed by Dr. J. A. Child. We had a very good time, and I trust that much good may result from it. The members present were much interested in the work of the Order. After adjournment we were taken to the Revere House.

September 2 Brother Child returned to Portland. In the morning Brother Allen and myself walked around the city. They have some good buildings, two banks, eight good church buildings, ten church organizations, and ministers. Several churches are closed for want of support. The interest in the Order runs low. Some wide-awake brother should visit them who can *pound* fraternity into them. The agricultural surroundings are fine.

AT ROSEBURG.

Brothers Allen and Woodman went with me to the train, and at twelve o'clock, M., I started for Roseburg, arriving at six o'clock, P. M. Was met at the depot by the Committee on Reception, and taken to the McClellan House. In the evening a public reception was tendered me at the Court House. Had a very large audience, a fine band of twenty-two pieces. The meeting was called to order by the chairman. Overture by the band, after which the address of welcome was delivered by Brother Hurst, to which I replied,. being followed by Grand Master Workman Davis in an able and interesting address, to whom marked attention was paid. The members seemed to take great interest in the Order; in fact, the members and people generally expressed themselves as greatly pleased with the proceedings of the evening. It is believed that much good will result from the exercises of the evening. On adjournment, the members and their ladies, with the band, repaired with me to the hotel, where a fine collation was in readiness, and was enjoyed by all present. At a seasonable hour all retired, much gratified with the entertainment. This is a live little town of about fifteen hundred inhabitants, some good buildings, banks, churches, schools, etc.

EUGENE CITY.

September 3, at quarter past five o'clock, A. M., took the train north, for Eugene City, arriving at nine, A. M., where a committee was in waiting at the depot, when we took a carriage and went to the St. Charles Hotel. In the evening was escorted by a committee to the hall, and after introductions and hand-shaking, a procession was formed and marched to the theater, where there were about one hundred fifty persons, of both sexes, assembled. The meeting being called to order, Grand Master Davis delivered a fine address of welcome, to which I replied, followed by Judges Bean and Walton. I found that the members here were alive to the work, which shows that the Grand Master Workman is out among them with his good cheer. I believe that a fine Lodge will grow out of the work of this day. This is a nice little city of two thousand inhabitants, having two banks, four churches, and a State University.

SALEM, OREGON.

September 4 Brother Davis and myself took the train for Salem, reaching that city at half past one o'clock, P. M. A Committee of Reception was waiting with a carriage at the depot. After entering the carriage we proceeded a few squares, to where the Lodge was drawn up in line, with a band, and we were escorted to Lafayette Park, there being

four or five hundred persons present. The meeting was
called to order, and the address of welcome was delivered
by Dr. C. H. Hall in a very able manner. On being introduced, I addressed the audience for three-quarters of an
hour, trying to convince them that our Order was *the* Order
for the people, its beneficiary features the cheapest and best
of all the many organizations that have taken pattern after
us. Grand Master Davis then followed in a very instructive as well as entertaining address, pointing out to them the
great importance of securing to their loved ones two thousand dollars, the amount guaranteed to the widow and
orphans of any deceased member. Between each speech
there was fine music rendered by the band. The audience
seemed to be well pleased, judging from the repeated
applause, and some of them asked to be proposed for
membership in the Order at once. On leaving the park,
others expressed themselves as being well pleased with the
meeting. The audience being dismissed, we were driven
through the town. It is a very nice little city, with numerous fine buildings, consisting of the State House, Court
House, prison, and insane asylum, with the largest grist-
mill in the State. At certain seasons of the year the
stream is navigable to small steamers up to this point. It
is a fine agricultural district. I stopped at a hotel whose
name I failed to get. This is a city of some five thousand
inhabitants, and business is very good, excepting at the
hotel where I stopped.

September 5 took the train for Portland at a quarter to
seven o'clock, A. M. Went about seven miles and found a
woodpile on either side of the track on fire, the ties being
burned and rails twisted up for a hundred yards. We
backed up to Salem, having to lie there until half past two

o'clock, P. M. I expected to take the afternoon train on the Northern Pacific, for Montana, but being too late, I had to lie over. Reached Portland at half past four o'clock, and stopped at the Gilman House. I called on Dr. Child on the morning of the 6th. The Doctor was twenty dollars short in purchasing a ticket to St. Louis, which I furnished. I was much disappointed in Oregon. Some of the previous officers have certainly misled the people, but I believe that a great many see their error, and will erelong go to work with renewed energy. There are some who are doing all they possibly can to get up an interest among the members; and when that is accomplished, the Order will become a grand and prosperous organization.

LEAVING OREGON.

September 6 went to the ticket office and ferry-boat alone. Took the train at East Portland, striking the Columbia about five o'clock, P. M., and followed its southern bank, seeing some five or six rock pyramids, about twenty-five feet high and about seven feet across at the base, running up to a point. The train stopped fifteen minutes to give passengers a view of Multnomah Falls, which are eight hundred and fifty feet high, falling over an almost perpendicular rock. The stream is small, and the water falls into a basin. From here it has another fall of about thirty feet. There is a bridge across the gorge about three hundred feet high, from which a grand view of the falls can be had. Took supper at Bannerville. Here are the cascades of the Columbia. The river is full of rocks, but deep; many persons have lost their lives by attempting to cross the stream in boats. At Cascade Falls, a ship canal and locks are being built by the Government. Those works are under the charge of a son of Brigham Young. He is a graduate of West Point, and employs Mormons almost exclusively. I was told that if a Mormon applies for work, a Gentile is sure to be dismissed, if there is no other plan.

THE DALLES.

At The Dalles I got off the train, where a number of members were in waiting to see me and shake my hand. All seemed to regret very much that I could not stop over and speak to them, they having made arrangements to give me a reception, and show me the surrounding country.

September 7, in the morning, saw nothing but a vast desert with ledges of black rock capped with snow. Eight o'clock saw a few cabins, with some dismal-looking horses on the prairies. Ritzville lies on the open prairie, having two hotels, land office, church, and several stores. Some land is in cultivation. A few miles east of Ritzville, is Sprague Lake, a fine sheet of water, with a number of small islands. The lake is five miles long and from a half to three-fourths of a mile wide. There are fine fish and fowl in this lake. Along its outlet are cottonwood and willow timber, with some few ranches upon its banks. The town of Sprague is a nice little place of about twelve hundred inhabitants, having a good hotel and several business houses. John Robinson had his show bills up for the 10th of September. There are a number of saloons, four churches, a band, and a fine depot. An attempt is being made to have a city here.

Cheney is a pretty little town of twelve or fifteen hundred inhabitants, and is said to be quite a business place. It has a number of good buildings, and is situated among the scrub pines, with two medical springs a short distance from the place. There is some fine wheat land. I saw some wheat that was five feet high and was told it would average thirty-seven bushels per acre.

Spokane Falls is considerable of a town, said to have some sixteen hundred inhabitants. The falls are not in view of the railroad. It has some large buildings of brick, a steam flouring-mill, and a railroad repair shop.

IDAHO.

Pend d'Oreille Lake, Idaho, is a fine sheet of water, ninety-one miles long and fifty miles, at some points, across. At Sand Point there is a pretty fair depot. Here I saw eight or ten Indians dressed in fancy colors. There are only six families in the town; and I suppose they wish they were somewhere else. Saw a great many ducks, geese, and swans on the lake. Here we struck the Rocky Mountain Range, about one thousand feet high.

Hereon is a little town with one hotel, called the Mountain House, a fair depot, and a number of small box houses. I think the Chinaman has the majority here. The mountains loom up all around this place, some of them from ten thousand to twelve thousand feet high.

AT HELENA, MONTANA.

September 8 I arrived at Helena, Montana, at eight o'clock, A. M. A Committee of Reception was in waiting, composed of Past Grand Master Workman Kinsley, Grand Master Workman Sullivan, and others; also a company of Select Knights on horseback, who escorted me to the Grand Central Hotel. Here I met and shook the hands of a great many members and friends of the Order.

[From the *Daily Independent*, Helena, Mont.]

"Yesterday was a gala day with the Ancient Order of United Workmen of this city. There was a grand parade, and a most cordial reception extended to J. J. Upchurch, the founder of the Order.

"The distinguished visitor arrived on train No. 2, yesterday morning, and was escorted to his hotel by a large delegation of Select Knights, under command of Commander Evans.

"At ten o'clock a special session of the Grand Lodge was held at the hall of Capitol Lodge, No. 2, when the Grand Lodge degree was conferred by the following, James Sullivan, Grand Master Workman, presiding: Past Supreme Master J. J. Upchurch, as Past Grand Master Workman; Past Grand Master Workman J. W. Kinsley, as Grand Lecturer; Past Grand Master Workman W. M. Bullard, as Grand Recorder; Deputy Grand Master Workman H. C. Yeager, as Grand Foreman; Past Grand Master Workman J. A. McDonald, as Grand Overseer; Past Grand Master Workman Wm. Zeastrow, as Grand Receiver; District Deputy Grand Master Workman J. D. Conrad, as Grand Guide; Past Master Workman J. McKilligen, as Grand Watchman. The following received the degree: Messrs. Mann and Duff, of No. 2; Dickenson and Hartman, of No. 3; Riggs and Taylor, of No. 4; Coss, of No. 19; and Kirby, of No. 31.

"At two o'clock a procession was formed in the following order: Police—Chief Marshal, H. C. Yeager; Aids, John Bunton, G. White, William Hudnall, H. W. Child, Anton Kootz, G. W. Gibbs, S. H. Cromroe, J. H. McDougald, S. Duff, John Moffit, A. E. Bunker, O. C. Bissonette, W. R. McComas, A. J. Seligman, and W. Lorey; band; Select Knights, mounted; Visiting Lodges of Ancient Order of United Workmen; Protection Lodge, No. 15, Ancient Order of United Workmen; Capitol Lodge, No. 2, Ancient Order of United Workmen; carriages with body guard of Select Knights, containing Past Supreme Master Workman J. J. Upchurch, Grand Master Workman James Sullivan, Past Grand Master Workmen J. W. Kinsley, and W. M. Bullard.

"There were about three hundred Workmen in line, and many were the expressions of praise heard of their fine appearance and discipline.

"The column arrived at the Opera House at half past two o'clock, where the following exercises took place:—

"Past Grand Master Workman W. M. Bullard, presiding, introduced the first speaker, Supreme Representative J. W. Kinsley, who spoke as follows:—

ADDRESS OF J. W. KINSLEY.

"'MR. CHAIRMAN, LADIES, BROTHER WORKMEN, AND FRIENDS: The duty assigned to me on this occasion is one most pleasing. We are not here to celebrate an ordinary event. We are here to do honor to one whose name and work have already been made famous, and one whom future generations will no less love to honor than we, his present followers, brethren, and admirers.

"'Americans will never forget their Washington, and so long as the stars and stripes float on the breeze, the names of Lincoln and Grant will be spoken with reverence and admiration.

"'Wherever Masons flourish, whether on this continent or abroad, they will continue to impress upon their initiates the sterling qualities of, and urge them to imitate in, their daily life the virtues of their patron, St. John the Baptist, and the evangelist.

"'Odd Fellowship will never tire of paying fitting tribute to the memory of Wildey, and so on I might continue through a long list of mighty nations and benevolent associations, and enumerate scores of men, who, by their deeds and works, have endeared themselves to their followers.

"'I do not approve of man worship; I do not relish excessive gush and extravagant praises; but there are men whose acts in behalf of humanity have singled them out as public benefactors, and of whom the poet writes as asking no higher sounding titles, no greater honors than to be truly classed "as those who love their fellow-men;" and when the name of such a one is spoken, or his deeds rehearsed, I am only too willing to join the throng in rendering that praise and honor their characters warrant.

"'Why are we here, brother Workmen? What occasion has drawn together this large assemblage? Why these smiling faces and warm hearts, with welcome expressed upon every countenance? This is indeed one grand welcome, and to whom? It is a Montana welcome to our own dear Father Upchurch.

"'Seventeen years ago, in the city of Meadville, Pennsylvania, a little body of men were called together, and then and there, from the mind and hands of this venerable gentleman, the Ancient Order of United Workmen was inaugurated. The insignificant number of thirteen embraced the entire membership for that day. The plan there adopted, the principles there enunciated, and the bonds there consummated, had been maturely considered and carefully analyzed by our distinguished guest, for months, and it required just the elements of character he possessed, and the determination his will furnished, to set in motion a work that has to-day far exceeded his most sanguine expectations, and has developed into an Order that takes its place most deservedly with the grandest of the world.

"'From that small beginning, like the trickling stream on yonder Rockies, it has grown and expanded, until to-day, like a mighty river, it has assumed mammoth proportions, and contains within its fold one hundred and fifty thousand good and true men, and in all reasonable probability will, ere another seventeen years roll by, number not less than half a million members.

"'The Ancient Order of United Workmen seeks not to gratify curiosity by mystical parade or ceremonies; it seeks not to draw within its fold seekers after light amusement or triflers of any grade. Its objects are well defined, its work can easily be described, and its record is that of performing all its promises, and that, too, with promptness and in the spirit of fraternity and true brotherhood. When I tell you that within the short time this organization has existed it has paid to the widows, orphans, and legatees of six thousand of our deceased brethren, twelve million dollars, and over one million dollars to our brethren for sick benefits, I state facts that are borne out by our records. When I state to you that our membership is now scattered throughout every State and Territory of this Union, and also in the Canadas, and that in every city, town, and hamlet therein, faithful men, actuated by the same noble sentiments, by the noble attributes inculcated by this patriarch, and engaged in the work he first organized, I state that which is known to every Workman present.

"'What more appropriate occasion for rejoicing and praise? What so fitting as this demonstration at this time? Why, my brothers, we have right here with us upon this rostrum, in your very presence and within the sound of our voices, our dear old Father Upchurch. We have here with us our grand old founder, to whom we and those dependent upon us are indebted for the privileges we enjoy of being Workmen. Why should we withhold our sentiments of welcome, of praise, of admiration, to this Abou Ben Adhem, of the nineteenth century; this man whom the Almighty Father of the universe has made the humble instrumentality by which one of his noblest works for the amelioration of human suffering was given to us? Why should we restrain ourselves when the opportunity is afforded us of paying fitting homage to one whose philanthropic heart beat with restless emotions, until he had overcome all difficulties and matured a plan to dry the tears of the widow and the orphan; to provide for them without the intervention of charity; to set in motion an agency for good whose full work and its results can never be known until the last great day of accounting comes, when there will be written in letters of sparkling brightness over the archways of that celestial kingdom where are arranged the record of our world's greatest and best of men, that of J. J. Upchurch.

"'No, my brethren, we need offer no apologies for our words or actions in the cordial welcome to-day. Spare not the English language, Grand Master Workmen, in your words of welcome to our honored guest. This is our day; this is an event in our history which can never be repeated. The dread destroyer is abroad in our land, and even though our dear old brother may be spared for many years to come, yet it is not within the range of possibilities that all of us who to-day are enjoying the pleasures of this grand ovation, will ever meet here again; hence I say, Pull the valve clear open; let all heartily unite; let all restraint be gone, and with one accord enjoy this reunion and show our illustrious founder that we here in the mountains of Montana, have caught the inspiration; that we have interpreted his meaning correctly; that we are Workmen full-fledged, and that the interests confided to our keeping here are in safe hands.

" ' Grand Master Workmen, my task will be ended now, when I formally present to you, and through you to the brethren of Montana, our honored Father and Founder, Brother J. J. Upchurch.'

" Hon. James Sullivan, Grand Master Workman of this Jurisdiction, responded as follows:—

" ' MR. CHAIRMAN, LADIES, AND BRETHREN: This is indeed a momentous occasion. This vast assemblage, gathered from our mountains and plains, from our mines and plowshares, from the various portions of our Territory, and in *this* presence, is one few of us ever expected to witness and enjoy.

" ' The sounds of booming cannon and tolling bells have hardly died away, which demonstration betokened the departure of one of our country's noblest and bravest heroes. That event caused a nation to mourn, and in every city, town, and hamlet, patriots assembled to do homage to the memory of the departed.

" ' It has been truly said that there are occasions when it is meet for nations and communities to assemble and pay fitting tribute to merit and true worth. How eminently proper it is, my brothers, that we have congregated here to-day! How happily can we contrast our situation with that of our countrymen of a few weeks since!

" ' We are here to do homage to our living; one not honored with the title of a conquering hero on fields of battle, but one who has been worthily crowned with the glorious mantle of originating a plan that has contributed so much toward conquering the twin monsters—poverty and degradation; one who by his persistence has matured a plan that has driven want and distress from six thousand firesides, and erected in their place the standard of hope and protection.

" ' As Grand Master Workman of this Jurisdiction, and on its behalf, it becomes my province and pleasure to extend the hand of hearty welcome to our honored and revered Brother Upchurch.

" ' It has been said that a pebble thrown into the tide affects all the water in the ocean. The small mountain stream is the source of a mighty river; from the smallest spark is kindled the sweeping conflagration; and a single idea evolved from the mind of the most lowly, frequently permeates and astonishes the world.

" ' I do not suppose that the venerable founder of our glorious Order, who to-day is the guest of the Montana Workmen, ever imagined that his beneficent system of fraternity would grow to the magnificent proportions that it has attained; and that seventeen years from the time the first Lodge of United Workmen was organized, he would be the honored subject of a reception from his children among the mountains of this far West.

" ' From the hills of Pennsylvania the Order and the fame of its founder have spread with a growth unparalleled, until to-day, from the Atlantic to the Pacific, it enfolds with its fraternal blessings the representatives of every walk in life.

" ' The laborer of the East in all its diversity joins the brother laborer of the West, and the anchor and shield inspire alike the Workman at the spindles of New England, the toiler in the cereal fields of Ohio, the farmer on the wide acres of the Mississippi Valley, and the hopeful miner of these mountains and on the Pacific slope.

" ' The benefits of brotherly affiliation and solicitude increase the joys of a thousand homes and change the tears of widowhood to the hopeful assurance of security from pressing want.

" ' The term Fraternity, in its true and full sense, comprehends more than mere forms and ceremonies. It means the generous protecting arms of the many and the strong

12

about the weak and needy. It means fewer outcasts and paupers and more of civilization and progress. Show me a community where fraternal societies flourish, and I will challenge you to find crowded poor-houses or jails. Who ever heard of a member of a society of this class being carried "over the hills to the poor-house"? Who ever heard of a deceased member being buried in the potter's field or a pauper's grave?

"'Search our penal institutions for *faithful members* of our organizations, and you do so in vain. Therefore, I say to you, fellow-citizens, of all grades and classes, never go upon record, either by word or deed, as placing any obstacle in the way of progress of fraternal societies. Rather let your influence and example tend to increase their strength and usefulness, and thus assist them in their noble work. Do not allow yourselves to be deceived as to the objects and aims of these societies. They are substantially alike, and when I quote to you a brief extract from the preamble of the organization, I outline to you the general work of fraternities. It runs thus:—

"'Omitting all references to nationality, political opinions, or denominational distinction or preferences, but believing in the existence of a God, the Creator and Preserver of the universe, and recognizing as a fundamental principle of our Order, that usefulness to ourselves and others is a duty which should be the constant aim and care of all; to embrace and give protection to all classes of all kinds of labor, mental and physical; to strive earnestly to improve the moral, intellectual, and social condition of its members; to endeavor by moral precepts, fraternal admonitions, and substantial aid, to inspire a due appreciation of the stern realities and responsibilities of life,—these are the fundamental principles as taught and inculcated by the Order which you originated.

"'In behalf of this Jurisdiction, greater in area than any other, in age but an infant; in behalf of these Workmen, your followers, toiling with strong arms and noble hearts, nerved and supported by fraternal assurance; in behalf of the homes which they represent, in valley or in mountain glen—I extend to you, Brother Upchurch, father and founder of our Order, the heartiest welcome which feeble language can express.

"'We meet here as strangers by kin, but as brothers by honored ties. So many thoughts and hopes are common, so many impulses and aspirations, the same in character, move our hearts, that a formal introduction immediately grows into an intimate acquaintanceship, and adopting, to-day, the characteristic friendship imposed by the ritual, which you yourself formulated, which calls all to a common level, the rich from his mansion, the poor from his cottage, we cast aside all formalities existing between strangers, and welcome you to our hearts and homes.

"'You have traveled over our Jurisdiction, and have observed its magnitude, and are familiar with the progress we have made in so short a time.

"'You have probably been reminded that rare plants sometimes grow in obscure places; that flowers are blooming near snow-banks, and in rugged fastnesses of desolate mountains, forever unseen, except by the prospector or hunter. So the Workmen among the sage brush and the mountain-tops present to you a Jurisdiction permeated by the same zeal, the same philanthrophy and charity, which actuated you, its original founder.

"'We are reminded to-day by your work, life, and character, that all the elements of true manhood are not furnished by accident of birth, nor by advantages of education, nor even by social position. And it is, perhaps, fortunate that a discriminating public can and do place their own estimate upon many of our would-be leaders of society, who, having little else to stand upon, saving their assurance and conceit, the bare semblance of worth that wealth gives them, are too ready to forget their early past; that others, perhaps quite as deserving as they, are struggling to cover the ground which they have just compassed; that there is still undeveloped talent only waiting the opportune turn in the wheel of fortune to shine forth, that may be more brilliant than theirs.

"'Thank God, there are true and noble men standing

along the pathway of history, who were neither kings nor warriors, nor blue-blooded aristocrats. And so long as the world can point to a village Hampden, the master-spirit of a more liberal government; a Hugh Miller, the stone-cutter, who, while at his work, composed that masterpiece of English literature and science, "Foot-prints of the Creator;" so long as history records the fact that the great philosopher and statesman, Benjamin Franklin, arose from the humble calling of a printer; Henry Wilson, once a shoemaker, and late Vice-President of these United States; so long as a Webster or a Clay lives in the annals of the lowly great, so long will the humble strive, and the world lay its laurels at the feet of true merit.

"'You behold in this Western branch of your family a band of noble Workmen, living for the highest manly qualities. By the very conditions of our Western life and rushing enterprise, our society considers not rank nor pedigree, but recognizes the development of manliness, which it is ever ready to commend and reward.

"'We are all toilers; we are workmen engaged in the conquest of nature. Mountains yield to our bidding, and pour forth their treasures without stint, and the fruits of a permanent civilization are already ripening as the result of our industry.

"'It must, indeed, be a source of personal satisfaction to you, in this your Western pilgrimage, to know that even here your work has erected monuments which can never be effaced. The rich heritage of our present civilization is the product of innumerable minds and hands. In most cases their possessors are unknown and forgotten, and it is very seldom that from the ruins of oblivion history rescues an idea, a system of laws, or an institution with the name and character of the originator.

"'The waters of mighty rivers are mingled in a common ocean, and in no way, however sparkling, can their identity be traced. On Egyptian plains were built pyramids in commemoration of kings, and mounds of earth remain, together with only a shadow of tradition of those who reared them. But with you, honored sir, responding to the neces-

sities of an advanced civilization, with motives the purest
and the best, you have inaugurated a system whose increasing growth assures its everlasting permanency, and
which will need no printed page to preserve the history of
its purposes or the name of its founder. In six thousand
homes, preserved and cheered; in thousands of hearts comforted; in innumerable lives freed from despondency and
despair, strengthened by kind words and fraternal hopes,
will be perpetually engrafted the purposes, history, and ex-
emplification of our Order.

" ' In looking out upon the audience to-day, representing
so many homes our Order is protecting, composed of so
many who will sooner or later become the natural beneficiaries of the great work in which we are engaged, the
grandeur of our system is so impressed upon our minds that
the contemplation of possible results already compensates
us for the time and money invested; and the present satisfaction of being but an humble factor in so great an institution, is to us a full dividend from the standpoint of
duty, and the satisfaction of doing unto others as we would
that they should do unto us.

" ' Our work in this Jurisdiction is but begun, and should
your life be spared to return to us, even though your hair
be more silvered by the work of time, and with enfeebled
step you may come, you will always find the term " Montana Workman," to mean a warm fraternal heart, beating
within the breast of an honest man, with all that the terms
imply, and by whom you will then, as now, be cordially
welcomed.

" ' I cannot let this opportunity pass, my brothers, without saying a few words to you, suggested by this occasion.
The proud position which the Ancient Order of United
Workmen occupies to-day in the ranks of great organizations, is due to earnest, faithful, and persistent work, and to
maintain its present standard, and raise it to even grander
proportions, should prompt every one of you to increased
zeal and fidelity to the interests confided to your care. It
is not sufficient to promise faithfully to perform an act, and
then evade its burdens; nor that you have induced others,

either by personal solicitation or by example, to become
members of our Order, the meetings of which you seldom
attend, and of which you know but little, except by hearsay.
Can you reconcile such conduct to the duty you owe to
your family and loved ones?

" 'Your connection with this organization, which agrees
to pay over to your dependents the sum of two thousand
dollars, has led them to believe that the fear of destitution,
which might stare them in the face were you taken from
them, is no longer visible; that you have made a sure provision for them. Yet you would trifle with their dearest
expectations; you peril their interests; you deliberately deceive them, when you unnecessarily and wantonly neglect
to pay your assessments promptly when called upon, or
refuse to bear your share of the burden attendant upon the
proper working of your Lodge. Pardon me, my brothers,
if too severe; but I plead in the interest of those you should
love, and are bound by the strongest human ties to protect,
and I should be doing less than my duty in the position
which I now occupy, were I to do less than call your careful attention to this matter thus forcibly.

" 'If you will but study and live up to your obligations,
you will find that the light of true fellowship which this
organization so generously teaches has been a beacon to
many a brother tempted to wander from the paths of virtue
and integrity. It has shed a friendly ray of hope upon
thousands who might otherwise have drifted upon the rocks
of adversity. It has shone with unparalleled effulgence
upon the sorrowing widows and orphaned babes, and it will
gleam in the hearts of the bereft and unfortunate of its fold
until, like a glittering gas-jet, eclipsed by the more dazzling
rays of an electric spark, it is lost in the glories of the land
that is fairer than day, where the billows of adversity roll
no more, and the storm of life is succeeded by a holy calm,
to endure through the boundless expanse of eternity.'

"Father Upchurch then responded most feelingly, giving
free expression to his appreciation of the cordial welcome
extended him, and in the course of his remarks gave evidence of the earnestness and zeal with which his efforts in

behalf of *his* Order have been exerted. His remarks were frequently and heartily applauded.

"John W. Eddy, Past Master of Protection Lodge, then read the following

POEM.

When wisdom once had formed a plan
  Of vast concern, she saw
The need of one intrepid man
  To execute her law,

And so began a weary round,
  Determined she would find
Somewhere a man whose qualities
  Were suited to her mind.

And long she went her patient round,
  In eager, anxious search,
Nor rested till at last she found
  Our honored friend Upchurch.

When he was found the work was done,
  And now, from far and near,
The voices of his loving ones
  He may distinctly hear;

The voices of the friends who stand
  United, strong, and true,
And shed a luster on the land—
  A. O. U. W.

PENNSYLVANIA.

We're the Keystone State of the Union,
  Where you in your manhood's prime
Established fraternal communion,
  To grow through all coming time.
    In love we address you,
    And all say, God bless you,
      Again and again,
      Amen and amen!

OHIO.

And we are the Buckeye State,
   The second in point of age,
     In honor the second,
     Where honor is reckoned
As an earthly heritage.
   But you'll find us as true
   As the heavens are blue,
When the Master's final award is made,
When the Workmen's wages at last are paid.

KENTUCKY.

And we are Kentucky.
   If not large, we're lucky
To be counted worthy to stand
     'Mong the true and the good
     Of our grand brotherhood,
That surely is blessing the land.
   We're third in the line,
     And loyal and trustful and true.
   We gratefully twine
     The laurel and myrtle for you.

INDIANA.

Kind fortune we thank,
That we're fourth in the rank
   Of age in this glorious Order.
We're small, but we know
If we live, we shall grow,
   And lengthen and strengthen our border,
Though sometimes he is tardy,
A Hoosier is hardy,
   And stays like a November snow.

IOWA.

We are from Iowa,
And you'll never know a
More staunch Lodge of brothers than ours.
To be sure, the restrictions
Placed on Jurisdictions
We thought were curtailing our powers,
And made us rebel;
But now, joy to tell,
We're back 'mong the bowers and flowers,
And will never more trouble you,
Nor the A. O. U. W.,
While it shall protect us and ours.

NEW YORK.

We're the Empire State,
Magnificent and great,
And the largest beneficiary known;
And we're proud to be the guest
Of this Empire of the West,
For its grandeur soon will quite eclipse our own.
And from all the good and true
Here is royal homage due
To the venerable founder of our clan;
And we bring it now to you,
And we ask the world to view
And appreciate this kingly-hearted man.

ILLINOIS.

We're the State of Illinois,
And the third in point of size;
And our fifteen thousand boys
May the country yet surprise,
For we've set our aims as high
As our purposes are good;
And to stand the first will try,
In our noble brotherhood.

MISSOURI.

Like our mighty flowing river,
  We are following along
In a restless, growing column
  Fully fourteen thousand strong!
Not alone the great Missouri
  Is all worthy of our theme,
For our Brooks has won the honor·
  Master Workman now Supreme.
And at last, our honored father,
  You have sought our prairie West,
And within our Jurisdiction
  Found a peaceful home and rest.
And we trust you'll never leave us
  Till the day of life expire,
And you hear our all-wise Master
  Saying, " Brother, come up higher."

MINNESOTA.

And we are Minnesota;
Though we are a mere iota,
  In the aggregate display,
We hope next year to meet you
In our own State, and to greet you
  With an excellent array
Of names of added brothers,
Till our Lodge vies with the others,
  In the foremost rank to-day.

WISCONSIN.

And we are Wisconsin,
  With our hopes set high,
That we may rank proudly
  In the sweet by and by.
Our Lodge is as loyal,
  And as fondly true,
As flowers are fragrant
  That we bring to you.

TENNESSEE.

We are from the home of Frizzell
  In the good State of Tennessee,
And we've not a good story to tell
  For a people as thrifty as we.
    We've been unlucky,
    But still we're plucky,
And bound to make the future see
Our Order thrive in Tennessee.

MICHIGAN.

If you want to be rich again,
  Just come to Michigan!
Where the Order is healthy and strong,
  And there you will find
  The very best kind
Of spirits around you will throng.
    There is Baxter, whom you know
    Dealt the rebels such a blow
As brought them in a hurry into place;
    And come whene'er you may,
    We will celebrate the day
When you come to look our brothers in the face.

CALIFORNIA.

The sun lights the East till the hill-tops are burning,
  But ever delights in his haunt of the West,
And always again in his journey returning,
  He leaves his last smile on the land he loves best.
    Down in the Golden State,
    Through her bright "Golden Gate,"
  Shines the pure light of the Order we love.
    And may it ever grow,
    Till by its heavenly glow
    We all at last may know
Charity, Hope, and Protection above.

From the Golden State we hear
Voices of the gladdest cheer,
And from all in fond acclaim
Blessings on your honored name.

GEORGIA, ALABAMA, MISSISSIPPI, NORTH AND SOUTH CAROLINA, AND FLORIDA.

North and South Carolina
    And Georgia on the coast,
Florida and Alabama,
    The happy Southron's boast,
And Mississippi added—
    All these together are
The smallest Jurisdiction
    In the Order now by far!
Our gratulations are as true
    And hearty as the others;
We never mean to be outdone
    As loyal Workman brothers!

KANSAS.

Kansas is prosperous and healthy,
Becoming prominent and wealthy;
    Jayhawkers and Bushwhackers,
    And the ruffians of the border,
Have sunken into shadows
    In the pure light of our Order.
For the bow of freedom spans us,
And the peace of Heaven fans us,
And the love of country mans us,
    On the fertile plains of Kansas.

ONTARIO.

We're Englishmen from foreign soil,
    And wary O, and chary O, —
United brothers, sons of toil,
    From Province of Ontario.

Will drop our aitches, doff our hats,
Endeavoring, if we can,
To make all pride of name or birth
Merge in the brother man.

OREGON, WASHINGTON TERRITORY, AND BRITISH COLUMBIA.

We're Oregon and Washington,
Nevada's jealous neighbor,
Two years ago just twice her size;
But now, despite our labor,
She's grown to be
As large as we,
Our lively, lovely neighbor!
God bless her, and God bless us all.
The good of one is joy for all.

MASSACHUSETTS AND NEW ENGLAND.

And we are the Yankees,
But just where our rank is,
It might be hard to show.
We're always bound to shine
In the transcendental line,
And that all people know.
We're good at making shoes,
And at making shoe-pegs;
And its nuts for anybody
To crack our nutmegs!
We've always been original
As the aboriginee,
And doubtless from the Indians got
Our ingenuity.
If you don't believe we've got it,
Just inquire of Doherty!

MARYLAND, NEW JERSEY, AND DELAWARE.

New Jersey on the coast,
  And diamond Delaware,
A Jurisdiction make,
  With Maryland, the fair.
From the shore of the Atlantic
  Westward evermore
O'er the continent gigantic
  To Pacific shore,
With a history romantic
  Never known before,
Our Order that you founded
  Has spread from shore to shore.
Her Ægis now is honored
  The whole wide country o'er.

TEXAS, LOUISIANA, AND ARKANSAS.

Hard luck, no doubt, will often vex us,
And well we say it may vex Texas;
Three years ago we felt quite thrifty
With our eighteen hundred and fifty,
And we're certain we could now send
Names of more than our two thousand!
But alas! Time's a deceiver!
What, with all our yellow fever
And the trouble that came to us,
Threatening sometimes to undo us,
We've done very well, we're thinking,
That we saved ourselves from sinking.
Our Order yet may notice Texas
Standing where she least expects us.
Though fates may frown, we will not mind them;
Darkest clouds have light behind them.

NEVADA, MONTANA, UTAH, WYOMING, AND IDAHO.

And we are from Nevada,
  Than which you never had a

Fairer, brighter jewel in your sparkling crown.
Our motto is still onward,
And onward still and sunward;
And we'll add a gleam of splendor and renown
To the name we love the most
'Mong the loyal Workman's host.
Four Territories and a State
In this inter-mountain land,
Make one Jurisdiction great,
Which forevermore shall stand
As a bulwark to the right,
As a barrier to wrong,
And make living a delight,
And its end a crown and song.

COLORADO, NEW MEXICO, AND ARIZONA.

We're the baby Jurisdiction,
Born not quite a year ago,
Colorado, Arizona, added to New Mexico,
Have so soon a Grand Lodge gathered
That beholders all have wondered,
For in their babyhood they count
Two thousand and five hundred.
O father of us all! we bring
One voice from all these brothers,
May God reward you with the good
That you've conferred on others!

" On the conclusion of the poem, Dr. C. K. Cole gave some very interesting statistics, showing the date of organization, and progress made by the Order in this Jurisdiction, which wound up as follows:—

"'Last year we paid to the beneficiaries of our Jurisdiction twenty-eight thousand dollars. From the date of the institution of Alpha Lodge, No. 1, at Eureka, to the present time, we have, in this inter-mountain section alone, paid out to similar persons over one hundred thousand dollars; while our Order at large paid out something over two million dollars last year alone, and, as has been stated, our total payments of this character exceeded thirteen million. And now, my brethren, in conclusion, let me admonish you personally, to a continued fidelity to our beloved Order. May you be protected by the Watchman on high, who never slumbers. May you be directed by that Guide who will lead you in paths of rectitude and honor. May your account with the Great Financier always show you to be square on the books. May the Receiver always have a score of noble deeds to your credit. May the Recorder inscribe on the pages of your history, many, many valiant deeds of charity and protection. Let the Great Overseer see you are well instructed in the tenets of our Order. Constitute yourselves each a Foreman in all acts of love and kindness, and finally become Master Workman in that best and truest sense, excelling in all that goes to make true men and useful members of society.'

" In conclusion, the following letter was received and read:—

"' OGDEN CITY, Utah, September 5. 1885.

"' W. M. BULLARD, Chairman Upchurch Reception Committee—*Dear Sir and Brother:* All of us watch with deep interest the arrangements for the reception of Brother Past Grand Master Workman J. J. Upchurch, in your city, by ye Workmen of ye North, with the foreknowledge that the last "grand wind-up" by your father of his children on the Pacific slope, will not be excelled by any similar event in the history of our Order, and could not be equaled outside of the limits of this Jurisdiction.

"' Fraternally yours in C., H., and P.,
            D. THORNBURN, *Grand Recorder.*' "

The meeting then dispersed, I being escorted to the hotel by the Select Knights, headed by a band. A number of brothers came thirty miles in wagons——one brother coming one hundred and seventeen miles especially to attend this meeting. We were invited to visit the theater in the evening, which we did. At ten o'clock we visited the grand ball given in honor of the occasion. In the evening I was introduced to Thomas Powers, the largest stock-raiser in the Territory. He stated that he had always been opposed to secret societies, but something told him to go to the Opera House that afternoon; he must confess that I captured him on the first charge. He thought it was the grandest institution known, and was calculated to do the greatest amount of good.

I presented Alta Lodge, No. 4, and Union Lodge, No. 3, with a large-sized lithograph of myself, to hang in their hall.

September 9 Brother Burns called with a buggy for me; we drove around town. There are many fine, substantial buildings, with a United States Assayer's office, churches, schools, etc. We stopped at the residence of Brother Burns, where he presented me with a fine specimen of gold quartz; also his estimable lady presented me with some fine nuggets of gold to have bosom studs made of.

Grand Master Sullivan then came up, and we drove out to the Hot Springs, a nice place of resort. I took a warm bath. In the evening a number of brothers met in my room, and presented me with seventy dollars.

I was much astonished at my reception in this city, to see so much interest taken in the Order. They are full of fraternity, nothing being too great for them to do for the advancement of the principles of our beloved Order. The people of this Jurisdiction certainly descended from the same stock I found in California. The remembrance of the kindness received at the hands of the brothers here, will be ever held in remembrance.

13

ON THE WAY HOME.

September 10, in the morning, I was accompanied to the depot by Past Grand Master Workman J. W. Kinsley, Grand Master Workman James Sullivan, and Brother Burns. I bade farewell to the brothers, took a sleeper, and was soon on my return home. At ten o'clock, A. M., crossed the Missouri River, it being only sixty feet wide; vegetation in the valley green and fresh, while that on the hills was dry. Farmers were cutting oats, and it was quite green.

Maitland is a station in the midst of the finest valley in the Territory. Its yield of wheat is from fifty to sixty bushels per acre and oats from seventy to ninety. On the right, coming East, there is a long range of snow-capped mountains.

Bozeman is a fine little city, with some fine brick buildings, in the midst of a fertile valley from ten to thirty miles wide.

Livingston is where passengers take the branch road for the Yellowstone Park. A heavy storm was raging on the mountains, but did not reach the valley.

Billings is a small place. Wm. B. Webb, of Billings, Montana, I met on the train. He says the Lodge was instituted one year ago, with fifteen charter members. To-day they have forty members, who are very much interested in the work of the Order.

September 11 Glendive was reached at six oclock, A. M., a small town having a round-house. Passed through the Bad Lands, scenery very picturesque. There seems to have been a general washout, leaving many points standing in all conceivable shapes from ten to fifty feet high, and they extend into Idaho.

Dickens is quite a town; there being one firm that deals in

various kinds of furs, horns, and other curiosities. Almost fifteen miles east I saw the first and only antelope go bounding over the prairie.

Bismarck is a fine little city and is the capital of Idaho. The State House is built of brick and there are many other substantial brick buildings. It has a population of three thousand five hundred.

I reached Minneapolis at twelve o'clock, M., and sent a telegram home that I would be there on Monday. Took train for St. Louis at half past three o'clock, P. M.

September 14 I reached home on the three o'clock train. The following will show my reception there:—

HIS RECEPTION.

[From the *Crawford Mirror.*]

"As our readers are aware, Founder J. J. Upchurch, of the Ancient Order of United Workmen, has spent the last three months visiting in California and Oregon, whither he went on invitation of the Order on the Pacific Coast. His stay there was one continuous ovation, and no man ever received greater honor, or was more generally eulogized than has been our distinguished citizen.

"A telegram received a few days ago announced that he would reach here on Monday. The Founders Lodge determined to give him a welcome that would be no whit behind that tendered him by other members of the Order.

"The Cuba and Salem Lodges were invited to participate, and a reception and banquet were hastily arranged. On the arrival of the three o'clock train from Cuba, Father Upchurch was met by a committee of the Lodge, and the Steelville Cornet Band escorted him through town and then to his home, and an invitation was given him to be present at Davis & Hamill's Hall at seven o'clock, P. M. At that hour a large number of the members and ladies and invited guests assembled at the hall. The exercises opened with an eloquent address of welcome by Thos. R. Gibson, as follows:—

"'FATHER UPCHURCH: On behalf of and in the name of the Founders Lodge, No. 224, of the Ancient Order of United Workmen, I welcome you to your home, to your family, to your friends, and to the brothers of that noble and charitable organization, of which you are the recognized father and founder, from your grand tour of the Pacific States, and I sincerely assure you that we were highly gratified at the reception our brothers of the West accorded you in the many cities and towns you visited.

"'The honors bestowed upon, and the attention shown you, were worthy of any king, prince, or potentate, and fully demonstrated, beyond question, that your work in founding and establishing the Ancient Order of United Workmen is appreciated and cherished, not only by the brothers in the many Lodges throughout the Union, but by every citizen of this great and glorious Republic that holds near and dear those who are dependent upon him.

"'Your grand and triumphant tour of the golden States of California and Oregon was watched by one hundred fifty thousand Workmen, who vied with each other in the pleasure and gratification of beholding the father and founder of our noble Order the recipient of such marked attention and distinguished honors.

"'The Order originated and founded by you has well-regulated Lodges throughout the civilized world, and in each of them there is always a vacant chair awaiting your arrival.

"'The membership now exceeds one hundred fifty thousand, and over two million dollars are annually paid to the widows and orphans of deceased brothers. Little did you dream, a few years ago, when in Meadville, Pennsylvania, while following the vocation of a mechanic, you gathered around you a few of your fellow-laborers to plant the germ of this Order, that the society you were then organizing would in maturing touch a tender spot in the hearts of your fellow-creatures, and flash like electricity through the Christian world.

"'You founded and originated this Order from no selfish purpose, but with the sole view of assisting and bettering the condition of your fellow-workmen in their struggle through life, and as a protection to their families when called from this terrestrial globe.

" 'You had observed that the relation between the twin brothers, capital and labor, was not of a nature to promote the welfare and prosperity of those two great civilizers. One cannot exist without the other; capital is built upon and created by labor, and labor is fed and nourished by capital.

" 'Your good common sense, not polished with an academic education, conceived the idea of establishing an organization in which the employer and employé could meet on a level, and in social intercourse assist each other, adjust plans, and devise means whereby both could work in harmony and for their mutual benefit and protection.

" 'You can now behold the fruits of your labor. Your name is a familiar word in every home where peace and harmony prevail, and your picture adorns, not only Lodge rooms and parlors, but is engraved upon the heart of every true Workman, and few men are held in greater esteem than yourself.

" 'The good you have done is confined to and monopolized by no political party, no religious creed, select class, or clique of your fellow-beings, but is open for acceptance by all men, both rich and poor, who lead pure and upright lives, and pursue honest and honorable callings.

" 'We are rejoiced to welcome you again to your home, to our hearts, and to the fraternal circle of our Lodge. Our good wives, daughters, and sisters also greet you, and have prepared this banquet and reception as a slight indication of the kindly feelings they entertain for you, and a feeble reminder that though you have been royally received afar, there are affectionate hearts that beat as warmly for you here as in other lands, and that

" ''Mid pleasures and palaces, though we may roam,
　Be it ever so humble, there's no place like home.' '

" When Father Upchurch arose to respond, he was greeted with applause. He thanked the brothers for the cordial

greeting they had given him, and expressed his pleasure at
again being at home. At the close of his response the
company took their seats at the bountifully laden table, and,
after grace, did ample justice to the delicious viands so
temptingly displayed.

"The following toasts were then proposed: 'Our Order,'
by Mr. Charles Everson. Dr. J. F. Coffee was called on
to respond, and did so in an eloquent and graceful speech,
in which he reviewed the progress of the brotherhood. To
the sentiment, 'Father Upchurch,' Mr. Thomas Everson
made a graceful and fitting response, which elicited many
rounds of applause. 'Our Brothers of the Golden Shore'
was next proposed, and Mr. Frank M. Dunlavy responded
in a brief but eloquent speech, suited to such a sentiment.
'Our Wives and Sweethearts' was responded to in a happy
vein by Rev. P. D. Cooper. 'Our Visiting Brethren' was
the theme for a neat little speech by Mr. Noah L. Hawk,
which, with a bit of choice poetry, ended the exercises of
the programme, which was of unusual interest and remarkably
pleasant.

"Father Upchurch was then invited to give an account
of his visit to the Pacific Coast, which he did in a very interesting manner.

"The band, led by Dr. R. E. Jamison, interspersed the
occasion with excellent music. At a seasonable hour the
audience dispersed to their several homes."

SUCH is the simple narrative of the life and labors of Father Upchurch as prepared by himself. It only remains that we pick up the thread of the story where he let it fall, and, by the aid of such data as we have been able to procure, continue it to the end.

AT ST. LOUIS.

After the ovation tendered to him by the Lodges and populace on his safe arrival home, at Steelville, he quietly and unobtrusively resumed the business in which he was engaged before he started on his memorable journey, viz., dealing in agricultural implements, lumber, and undertaker. He had been home but a few days, however, when he received an invitation from the Sixth Regiment, Select Knights, to visit them at St. Louis. Accepting the invitation, he was met on his arrival at the depot by a committee of distinguished brothers and driven to his hotel, where an address of welcome was delivered by Hon. John I. Martin, to which he briefly responded, visiting two of the Lodges that evening. The two following days he received marked attention by eminent citizens of St. Louis, being driven about to the various points and places of interest. On the evening of one of these days, he was tendered a grand reception by about seven thousand of the brethren of St. Louis, a competitive drill by several of the Legions being held in his honor.

SWORD PRESENTATION.

He also attended by invitation the biennial conclave of Select Knights of Missouri, at Moberly, on the 27th of October. Here also he was the recipient of much respect and distinguished honor. The following is an epitomized account of his reception, taken from the *Watchman* of November 14, 1885:—

"At the session of the Grand Legion (Select Knights) of Missouri, at Moberly, on the 27th ult., Father Upchurch was present, and received much attention from the many present. There were many valuable prizes given to competing Legions for excellence in drill, but according to reports contained in the Missouri papers, 'the grandest gift of all' was awarded to the venerable father of the Order, J. J. Upchurch, who was present. The gift was a sword and belt, which was beautiful enough to grace any officer. This being the seventeenth anniversary of the founding of the Order, no more appropriate recognition of the father of the Order could possibly have been given.

"After the awarding of prizes, the members of the Grand Legion filed by and shook hands with Father Upchurch, after which he made a short speech, expressing the pleasure and gratitude he felt in being so honored. He also adverted to the early struggles of the Order, making a speech that is described as sound, sensible, and to the point."

VISIT TO WYANDOTTE.

Returning from these pleasant visits he spent about a month in quiet at home, receiving in the meantime an invitation to visit Wyandotte, Kansas, by Geo. W. Reed, Supreme Commander Select Knights, and others. Of this visit he speaks as follows in a letter written to the *Watchman*, after he returned home:—

"EDITORS *Watchman:* On January 1 I visited Wyandotte, Kansas, where I was received at the depot by a committee headed by Bro. Geo. W. Reed, Supreme Commander Select Knights and Grand Master Workman of Kansas. In the evening a large number of brothers assembled in Odd Fellows' Hall to install the officers of Lodge No. 30. A fine address was delivered by Grand Master Workman

Reed, who, with the assistance of Supreme Master Workman John A. Brooks and your correspondent, conducted the installation.

"After the ceremony about four hundred brothers and their friends sat down to a sumptuous banquet, prepared by the ladies, which was greatly enjoyed.

"January 4 I went to St. Joseph, Missouri, and was present next day at an informal reception tendered Brother Reed at the hall of No. 50. In the evening many members of the Order, including Select Knights in uniform, formed in procession and all marched to the Opera House, where a large audience had already assembled. There, addresses were delivered by Brother Reed, the undersigned, and others, and a secret meeting at the hall of No. 50 followed, in which the work of the two Orders was exemplified.

"On the 8th inst. I had the pleasure of visiting the good brothers of Centralia and talking to them, returning home from the trip on the 9th.

"Yours in C., H., and P.,   J. J. UPCHURCH."

THE GRAND LODGE OF KANSAS.

The Grand Lodge of Kansas was to meet at Topeka February 23, and a warm invitation had been extended to him to attend. Previous to that, however, he had been urged to meet the legions of Select Knights at Sedalia, Missouri. Of these visits also he has left an account in another letter to the *Watchman*, dated Steelville, Missouri, March 1, 1886.

"EDITORS *Watchman:* On the 19th of February I had the pleasure of visiting Sedalia, Missouri, by invitation of the Select Knights, and I take the liberty of sending you a brief account of the visit, for it was to me one of great pleasure. Met at the depot by a delegation of Knights in uniform, we proceeded to their hall, where introductions and an exchange of fraternal greetings took place. In the evening an audience of fifteen hundred at least assembled in the large rink, it being the only hall in the city large enough to accommodate the crowd. Preliminary to this, however, a banquet was enjoyed by about six hundred brethren and guests. Following this feast of good things came requests to address the friends, which it was a pleasure for me to do, as everybody seemed in sympathy with our Ancient Order of United Workmen sentiments of fraternity.

" On the following evening I went to Independence and there had the satisfaction of being warmly greeted by many brethren and invited guests, and of speaking to them briefly on the principles of Workmanship. The members of the Order there are alive to its interests.

" On the 23d I proceeded to Topeka, where the Grand Lodge was in session, and spent a delightful time with the members of that body and other brothers in attendance. Grand Master Workman Reed (who is also Supreme Commander of the Select Knights), joined with the other Grand officers in extending to me every courtesy. On the first evening of the session the Grand Master Workman and your correspondent were escorted to the Opera House by a delegation of uniformed Knights, where a fine programme of exercises was carried out, including addresses by Brother Reed, Grand Foreman Miller, and your correspondent. The audience was a very fine one, representative, I believe, of the members of the Order generally in Topeka.

"Yours in C., H., and P.,   J. J. UPCHURCH."

Another report has the following in relation to the founder's visit to the Grand Lodge of Kansas:—

"The Grand Lodge of Kansas met in Topeka in eighth annual session on the 23d of February, one hundred and eighty-nine delegates being present. The session was opened by Geo. W. Reed, Grand Master Workman. The report of the Grand Recorder, E. M. Forde, shows that thirty-four deaths occurred in the Jurisdiction during the past year. A pleasant incident of the first day's session was the presentation to Grand Master Workman Reed, on behalf of the Grand Legion of the Select Knights, of a beautiful gold badge, suitably inscribed.

"Father Upchurch was present by invitation of the Grand Lodge, and on the evening of the opening day he was accorded a grand reception at Crawford's Opera House, the hall being crowded. Addresses were made by Brother Reed, Grand Master Workman Father Upchurch, and Hon. J. M. Miller, Grand Foreman. In his introductory address, the former thus referred to the honored and venerable guest of the evening:—

" 'To-day, in unfeigned happiness, we extend the hand of welcome and fraternal greeting to our brother, who not only moulds his own nature to the best conformation of which it is susceptible, but by his teachings and example influences many others to work in harmony for the uplifting and improvement and relief of needy humanity. We are proud to listen to a man whose whole inward life is an upward life, a progressive life, a life devoted to right. We are proud to welcome a man who is so truly worthy of reverence. Thousands of the best and noblest men in our land hasten to do him honor. We welcome him, while we thank him in grateful affection for the great and glorious work he established and has helped with fatherly care to guard and maintain.'

"The reply of Father Upchurch was unusually full and admirably expressed. We have space for but brief extracts. Referring to the early struggles of the Order in Pennsylvania, and to the recent disincorporation of the Grand Lodge of that State, he said:—

" 'Dissension arose in the Order. About one-half of our members seceded and formed an opposition Grand Lodge. This second Grand Lodge procured an act of incorporation which has given us more trouble than everything else that has been brought to bear against us.

" 'I thank God that the mother of our Order has had independence enough to cast off the incubus and assert her rights to do business under the charter of the Supreme Lodge, and I sincerely trust that every other Grand Lodge will do likewise. This separation continued for two years, when in January, 1873, a union of the two wings of the

Order was affected. At this time there were only about eight hundred members in both wings of the Order. The ratification of the union was held in New Castle, Pennsylvania, about January 25, when every member present gave evidence of his approval that we were again a united Order. Old Brother McNair, Grand Recorder of Pennsylvania, arose and proposed that we sing, ' Praise God, from whom all blessings flow,' which was done with enthusiasm, and I am yet to be convinced that there was a dry eye in the hall.'

" Again he said:—

"' It is not sufficient to promise faithfully to perform an act and then evade its burden, or that you have induced others by personal solicitation or otherwise to become members of our Order, the meetings of which you seldom attend, and of which you know but little, except by hearsay.

"' How can you reconcile such conduct to the duty you owe your families and loved ones? Your continuation with this organization, which agrees to pay over to your family the sum of two thousand dollars, has led them to believe that the fear of destitution which might stare' them in the face were you taken from them, is no longer visible; that you have made a sure provision for them. Yet you would trifle with their dearest expectations; you peril their interest; you deliberately deceive them when you unhesitatingly or wantonly neglect to pay your assessments promptly, or refuse to bear your share of the burden attendant upon the proper working of your Lodge.' "

CALIFORNIA GRAND LODGE RESOLUTIONS.

The Grand Lodge of California convened in San Francisco, April 6, 1886. We cull the following from the minutes of the third day's proceedings of that body, to show the appreciation in which the recent visit of Father Upchurch was held by the Grand Lodge and the brothers on the Pacific Coast.

Bro. A. T. Dewey offered the following resolutions, which were adopted:—

" WHEREAS, The visit of Father Upchurch to this coast last year was an event of great importance in the history of the Ancient Order of United Workmen on the western slope of the continent;

" *Resolved*, That this Grand Lodge return to the grand old founder of our great Order, J. J. Upchurch, Past Supreme Master Workman, its grateful acknowledgments and most sincere thanks for his visit to our fair State.

" *Resolved*, That by his modest and noble bearing, and his wise and kindly counsel, he won the respect and love of all our brotherhood and helped to cement more firmly the fraternal ties that bind the Ancient Order of United Workmen into one great co-operative body for the elevation and protection of its members and their dependent families.

" *Resolved*, That Father Upchurch's visitations to different portions of our Jurisdiction afforded the brethren who had the opportunity of seeing and hearing him a privilege that will always be cherished as one of the pleasantest memories of true Workmen.

" *Resolved*, That this Grand Lodge sends warm fraternal greetings to the venerable founder, who, in his humble home, still contributes his influence to the support of the Order he brought into life, and congratulates him upon the fact that he has lived to see the Ancient Order of United Workmen grow into a star of the first magnitude, fixed in the grand center of a new and wonderfully progressive system of beneficiary fraternities."

PREPARING HIS BOOK.

In the meantime he had been utilizing all his spare time in collecting and arranging the manuscript for his biography, according to the agreement* entered into with Brother

---

* The following extract, from the report of the Upchurch memorial services in San Francisco, briefly explains how Father Upchurch came to write his book, and, finally, his last letter to accompany the sam :—
" With the letter in hand, Past Grand Master Workman Barnes advanced to the foot-lights at the close of the regular services in San Francisco, and in a voice and manner betokening the deepest emotion, spoke, before reading, a few words to the brethren, mentioning the matter of Fa her Upchurch preparing his book for publication, and the circumstance that while here he was induced by Bro. Past Master

Dewey, while he was in San Francisco. This was a work of considerable labor, the earlier portions of the narrative being supplied entirely from memory. Nevertheless, by applying himself diligently to it, he was able to forward a considerable portion of it in May, 1886.

The Supreme Lodge of the Ancient Order of United Workmen met at Minneapolis, June 15, 1886, and there, in his capacity of Senior Past Supreme Master Workman, he attended.

HIS LAST "PILGRIMAGE."

Towards the latter part of October he started on what proved to be his last pilgrimage, going East in response to pressing calls from Boston and Philadelphia, by the way of Niles, Michigan, whence he had also had a pressing invitation.

LETTER TO PAST GRAND MASTER BARNES, OF CALIFORNIA.

At this time Past Grand Master Workman William H. Barnes, of California, was on a round of visits to the Lodges of the Southern and Middle States, by invitation of the Grand Jurisdictions there. From Toledo, Ohio, he addressed a letter to Father Upchurch, October 6, 1886, and received the following answer at Cincinnati, October 17:—

"STEELVILLE, Mo, October 16, 1886.

"MY DEAR BROTHER BARNES: Your kind letter from Toledo received. You are going to Tennessee for the aniver-

---

Workman A. T. Dewey to promise to write a history of his life and work, for publication, in book form, by the *Watchman* Publishing Co., the same to be sold throughout the world for the benefit of the honest old founder. Fortunately for all our brethren, and the many thousands who shall yet swell our ranks, and their families as well, Father Upchurch kept his word, and the precious MSS., largely in his own handwriting, were duly prepared, and thus will be preserved, to the Order and the world, one of the most significant of all life histories. Urged to add a few words more to his book, by way of benediction to his children of t e Ancient Order of United Workmen, he complied, and sent to his fellow-Workmen, from his good old heart and brains, a last blessing so characteristic of the dear, good man, and so appropriate to this sorrowful occasion, that it should not be withheld longer from those who so love and cherish his memory."

sary celebration, and I am going to be in Boston. Wherever you go, Brother Barnes, God be with you and bless you for your noble efforts for humanity. I shall never forget you or any of my dear California brethren. Give my sincere good wishes to the brethren everywhere. I often think of my grand trip to the Pacific Coast. Everybody is kind to me everywhere, but there is but one California, and I hope some day to see you all again. Praying that our work may spread and increase, I am

"Faithfully yours, John J. Upchurch."

As we prefer to have him tell the story of his life and travels himself whenever it is practicable, we transcribe the following letter written to the *Watchman*, from Steelville, Missouri, November 20, detailing his reception at the various places visited:—

VISITING EAST—THE PREDICTION OF CONTINUED PROSPERITY FOR HIS FAITHFUL FOLLOWERS.

"Steelville, Mo., November 20, 1886.

"Editor *Watchman:* According to promise I send you a few items concerning my trip East. On October 27, I attended the eighteenth anniversary of our Order at Niles, Michigan. There was a procession of Knights and Workmen in the afternoon. In the evening there was a meeting in the Grand Army of the Republic Hall, where the Workman Degree was conferred under the new ritual by the Grand Officers with good effect. The Lodge and visitors repaired to the banquet hall and partook of a sumptuous spread prepared by the wives and daughters of the members. At seven o'clock all returned to the hall, where Bro. W. Warne Wilson delivered the address of the day, which was followed by the Grand Master Workman, myself, and others. At half past ten o'clock, the meeting adjourned, when I took the train for Boston, and was met at the depot by Supreme Medical Director Doherty, and conducted to the hotel.

"In the evening we had a fine meeting in Tremont Temple, which was well attended, considering the heavy rain that had fallen during the day and night. The meeting was addressed by Brother Loomis, of Buffalo, myself, and others.

"On November 1 I visited Everett Lodge, No. 7. The meeting was well attended, and a banquet was indulged in, and a number of well-directed, enthusiastic speeches made.

"On the 4th of November we visited Hallowell Lodge, of Maine, and assisted the Grand Officers in dedicating a new hall. There was a fine attendance, and a number of appropriate addresses. On the 5th, visited Salem. In the evening had a large meeting of the members; there was a banquet, and many fine speeches were made. On the 6th, took in the city, which was very interesting.

"In the evening I took the train for Pennsylvania. On the 7th visited Industry Lodge, No 2, of Wilmington, Delaware. A large meeting of the members and their families was held, many fine addresses, music and recitations, and a good time generally.

"On the 10th I took the train for Philadelphia, and was met by Brothers Past Master Workmen Smith and Jones. In the evening met with Quaker City Lodge, No. 110, in their hall. There was a fine attendance, and a number of enthusiastic speeches by Past Grand Master Workmen Smith, Jones, and others, and myself. On the 11th took in the city. The work is growing everywhere I visited, both in numbers and interest. I predict that the Order will approximate two hundred thousand by the next meeting of the Supreme Lodge.

"Fraternally yours, in C., H., and P.,

J. J. UPCHURCH.

IN BOSTON.

The following in relation to his Eastern visits is epitomized from New England papers:—

THE BOSTON CELEBRATION—A ROUSING RECEPTION TO FATHER UPCHURCH.

"The Grand Lodge of Massachusetts and the Workmen of that Jurisdiction, decided early upon a proper celebration of the eighteenth anniversary of the founding of the Ancient Order of United Workmen, with the result that the occasion was one of the most gratifying and profitable in the history of the Jurisdiction. Father Upchurch was the special guest of the Grand Lodge. Tremont Temple had been secured, and though the weather was not the most propitious, there was a large attendance and the greatest enthusiasm prevailed. The exercises were opened by an organ recital. Grand Receiver Temple, Chairman of the Committee of Arrangements, welcomed the audience, and called upon Grand Master Workman Hon. James Weymouth, of Old Town, Maine, to preside, who, after a brief speech, introduced Father Upchurch, who was accorded a genuine New England welcome.

"Brother Upchurch gave a brief account of the origin of the Order, the obstacles he met and overcame, and the progress made in the first few years of the existence of the Order. He explained the cause which brought a division of the Order, and the harmonious reunion, which was acknowledged by the convention of the two bodies singing, ' Praise God from whom all blessings flow.' He was very enthusiastic as to the future of the Order, and thought that ten years more would see a membership of five hundred thousand.

"Past Grand Master Workman Hobart B. Loomis, of New York, was also a guest of the Grand Lodge, and being called upon delivered a clear-cut exposition of co-operation as exemplified in the mutual plan of the Ancient Order of United Workmen, and showed, to the evident satisfaction of all present, that fraternity was the foundation-stone of the Order. The evening's entertainment included vocal and instrumental music by celebrated artists, and the whole affair was one of the most successful ever given in the Order, in every way except in the attendance, which, as said above, was limited somewhat by inclement weather.

"Sunday afternoon Brothers Upchurch, Ingalls, and Doherty 'went to college' in Cambridge. Monday was spent in sight-seeing. Tuesday evening Brother Upchurch was the guest of Everett Lodge, of Dorchester, where he had a royal reception.

14

"Wednesday evening he dedicated the new hall of Crescent Lodge, in Hallowell.

"Thursday morning the train was taken in a homeward direction. On arriving at Salem, a committee of John Endicott Lodge received the Upchurch party. In the evening Brother Upchurch witnessed the work as it was beautifully rendered by the officers of the Lodge. Representatives of fifteen Lodges were present. A collation and a pipe of peace followed the Lodge meeting. After a farewell to the brethren in Salem, cars were taken for Philadelphia, where Brother Upchurch met Quaker City Lodge, who gave him a warm reception, and saw him safely on his way home."

IN PHILADELPHIA—HIS LAST SPEECH.

Of his warm reception in the city of brotherly love we take the following account from the *Protector*, and as his response was the last recorded speech of the grand old man, we make no apology for giving it entire.

FATHER UPCHURCH IN PHILADELPHIA—HIS RECEPTION BY THE LODGES OF THAT CITY AND VICINITY.

" Large delegations from the Lodges in Philadelphia and vicinity, including Wilmington, Camden, Haddonfield, and Baltimore, assembled in the hall of Quaker City Lodge, No. 116, on Wednesday evening, November 10, to welcome Father Upchurch and make him feel how well beloved he is by the brothers of the Order here. It being the night of the regular meeting of the Lodge, the routine business was concluded with dispatch. The honored visitor was admitted to the Lodge under the guidance of the chairman of the committee, Past Grand Master Workman Wm. H. James, escorted by Past Grand Master Workman Jos. C. Smith, Grand Overseer Alfred Frank Custis, and Past Grand Master Workman F. J. Keffer. The Lodge room was crowded, and all testified their respects by giving the honors of the Order.

" Under the call of 'good of the Order' Past Grand Master Workman Wm. H. James arose and said:—

" ' It is of course to me a matter of great pleasure to introduce to you Brother J. J. Upchurch, the founder of our Order. Brother Upchurch is a man of modest demeanor, but he is a true Workman—a mechanic by profession. His idea was to form a society wherein the employé and employer could meet face to face as brothers, upon the same plane, upon the same platform, and obligated to the same principles. He also provided in his original constitution that the members were to do all they could for the elevation of the laboring class, in that they should provide for lectures and essays in the Lodge room, present new inventions as they came out, and provide a library for the members. He also provided for the payment of sick benefits and the system which has become the great item of our Order—the payment of a fund to the family of a deceased brother. We here to-night, meeting as members of the Ancient Order of United Workmen, welcome Brother Upchurch with the heartiest good wishes for long life and prosperity.

" ' I now introduce Brother Upchurch to you, that you may hear some remarks from him.'

"Brother Upchurch said: 'MASTER WORKMAN AND BROTHERS: It gives me a great deal of pleasure to be able to meet with you on this occasion, especially in this grand old hall. You are my first love, being in this Jurisdiction where my first labor was devoted to the Ancient Order of United Workmen. I am not much of a speaker. At the time when I should have been studying elocution in order to become a public speaker, I was studying mechanics and the wants of the people, otherwise you might not have the Order of United Workmen. I feel proud to-day that I am permitted to meet you here in this city, to meet the brothers of other Lodges here with those of Quaker City Lodge, the largest Lodge in the world. Perhaps I had better give you some of the incidents that caused me to think and act in building up our Order. It is known by a great many that in early times it was thought that all mechanics should belong to some trades-union. I thought so at one time. I went into the union, and I soon discovered that they were not doing what they professed to. They were selfish; they were envious. The blacksmith was ready to sacrifice the business of the machinist and to build up his own interest; so all the way down. It occurred to me that it was wrong that there should not be a union of the whole for the greatest good of the greatest number. It is true that while I was thinking about this matter, I formed no plan for the organization until 1864. I was master mechanic of the Mine Hill & Schuylkill Haven Railroad. Many of you know that in Schuylkill County the train hands demanded an advance of fifty cents a day, and I wrote to President Johnson, of Philadelphia, who directed me to give them forty cents a day advance, which made the engineer's wages four dollars a day. I notified the committee of train hands. They hooted at the idea and said that the society had directed them to demand fifty cents a day and take nothing less, and unless they were paid that fifty cents a day they would strike. They went on a strike and were out four weeks. The Secretary of War sent on a corps of engineers and firemen, and I ran the road in the interest of the Government of that time. At its expiration these men were ready to go to work at what I offered them in the first place.

"'Then it occurred to me what an outrage had been committed by this society on these poor laborers. It had deprived them of a whole month's wages that never could be regained, and some of these men were not able to lose three days in a month without depriving their families of the comforts of life. Brothers, it made such an impression upon my mind that it was impossible to cast it off, and I finally came to the conclusion that if it was possible I would do something to harmonize labor and capital. I was filled with the idea and went to the oil regions next year, and there became acquainted with Brother Keffer, to whom I disclosed my plan for harmonizing the two great interests. Brother Keffer encouraged me to perfect the work and introduce it on the night of the 27th of October, 1868. I reported that I had a constitution and the first degree ready. We then organized the meeting and I read the constitution, which was adopted by sections, and I administered the obligation of the first degree to thirteen members beside my-

self. We elected our officers and we all went away highly
elated at the prospects of the new Order. On the morning
of the 28th, not twelve hours after the institution of the
Lodge, a number of members came to me to demand that
the words "white male" be stricken from the constitution.
You will remember that the article on eligibility to membership says all white male persons of good moral character
are eligible to membership in this Order; they wanted the
words "white male" stricken out. I told them that I would
never do anything to degrade a white man. I said if the
negroes want to get up an organization for their own elevation, I will do all in my power to assist them; but that was
not what they wanted; they wanted it a mixed society, and
I do not feel like mixing too much. I do not believe in
too much mixture anyway. The Recorder took it upon
himself to refund to every member his initiation fee.

"'On the 3d of November, the second meeting night, I
went to the hall, not knowing whether there would be one
of them there, but I did not wish any of them to go there
and not find me. But, fortunately, six of the thirteen came
forward and paid their initiation the second time, and,
brothers, we then and there renewed our obligation that we
would go to work with more energy and determination to
build up the Ancient Order. We had a great deal to con-
tend with. We were opposed by the business men of the
city, by mechanics and laborers, and it was supposed that it
was a trades-union of the ordinary type gotten up to fleece
the workingmen out of their wages. We labored zealously,
earnestly, and faithfully for nine months, and in that time we
got twenty members; and, brothers, we thought we were doing very well. Everything seemed to go along harmoniously,
but at last, unfortunately, a division arose in the Order and
there were two Grand Lodges; but I thank God, in February,
1873, all those differences were removed and we again had
a United Order. Everybody's soul was in the work, and
they were rejoiced that there was no division; that we
were again united for the purpose of making men better,
teaching them high and noble aspirations; and on the 11th
of February the Supreme Lodge was organized in Cincin-

nati with eleven members. At this time we had about
eight hundred members in both wings of the Order. From
that time the people seemed to take an interest in the Order;
they saw that its members were doing all they could to benefit their fellow-members; they investigated its principles and
they saw that there was a feature in our Order that never
had been presented before, that of making men better, of
providing for their families, their loved ones, when they
were gone. Brothers, that feature to-day should fill our
every heart. From that time forward the Order spread
with unprecedented rapidity; it leaped the bounds of States,
it crossed the Rocky Mountains, and to-day I am proud to
say that almost every State and Territory in our country,
and in the Dominion of Canada, has Lodges permanently
located, and in a flourishing and prosperous condition.

" ' A few years ago we were looked upon with suspicion.
It was thought, as I said before, that we were a trades-union.
To-day our society is composed of the best men of the
country. We have members from the highest professions
and the lowest grades of mechanical labor. We come into
this organization on the same great level. It is not money,
but it is purity of character and uprightness that bring us
here, and we can take each brother by the hand as an equal.
Brothers, in this organization we have done more to harmonize the human family, high and low, than all the other
organizations that ever existed.

" ' It is true that some object to the word "Workmen," but,
brothers, are we not directed to earn our bread by the sweat
of our brow? It matters not whether a man works with the
brain or the hand, it is all work. Brothers, I have had experience in my life of both, and I must say that brain labor
is the hardest labor that I have ever done. He who is
ashamed to be called a workman should be ashamed to reap
any of the benefits produced by labor. I am proud to say
that our Order is composed of Workmen who are ever
ready to do anything to advance a fellow-man in the scale
of civilization and usefulness. This is why we have met
with such unprecedented success. We have worked to
make men and women better, to make them more honorable

in all their dealings with their fellow-men. The proud position which the Ancient Order of United Workmen occupies to-day in the rank of great organizations has been brought about by earnest, faithful, and persistent work, and to maintain its proud standard and to raise it to even grander proportions, increased fidelity must be brought to the interests confided to our care.

" 'Our Order has contributed more toward curing the great monsters, poverty and degradation, than any other. It has driven want and distress from thirty thousand firesides and erected in their stead the standard of hope and protection. The widow's tears have been dried and the wail of the orphan hushed.

" 'Fraternity, my brothers, is the foundation upon which our Order stands. It is the mainspring that prompts us to action and propels us forward in the noble work of Charity, Hope, and Protection. Its principles are like unto the ceaseless fountain of pure waters, charity widening out of the broad stream of hope, flowing on to the broad ocean of liberty. Upon the bosom of this ocean, my brothers, to-day ride one hundred and seventy-two thousand Workmen, and their loved ones shudder less and less as the advancing difficulties of the commercial world sweeps over their heads.

" 'Fraternity in its true and full sense amounts to more than mere forms and ceremonies; it amounts to giving protection to the weak and money to the needy. It means a better state of society; it means fewer outcasts and paupers and more of civilization and progress. Show me a community where fraternal societies flourish, and I challenge you to show me crowded poor-houses or jails. That is something important. Who ever heard of a Workman being carried over the hills to the poor-house? Who ever heard of a member of our noble Order being buried in the potter's field or in the pauper's grave? I never did, and I have traveled over a great deal of the country. I have had a great interest in our noble Order, and that is one thing I have never heard said about it.

" 'The first death occurred in 1871, and the widow received one hundred and sixty dollars. Since that time there has been more than fifteen millions of dollars paid to the widows of the deceased brothers of our Order; that does not include the sick benefits, or local benefits, or charity. Brothers, can any of us estimate the vast amount of suffering that has been relieved by the distribution of this sum? I confess that I cannot comprehend it to this day.

" 'I was in Boston last Friday week. We had extremely bad weather. Our meeting was held in Tremont Temple, and I suppose that there were one thousand people in the audience. The Order is growing remarkably fast in the jurisdiction of Massachusetts, which has now about ten thousand members. I believe that our Order at the next meeting of the Supreme Lodge will number two hundred thousand, and I expect to live to see one million members in this Order. I do not know that I will want to die then, but probably I shall want to see another million. I do not believe my work is ended yet.

" 'I feel proud of the Ancient Order of United Workmen, and why should I not? There never was a man who lived that had such a family. I must say that wherever I have been I was treated by the Workmen as a father. I am proud of it. I appreciate the honor, and to-night I am glad to meet with you. Brothers, let us live up to the principles of our Order and meet in that Grand Lodge above.'

"Eloquent and appropriate speeches were made by Grand Overseer Alfred Frank Custis; Grand Master Workman John J. Gallagher, of Maryland, New Jersey, and Delaware; Bros. John B. Moffitt, of Spring Garden Lodge; Geo. B. Carr, of Mt. Vernon Lodge; Morton R. Morris, of Integrity Lodge, and Past Grand Master Workmen Jos. G. Smith and F. J. Keffer. After the addresses Father Upchurch held a reception. Each brother was introduced to him and shook him warmly by the hand, expressing his pleasure in meeting him."

RETURNS HOME.

He took advantage of this visit to Pennsylvania to visit, in company with his wife, relatives and old friends in

Mauch Chunk and Bethlehem, staying with them a few days before finally returning to his home in Steelville. These last visits to the Lodges in Boston and Philadelphia were exceedingly gratifying to him. He felt that the grand organization which he had founded was away beyond the region of experiment, that it was one of the fixed institutions of the country, and that its principles were so firmly rooted in the hearts of the people as to give assurance of its permanence and success. At the same time he felt that he was getting to be an old man, and he expressed the prediction that this would probably be his last visit East.

He arrived home about the middle of November, and spent the next three months about his ordinary avocations, apparently in his usual health.

HIS DEATH.

About the 9th of January, 1887, however, he was taken sick with pneumonia, but no great danger was apprehended till the 17th, when he grew seriously worse, and died next morning at fifteen minutes past one, surrounded by his wife and the surviving members of his family. Of these, five sons out of fifteen children only remain,—Theodore F., Horace C., William A., Curtis L., and John C. His honored wife, the good mother of his numerous children, for forty-six years his faithful companion and helpmeet, considering her age, the vicissitudes of her life, and her great bereavement, remains in tolerable health and circumstances.

NEWS OF HIS DEATH.

And so, in peace and content, the great work of his life fully accomplished, surrounded and attended by the loving ministrations of his affectionate family, passed away the gentle spirit of the great founder and father of our Ancient

Order of United Workmen. Great men, who by reason of fortuitous circumstances have filled exalted stations, and occupied conspicuous places in the world's regard, are continually passing away; but few men having so few advantages have ever attained such universal respect during their lives or been so sincerely mourned at their death.

The morning following the sad event, wherever the telegraph could convey the sorrowful announcement, a feeling of regret akin to that experienced at a personal loss, filled the hearts of every Workman, and in a thousand Lodge rooms, from Maine to California, and from Texas to Canada, before any official order had been promulgated, there was a spontaneous desire to drape their altars in the emblems of mourning. Telegrams and letters of condolence from all kinds and conditions of people, and from all quarters of the continent, poured in upon the stricken widow and bereaved family.

MESSAGES OF CONDOLENCE.

Some of these, as samples of numerous others, we insert. They were sent direct to the family, or through Bro. H. L. Rogers, Grand Master Workman of Missouri.

"TORONTO, Ontario.

" H. L. ROGERS, Grand Master Workman: Regret prior peremptory engagements render my attendance at funeral impossible. The sudden demise of dear Father Upchurch has created a profound sensation of grief throughout the great jurisdiction of Ontario, as it will have over this vast continent. I have directed general order of condolence to be issued; fail not to do full honor to the memory of our lamented Father.   G. W. BADGEROW,
Supreme Master Workman.

"ASSEMBLY CHAMBER, SACRAMENTO, Jan. 18, 1887.

"H. L. ROGERS, PAST GRAND MASTER WORKMAN, St. Louis, Missouri—*My Dear Brother:* Your telegram announcing the sad news of the death of Father Upchurch was received by me during the morning session, and I cannot express to you the surprise and sorrow it brought me. At half past twelve o'clock, P. M., I called the speaker *pro tem* to the chair. I took the floor, and after saying such fitting words as I could command, introduced the following resolution, which was unanimously adopted, after which the House adjourned for the day:—

"'*Resolved*, That when this House adjourns to-day, it does so out of respect to the memory of Father J. J. Upchurch, founder of the beneficiary fraternal institutions of America, who died this morning at St. Louis, Missouri.'

"A press of business and my own strong feelings renders it impossible to write you at length to-day. Please accept the sympathy which I feel we all need, and express to the Workmen wherever you may meet them my share of our common sorrow. Fraternally yours,

WILLIAM H. JORDAN, *Supreme Foreman.*"

"CHICAGO, Illinois.

"MY DEAR MRS. UPCHURCH: I saw in the morning paper an account of the death of your husband and my friend, Father J. J. Upchurch. His death will fall heavily upon the members of the Ancient Order of United Workmen everywhere, and you will have the sympathy and kindly aid if necessary of every brother. Hoping God will deal kindly with you and yours, I am very truly yours,

WM. C. MORRIS.
Past Supreme Master Workman.

MEADVILLE, Pennsylvania.
"*To the Members of the Family of Father J. J. Upchurch:*—
One hundred and seventy-five thousand members of the Workmen help to mourn the loss of Father Upchurch and extend their sympathy to you in your bereavement.

M. W. SACKETT, *Supreme Recorder.*

"SELECT KNIGHTS, A. O. U. W. ⎫
HEADQUARTERS SUPREME LEGION, ⎬
Topeka, Kan, January 19, 1887. ⎭

"MRS. J. J. UPCHURCH, Steelville, Mo.: I have just learned by telegraph of your sad bereavement, and the loss our Order has sustained in the death of our beloved founder, Father J. J. Upchurch.

"We mourn with you the loss of one of the purest and noblest of earth, whose whole life has always been a progressive life, a life devoted to the right.

"Accept the sympathy of the Select Knights from Maine to California, and their pledge that you shall never want for home and friends.   Fraternally,

GEO. W. REED, *Supreme Commander.*"

"SAN FRANCISCO, California.

"H. L. ROGERS, Grand Master: California, in union with her sister Jurisdictions, mourns the death of Father Upchurch, and places a wreath of immortelles on his grave.

EDWIN DANFORTH,
Grand Master Workman.

SALEM, Missouri.

"DEAR 'GRANDMA' UPCHURCH AND FAMILY: I cannot tell you how my heart ached for you all, at the loss of the dear loved one.   I long to be with you and soothe your aching heart, but we must look higher.   God will give comfort that no earthly friend can.   Let us look to him in this dreadful trial.   May he be your guide and comforter in this hour of trouble.   Your true friend,

MARY A. WALKER."

"CUBA, Missouri.

"MY DEAR MRS. UPCHURCH: It was with the deepest sorrow and regret that I learned of the death of Mr. Upchurch, and hasten to assure you and your family of my love and sympathy in this your greatest affliction.   I desire to commend you to Him who said, 'Come unto me all ye that are heavy laden, and I will give you rest.'   What comfort indeed to feel we have a kind and gentle Saviour to lean upon and enable us to say, ''Thy will be done.'

MRS. S. M. WALLACE."

OFFICIAL ANNOUNCEMENTS.

The following official announcement and request were issued by the Supreme Master Workman the day after his death:—

"TORONTO, Ontario, Canada, January 19, 1887.

"*To the Grand Master Workmen of the Various Grand Lodges of the Ancient Order of United Workmen:*—

"BROTHERS: It is with feelings of deepest sorrow, that I officially announce to you, and through you to the Order at large, the death of Father Upchurch, the founder of our noble Order.

"He died at his home in Steelville, Missouri, on the morning of the 18th inst., after a short illness.

"Details of his personal history and of his connection with our Order are well known to the membership, and universal sorrow at the announcement of his death, will testify to the high appreciation in which he was held by the brotherhood.

"Rare are the occasions when the hearts of so vast a number are touched with deep emotion at the death of one who, without heralded fame, but in the humbler walks of life, conceived, and successfully matured a plan of systematic charity and benevolence, the results of which to-day command the respect and admiration of the world.

"Father Upchurch has gone, but the great work which his mind conceived still lives, and will endure as a lasting monument to testify to the nobleness of his mind and heart.

"It is my request that you direct all Subordinate Lodges in your Jurisdiction to drape their charter, altar, and Lodge room for the term of six weeks, in respect to the memory of Father Upchurch, the founder of our noble Order.   Yours in C., H., and P.,

GEORGE W. BADGEROW,
Supreme Master Workman.

"ATTEST:

M. W. SACKETT, *Supreme Recorder.*"

Of the announcements and recommendations by the Grand Masters of the various Jurisdictions we insert, because most convenient, that of Grand Master Edwin Dan forth, to the Grand Jurisdiction of California:—

"SAN FRANCISCO, Cal., January 24, 1887.

" *To the Subordinate Lodges of the Ancient Order of United Workmen of California:—*

"You are hereby officially notified of the death of the founder of our Order, Past Supreme Master Workman J. J. Upchurch, which occurred Tuesday, January 18, 1887. We mourn the loss of our father and friend. It is meet and proper that the California Jurisdiction should do something to commemorate the sad event. Our father was with us a few months since. We little thought that the Master would take him hence so soon; but such is the case. When it was thought necessary to make him a present some time ago, the California Jurisdiction gave one-third the entire amount, and it is believed that now we will do as much or more than any other State in the Supreme Jurisdiction. It is for you to decide whether we shall hold memorial services, erect a monument, or adopt some other way of perpetuating the memory of FATHER UPCHURCH. At a meeting of the Grand Officers and delegates of the various Subordinate Lodges of this city, held on Friday evening last, it was—

" *Resolved,* That we believe it to be due to the memory of Father Upchurch, that a monument should be erected in California, and we respectfully submit the idea to the brethren of this Jurisdiction, and ask them, while at their Lodge meetings, to debate the question, and send the result of their deliberations, at the earliest moment, to the Grand Master Workman.

"The Grand Master desires and requests that the various Subordinate Lodges throughout this Jurisdiction, drape their charters, gavels, emblems of the Order, and officers' jewels in mourning for a period of thirty days. Hoping

that immediate action will be taken on above resolution, and
the results forwarded to me, I remain

"Fraternally yours, EDWIN DANFORTH,
Grand Master Workman.
" ATTEST:
H. G. PRATT, *Grand Recorder.*"

RESOLUTIONS OF RESPECT.

Of In Memoriam Resolutions we accord the first place
to those of the founder's Lodge, Jefferson, No. 1, of
Meadville, Pennsylvania, the first Lodge of the Order ever
instituted.

"*To the Master Workman, Officers, and Brethren of Jeffer-*
son Lodge, No. 1, Ancient Order of United Workmen:—

" The undersigned, a committee appointed to prepare and
report to the Lodge a proper tribute of respect to the memory of our lately deceased brother, John Jordan Upchurch,
beg leave to present the following

MEMORIAL.

" In the year of our Lord, one thousand eight hundred
and sixty-eight, John Jordan Upchurch, a resident of the
city of Meadville, Pennsylvania, gathered together a few of
his fellow-workmen, and submitted to them a plan that he
had conceived for the establishment and organization of a
Mutual Beneficial Society, which was to have for its object
the honor and protection of labor, the improvement of the
moral, intellectual, and social qualities of its members, the
destruction of any unnecessary existing social barriers between labor and capital, the uniting of employer and em-
ploye in one sacred bond of brotherhood, and the creation
and disbursement of a fund for the benefit of sick and disabled members, and for the benefit of the widows and
orphans of deceased worthy members.

"The plan and object met with favor, and it was resolved
by himself and friends to establish such a society, and on
the 27th day of October, A. D., 1868, the Ancient Order of

United Workmen was organized in the city of Meadville, Pennsylvania, and Jefferson Lodge, No. 1, was duly instituted. Brother Upchurch, the author of the Plan, Constitution, and Ritual of the Order, became the first Master Workman of Jefferson Lodge, No. 1, the first Lodge of the Order. He was afterward made Provisional Grand Master Workman of the Provisional Grand Lodge of the United States, and finally, on the 6th day of October, A. D. 1869, the Grand Lodge of Pennsylvania was duly and formally organized in the city of Meadville, and then Brother Upchurch was duly elected and installed the first Grand Master Workman of the Grand Lodge of the Ancient Order of United Wor':men of Pennsylvania. Upon the subsequent organization of the Supreme Lodge of the Ancient Order of United Workmen of the United States and Canada, Brother Upchurch was honored by receiving the highest dignity in the Order, that of Past Supreme Master Workman.

" In the history and development of great enterprises, the credit and honor of their origin and formation often become the subject of contention by pretenders and false claimants, and so was the case in the history of this Order. It was sought by envious and uncharitable persons from time to time, to deny to, and deprive Brother Upchurch of his well-earned credit in this respect, but they were silenced by evidence, and after the fullest and most thorough investigation of the subject, the Supreme Lodge of the Order has formally placed upon its records and among its archives, the absolute and unequivocal fact that to Brother John Jordan Upchurch belongs the honor and renown of being the founder of the Ancient Order of United Workmen.

" For some time after the Constitution of the Grand Lodge of Pennsylvania, Brother Upchurch remained within this Jurisdiction, and a few years ago he removed with his family to the State of Missouri, where he died on the 18th of January, A. D., 1887.

" He was buried under the rites and with the honors of the Order, and under the auspices of the Grand Lodge of Missouri.

" It was most fitting that, at these last sad rites, the parent Lodge of the Order, and which was formed by Brother Upchurch and the Grand Lodge of Pennsylvania, of which he was the first Grand Master Workman, as well as the Supreme Lodge, of which he was a Past Supreme Master Workman, should be duly represented, and therefore, among the thousands who followed the mortal remains of Brother Upchurch to their last resting-place, were to be found the Recorder of this Lodge, who is the Grand Master Workman of the Grand Lodge of Pennsylvania, and the Supreme Recorder of the Supreme Lodge of the United States.

" The sphere of Brother Upchurch in life was, as the world reckons it, humble, unpretending, and yet of how few in any condition can it be said that so honorable a position has been attained, as he gained in the hearts of his fellow-men; how seldom can it be said that so much of real benefaction, of practical charity, and of ennobling deeds of good-will have been accomplished in so short a period of time, as is seen in the growth of this great Order, springing, as it did, from the seeds of love, benevolence, and philanthropy, sown in the tender heart and practical mind of Brother J. J. Upchurch, the modest and unassuming founder and father of this Ancient Order of United Workmen. Well did he understand and follow the tenets of those cardinal virtues of Charity, Hope, and Protection, those endearing watchwords of our beneficent Order.

" Brother Upchurch needs no tablet of brass nor monument of marble to perpetuate his virtues and to eternize his memory. His epitaph is written in the records of the Supreme Lodge and of every Grand and Subordinate Lodge of the Ancient Order of United Workmen, and the memorial of his good and beneficent deeds will forever find lodgment in the hearts of hundreds of thousands of his surviving brethren, and hundreds of thousands of the widows and orphans of those of his brethren who have gone before, and of the beneficiaries of those who, in their turn, shall follow him.

" This Lodge takes a mournful pleasure in thus placing upon record its high esteem for the benevolence, kind-heart-

15

edness, and far-reaching charity of our deceased brother, John Jordan Upchurch, the founder and father of this, the parent Lodge of the Ancient Order of United Workmen. And therefore, it is ordered that this memorial be entered upon the records of the Lodge, and a duly attested copy thereof be sent to the widow of our deceased brother, and as an evidence to the Order, and the world at large of the action of this Lodge, it is further ordered that a copy of this memorial be furnished for publication in the journals of the Order and of this city.

PEARSON CHURCH,
W. A. DOUGAN,
J. H. LENHART,   *Committee.*
M. P. DAVIS,
J. B. McFADDEN,

" ATTEST:
  W. A. DOUGAN, *Recorder.*
" *February 1, 1887.*"

RESOLUTIONS OF RESPECT.

We could fill a volume with Resolutions of Respect from the minutes of the Subordinate Lodges throughout the country, but limitation of space permits us room for only one set, and we insert those of Keystone Lodge, No. 64, of Oakland, California (among the first adopted), as an indication of the feeling of all the rest:—

"HALL OF KEYSTONE LODGE, No. 64, A. O. U. W.,
OAKLAND, Cal., January 25, 1887.

"WHEREAS, It has pleased the Supreme Grand Master in Heaven to remove from our Order our beloved brother, Father J. J. Upchurch.

"WHEREAS, As the founder of the Order, Ancient Order of United Workmen, he has always exhibited the greatest meekness and humility with the gathering laurels of its marvelous growth and prosperity, an earnest friend of labor, pure and honest in every thought, true in his friendship, warm in his attachments, modest and unassuming in his conduct, he commanded and possessed in the fullest degree the love and confidence of that mighty brotherhood he had created with the most unshaken faith and unclouded hope, and whose daily life was a simple but beautiful embodiment of the fraternal sentiment; therefore be it

"*Resolved*, That this Lodge deeply mourns the death of our venerable founder and brother, and feels that in his removal the Order has lost its most distinguished member, the community in which he lived one of its noblest citizens, and his family their best friend.

"*Resolved*, That we tender to his faithful widow and bereaved family our sincere sympathy in this, the hour of their great affliction, and commend them to the care of Him who doeth all things well.

"*Resolved*, That in token of our deep grief at the loss we have sustained, that the charter of our Lodge be draped in mourning for ninety days.

"*Resolved*, That the foregoing resolutions be spread upon the minutes of our Lodge; that a copy be sent to the family of our departed brother, and that they be furnished for publication in the *Pacific States Watchman*, and the Oakland *Tribune*, *Times*, and the *Enquirer*.

A. T. DEWEY,
C. E. ALDEN, } *Committee.*"
D. T. FOWLER,

PREPARATIONS FOR THE FUNERAL.

Preparations were immediately made to give the remains such a funeral as would, in a sad sense, express the high regard in which he was held by the brothers of the Order. The Lodges of Workmen and Select Knights of Steelville offered their services in any way they could be of use. Jefferson Lodge, No. 1, of Meadville, Pennsylvania, the first Lodge of the Order ever instituted, and Franklin Lodge, No. 3, also of the same Grand Jurisdiction, the Lodge of which he was a member at the time of his death, requested the honor of having his remains interred in the town where the pioneer Lodge was inaugurated. But after consultations between the local Lodges of Steelville, the officers of the Grand Lodge of Missouri, and members of his family, it was finally decided that he should be buried at St. Louis. Accordingly, the Grand Lodge of Missouri undertook the management and details of the funeral. A burying plot was secured in the most beautiful part of that most beautiful of the cities of the dead, Bellefontaine, near St. Louis; and it was determined that there should be two funeral ceremonies, one at his late home in Steelville, and a more imposing one at St. Louis.

On Friday morning, January 21, H. L. Rogers, Grand Master of Missouri, and a number of prominent members of the Order went to Steelville to conduct the ceremony there. And there, in a beautiful casket, surrounded by those he loved so well, lay all that was mortal of him, of whom it might be so truly said, "None knew him but to love, none named him but to praise." The coffin was trimmed with gold and silver ornaments, and on a silver shield was the inscription,—

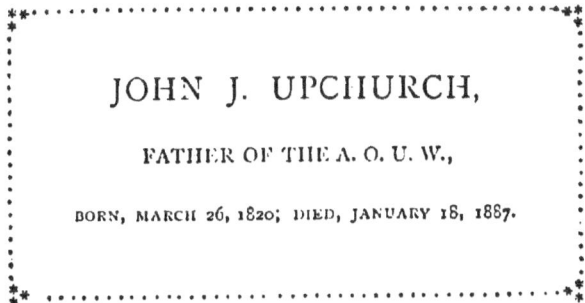

JOHN J. UPCHURCH,

FATHER OF THE A. O. U. W.,

BORN, MARCH 26, 1820; DIED, JANUARY 18, 1887.

At two o'clock the Lodges of Steelville, Cuba, Salem, and Rolla marched to the family residence headed by the

Steelville band, playing a funeral dirge. From there the remains were escorted to the Methodist church, the following acting as pall-bearers: Brothers Samuel Wyckoff, Charles Bangert, Patrick Stacks, Samuel Durst, Andrew Pabst, William Voss, John Hartfee, Andrew Pines, John Surch, John Guffy, Thomas Mercelle, Thomas Holmes, John Houston, and A. D. Day.

The exercises were opened by the choir singing, " Rest, Weary Heart." Rev. John D. Vincil, Supreme Trustee, read the ninetieth psalm, and the choir sang, " Jesus, Lover of My Soul." Rev. T. A. Bowman offered a prayer. The second Scripture lesson was read from the fifteenth chapter of Corinthians, and the choir sang, " It Is Well with My Soul." Dr. Vincil then delivered the funeral discourse, taking his text from Proverbs, fourth chapter, eighteenth verse: " But the path of the just is as the shining light, that shineth more and more unto the perfect day." The discourse is said to have been one of the most impressive ever delivered in the town of Steelville.

At the close of the address the funeral procession commenced forming. All passed by the remains and gave a last look at the venerated dead, and the coffin was then carried from the church and conveyed to Cuba and accompanied to St. Louis for final interment.

On arriving at the Union Depot in the morning, the remains were escorted by a company of Select Knights to the undertaking establishment, where they remained under charge of a guard of honor until Sunday morning.

LYING IN STATE, ST. LOUIS.

At ten o'clock next morning (Sunday), the body was taken from the undertaking establishment of Smithers & Waggoner and deposited in the center of Masonic Hall;

and here it lay in state from ten o'clock until one o'clock in the afternoon. Throngs from the various Lodges moved slowly through the great Lodge room. The hallways of the Temple were crowded, and the streets in the vicinity were filled with people. It is estimated that ten thousand people passed by the coffin. Upon the casket in the center of the Lodge room lay the cap and sword of the venerable founder of the Order and valiant Sir Knight, and a floral wreath from the Founders Lodge at Steelville, and an anchor from Rolla Lodge. Numerous beautiful floral offerings graced the Lodge room. On the platform at the end of the hall stood four handsome pieces. One, in the form of a shield, three feet in height, bore the inscription, "Sixth Regiment Select Knights—Father Upchurch, Farewell." A pillow, made for the Grand Lodge of California, was composed of white and yellow roses, with the word "California" in blue immortelles across its face. Anvil Lodge, No. 75, contributed a pillow made of white flowers, with the name of the Lodge in purple immortelles. The fourth piece was made for the Grand Lodge of Missouri, and was a magnificent tribute. The central figure was a large anchor passing through a shield, with an arched bar above and a straight bar below, all composed of the choicest of cut flowers and roses of the purest white, egded with ivy leaf. On the arched bar at the top were the words, "Grand Lodge of Missouri;" on the shield, "A. O. U. W.;" on the bottom of the anchor, "C. H. P.;" and on the straight bar at the base, " He Rests Well." The lettering was all done in purple immortelles.

ADDRESS OF GRAND MASTER WORKMAN ROGERS.

At intervals while the procession was passing through the hall, the band played solemn dirges. At two o'clock the bereaved family were conducted to seats, and Grand Master Workman Rogers ascended the rostrum and delivered the following address:—

"BRETHREN AND FRIENDS: A sad duty has devolved to-day upon the brethren of Missouri. We esteem it a high privilege that it falls to our lot, when the time has come, to lay away in the still, narrow house of death, with loving hands and sorrowing hearts, our father.

"This is not a time for many words from me, called as I am to introduce the ceremonies of this occasion as the representative of the Grand Lodge of Missouri.

"Away back in sacred history we read of a time when the Saviour of the world was on earth, that he stood beside the grave where friends were laying their loved one in its last resting-place; and it is not recorded that he delivered a funeral oration on that occasion, or that he pronounced any eulogy upon the dead, but we have only the record in these simple and touching words, ' Jesus wept.'

"We come here to-day to mingle our tears with the tears of those who are most bereaved; we come to burn incense over the bier of the departed. Gathering as we do under our protection and sympathy the widows and orphans of our brethren all over the land, we come with them to tender our thank-offering and heart-felt gratitude that he has lived.

"With us to-day gather three groups of mourners. First, the multitude of widows who in the darkest hour of their bereavement, in the day of their deep and hopeless desolation, saw the first silver light of hope through the works of our departed brother, Father Upchurch. Then come the thousands of orphans, who see others weep, but know not the reason why, not knowing how great has been their loss. These, in a later day, when they have passed the dangers incident to poverty and want, when they realize the benefits they have derived from the work of this good man, that they have been saved to useful manhood and womanhood by the instrumentality of the work he began, then their thanks will rise up as sweet incense forever, in memory of the works of our beloved and now departed father.

" And there comes another throng to-day, a stalwart band, to mingle their tears with ours. Time was when the countless multitudes of workers in this land, struggling to provide food and shelter for wife and children, looked forward to the day of their dissolution, and beheld only darkness and a hopeless pall hanging over them; and the thought came to them with agony: If I die what will become of this wife and these little ones? This question agonized their hearts whenever the thought of death would come; but their cry was heard, and this quiet, thoughtful man rose from his lathe in the machine shop at Meadville, Pennsylvania, and said: 'This is the way the poor man may have hope,' and when these words were spoken this dark veil was rent in twain, and the glorious light of hope beamed through the rift, shining before the toiling millions, to light their pathway for all ages to come. These countless thousands come here to-day to mingle their tears with ours over the death of him who has given hope to the poor man.

"As I said in the beginning, I will not mock the solemnity of this scene by further words. We, his brethren, with the widows and orphans, who have felt his kindly benefactions; these men, not only those connected with our own Order, but all that have grown up since these magic words were spoken, meet together around the grave of our venerated and beloved Father Upchurch, to weep.

The choir then sang, "Asleep in Jesus," and Past Grand Master Workman Vincil followed with an oration.

ORATION OF PAST GRAND MASTER WORKMAN VINCIL.

"BRETHREN AND FELLOW-CITIZENS: Day before yesterday, in the quiet town of Steelville, Missouri, I enjoyed the distinguished privilege of delivering a funeral sermon over the remains of our departed friend, Brother Upchurch.

"I had thought the performance of that duty sufficient to exempt me from further responsibility in the matter, but my friend and brother, Grand Master Rogers, ordered it otherwise; hence I am before you here to join with my brethren in offering a further tribute to the memory and worth of the departed. And I feel, gentlemen, that I voice the grief and the sorrow of a million people at this hour. He whose remains lie before us now, belonged, not to our own State, nor the State of Pennsylvania, but, when he organized the Ancient Order of United Workmen, he became cosmopolitan in principle and in character, and belonged to humanity. No place should claim him, no State can arrogate to itself the honor that he was ours exclusively, as he belonged to humanity. The fact being known to thousands, that at this hour we are performing funeral obsequies in the presence of his remains, I but voice the feelings of those thousands when I join with you in this tribute of sorrow, mingled with their griefs that our patriarchal friend has been taken. We shall see his face no more. In the home circle, where his sweet and quiet presence was a benediction, in the Lodge, where he was honored, in our Supreme Councils, where he was venerated —in all these relations and places there will be a sad vacancy. In the touching strains of the war lyrics:—

'We shall meet but we shall miss him,
There will be one vacant chair.'

"I congratulate the Workmen of Missouri, the citizens of St. Louis, and the brotherhood of this city on the fact that our departed friend and brother has been left, by the choice of his family, to sleep among us. Steelville, the place of his last residence, where his departing spirit went hence; Missouri, as the commonwealth of his adoption; St. Louis, as the place where he is to receive honored sepulture, may be congratulated that Brother Upchurch lived, and died, and sleeps among us. In Steelville went out a life that was a blessing to humanity; in the soil of Missouri his remains shall sleep, and the Workmen and citizens of St. Louis have the privilege and the honor accorded them of laying his body to rest in the dreamless quietude of our beautiful Bellefontaine. I prize the honor, I cherish the fact.

"It was said by one of the wisest men of all time, that 'a good name is rather to be chosen than great riches.' I believe it. For be it known unto you, fellow-citizens, that

that good name has been accorded to J. J. Upchurch by
thousands multiplied, and the verdict has never been ques-
tioned.

"It was the dream of Charlemagne to restore the empire
of the Cæsars, and the hope of King Arthur to revive the
ancient civilization, and embrace humanity in one brotherhood, represented by the 'Round Table.' With his good
sword, 'Excalibur,' Sir Arthur went forth, followed by his
noble knights, seeking to break the shackles that bound the
masses, redress the wrongs of the oppressed, and lead
humanity to a higher plane of development. Brother Upchurch never wielded a sword, in the carnal sense of that
word. Brother Upchurch never founded an empire, or led
armies to battle, or reared grand structures to live on the
map of time, through the coming years. And though he
may have builded wiser than he knew, he reared one structure
within whose sacred precincts thousands have found sanctu-
ary, realizing the rich fruitage of benefaction and of good.
And to-day, not only a hundred and seventy-five thousand
warm-hearted and heroic Workmen follow in his footsteps,
but thousands of widows and orphans that have been the
recipients of his benefactions, indirectly, rise up to call him
blessed, and to honor his name—a name rather to be chosen
than great riches; greatly to be preferred to gold and silver,
because of the loving favor with which that name is
cherished.

"Thus, brothers and citizens, I offer to-day, in brief, a
personal tribute, and accord to the memory of the deceased
my warm appreciation, which was the result of personal
association, springing from the very tender relationships between the deceased and myself. I am glad that on this
occasion, so memorable in the history of the Order of
United Workmen in this country, one of the very first men
enlisted in the work of that Order, at Meadville, Pennsylvania, Bro. M. W. Sackett, Supreme Recorder, is here to bear
his part in offering this tribute, and laying upon the coffin
of our departed founder his wreath of honor. I would that
some man had been here from among the earlier associates
of Upchurch, and chosen to fill my place. As one of the

younger and later accessions to the Supreme Lodge of that Order, which was founded by him in 1868, I feel that another should have performed this delicate task. There seemed to be, in those times when our Order was started, a demand for a man to meet given conditions, and God prepared and brought forth the man, and placed him before the thought and the attention of the American people. And I say to you, fellow-citizens, that the time never was more auspicious for the uprising of a leader, and the development of a character to make its impression upon and give direction to a beneficent Order, than at that period. Then the quiet but active and unpretending workman, amid his toils, framed and formulated a system of benefaction for our people, that came within the reach of the thousands and hundreds of thousands of his countrymen, whose hands were hardened by toil, and whose lives were spent in the earnest endeavor to make ends meet, and to provide a precarious subsistence for their dependent ones.

"You know, gentlemen, that the time has been, and is yet upon us, when an unfortunate conflict between capital and labor that produced abrasions, and frictions, and contests to be deplored, and out of a pernicious, as well as false conception of social life has grown up a feeling that has caused thousands to look down upon the multitude of common mortals as mere hewers of wood and drawers of water. The consequence has been that the toiler, the laboring man, has been placed at a disadvantage, and has been forced to look around him for sources of protection and of guaranty for his family. As a result, such organizations as we represent to-day, born in the brain of an Upchurch, cradled in the loving arms of those who united with him in the formation of the Supreme Lodge, spread through the agencies of the Grand Lodges, from the rising of the sun in the far East to where it sets in golden splendor on the coast of the Pacific.

" This organization, through the agencies thus put to work, has accomplished grand and magnificent results for the laboring people of the country. In its incipient history it was unpopular, because capital, always jealous, and sensi-

tive, and suspicious, looked down upon the name we had
assumed, and thought because we bore the cognomen of
'Workmen,' we belonged to that irrepressible class of an-
archists and destructionists that would strike down prosperity, burn up our cities, and eclipse forever the glories of
our institutions with the smoke of desolation.   They looked
upon us with contempt; we were called the 'Workingmen's
Society,' the 'United Workingmen,' and were scorned because of that title.   But it was not long until other associations sprang into being with the same idea, the beneficiary
feature, and took on all that was peculiar to our society.
And to popularize their imitations of our Order, they
assumed foreign titles, and hence it was 'royal,' and
'knights,' and the 'superb,' and 'legion,' and everything
else that was taking.

"I am proud to-day, fellow-citizens, that I belong to an
organization that bears the simple name of 'Workmen,'
and that it was christened by working men whose hands
were hardened by toil, and whose muscles and bones grew
weary under the restraints of labor.   The Ancient Order of
United Workmen had, as primary objects, the elevation of that
class of men whose time was occupied in labor, improve
their morals and their minds, bring them into closer relationship with each other, and make what never seemed
possible before anywhere on the globe, a brotherhood united
by the trinity of links, Faith, Hope, and Charity.   And
underlying this beautiful trinity, comes that which was the
watchword of Upchurch, Charity, Hope and Protection.
This was his work.   In the years that we have passed
since this conception and inspiration, more than one
hundred and seventy-five thousand have enrolled under its
banners; more than three hundred and fifty millions of
dollars to-day stand pledged as guarantee for the families of
these one hundred and seventy-five thousand members, and
the amount of money already paid to widows and orphans
since the organization was brought into being, added to
that which is guaranteed as benefits to members' families,
would amount to four hundred millions of dollars.   What
hath been wrought in these few years!   Charlemagne might

dream of empire, and Arthur hope for the unity represented by the 'Round Table,' but here, gentlemen, is practical work, resulting not only in brotherhood and fraternity, but in real positive benefactions to hundreds of thousands. And with such wealth as this and these important results accruing, wherever there are tears of sorrow to dry, and throbbing hearts to quiet, we are glad to remember him who is taken from us so unexpectedly.

"It remains for us who are living, to bear him to his silent resting-place in Bellefontaine, to lay him gently down to sleep, remembering that he sleeps well because he sleeps in Jesus. I would be untrue to myself, to the occasion, and to the character of the man I honor, did I not speak a word here of his *religious* character. Brother Upchurch, while he was a humanitarian and a philanthropist, was the highest style of man—a Christian gentleman. A little over forty years ago he professed faith in Christ, connected himself with the Methodist Church, and held the profession of his faith and Christian character and standing through all the intervening years. The rounding up of that amiable, gentle and pure life was to have a minister of Christ kneel at his bedside and commend him in prayer and faith to the God he loved. Loved in life, revered in death, glorious in immortality, his works do follow him. In this Jurisdiction, where his name is honored and his memory revered, we will place our loving tributes upon his grave, and say: 'Sleep, patriarch, sleep on—we would not break thy slumber by a sigh.'

"If the beautiful statue of Memnon, in response to the kiss of a sunbeam, sent forth its sweet tremulos and resonant music, will there not be evoked from the living statues of human hearts and tender affection, sweeter melodies and more dulcet strains as the name of Upchurch is mentioned or remembered in the coming time, when the sunshine of charity falls upon grateful natures. And though the statue we may erect in Bellefontaine be nothing but cold, insensate marble, yet every morning sunbeam that crowns it with beauty shall but portray the simple beauty of his life, and furnish a living prophecy of his immortality. That statue

we propose to raise by the voluntary contributions of one
hundred and seventy-five thousand of his brethren; and on
its base we will carve a name, simple, yet significant, ' Upchurch.' Upon its shaft we will carve an open Bible, and
above it inscribe in golden letters, ' Charity, Hope, and
Protection,' and on the obverse side write that sweet, gentle
expression that was characteristic and descriptive of his life:
' Peace on earth, good-will to men.' With a happy group
of widows and orphans, whose smile shall brighten with
every sunbeam, the work will be complete. And when the
sun rises and throws its sheen of beauty over the lovely
city of the dead—Bellefontaine—let its first kiss touch the
apex of the Upchurch monument, bathing it in light and
clothing it in glory—when the golden king of day shall ride
through the heavens in his chariot of splendor, let the last
coronation of the Upchurch monument be the sunbeam's
simple light.

" Beautiful his life, Christian his character, solid his fame;
and down the coming years that name, coupled in grand
unity with simple deeds, shall point back to the epoch in
which true philanthropy was born, an Order projected by a
laboring man, and humanity in the coming centuries, rise up
and thank God that Upchurch ever lived."

The casket was then removed by the pall-bearers as follows:
M. W. Sackett, Supreme Recorder; W. W. Hanscom, of
California; L. L. Troy, Past Grand Master, Illinois; B. F.
Russell of Steelville; Wm. A. Dugan, Grand Master Workman, Pennsylvania; Geo. W. Reed, Past Grand Master
Workman, Kansas; D. H. Shields, Past Grand Master
Workman, and B. F. Nelson, Missouri. Then followed the
mourners, members of the Grand Lodge of Missouri, and
visitors. Among the latter were M. W. Sackett, Supreme
Recorder of Pennsylvania; E. W. Tanner and Thos. Erwin,
representing Jefferson Lodge, No. 1, of Meadville, Pennsylvania, the original lodge established by Upchurch in
1868; Ignatz Baum, Grand Master Workman; Fred Beck,

Past Grand Foreman, and W. C. Gallaway, Chairman Finance Committee of the Grand Lodge of Illinois; M. H. Fuqua, Jas. H. Tiefenbrun, R. L. Wilson, of St. Joseph Lodge, No. 249, and W. A. Wyatt, Chas. T. Minturn and Wm. Page, Pride of the West Lodge, No. 42, of St. Joseph, Missouri; T. D. Smith, Newburg, Missouri; C. A. Herb, N. L. Winter, W. H. Helmein, L. Fager, A. Sotier, A. F. Erbeck and J. G. Quigley, of Alton, Illinois. Steelville, Missouri, the home of the deceased, was represented by B. F. Russell, Thos. Everson, E. A. Bass, J. T. Haley, Chas. Adair, A. J. Pinas, T. R. Gibson, J. F. Evans, J. A. Headrick, P. D. Cooper, J. W. Houston, and John Hanafin.

The hearse was drawn by four horses caparisoned in black. The funeral car proceeded from Seventh and Market to Walnut, on Fourth to Washington Avenue, Fourteenth to Locust, and on Locust to Leffingwell, where carriages were in waiting to convey delegations from each Lodge to Bellefontaine, where the body was laid to its long rest.

CONCLUSION.

There have doubtless been grander funerals, and more imposing pageants than that which followed the remains of the venerable founder to their last resting-place. But it has seldom fallen to the lot of mortal, to have more sincere mourners than those who gathered round the grave in beautiful Bellefontaine, in the gathering twilight of that winter evening, to gaze their last on John Jordan Upchurch, the Father of The Ancient Order of United Workmen.

Incidents in the History of the Order.

John Jordan Upchurch, founder of the Order, was born in Franklin County, North Carolina, March 26, 1820.

Order established, Meadville, Pennsylvania, October 27, 1868.

Grand Lodge of Pennsylvania organized July 14, 1869.

Division among the Pennsylvania Lodges December 10, 1870.

Reconciliation of the Lodges January 14, 1873.

First Supreme Lodge convened February 11, 1873.

Grand Lodge of Indiana suspended September 17, 1875.

Grand Lodge of Indiana restored April 6, 1876.

Institution of the Order of Select Knights, by Clark D. Knapp, Buffalo, N. Y., 1880.

THE YELLOW FEVER INCIDENT.

In 1878 there were seventy-six deaths from the yellow fever epidemic; forty-seven in Tennessee, and twenty-nine in the Supreme Lodge Jurisdiction. To meet the extraordinary demand caused by this increased mortality, the Supreme Lodge authorized relief calls on all the Grand Jurisdictions. These were reluctantly paid by some, and refused by Iowa. Delays were requested and granted, till, on February 7, 1882, the Grand Lodge of Iowa, at Cedar Rapids, formally refused to meet the Supreme Lodge call.

March 1, 1882, Supreme Master Workman Wm. H. Baxter revoked the Charter and suspended the Grand Lodge of Iowa. May 16, 1882, Loyal Grand Lodge of Iowa re-instated at Marshaltown, Iowa.

April 10, 1885, Father Upchurch invited to visit California. Arrived at San Francisco June 23, 1885. Reached home September 14, 1885. Visited Boston and Philadelphia October, 1886. Died, Steelville, Missouri, January 18, 1887.

APPENDIX.

It would seem, that in the compilation of this book, the editor's task would be incomplete without some account of the memorial exercises held in respect to the subject of it. We shall therefore as a fitting appendix add some such account of services rendered in honor of his memory by his loving children of the Pacific Slope in the Grand Jurisdiction of California. On Tuesday, January 18, the news of his death was received in San Francisco.

Wednesday morning, Grand Master Workman Danforth, Past Grand Master Workman Barnes, Deputy Grand Master Workman Poland, Grand Recorder Pratt and Past Master Workman Dewey representing the *Pacific States Watchman*, met in the office of the Grand Recorder, and after a brief informal talk, Grand Master Workman Danforth decided to issue a call for a meeting to take proper action on the death of Father Upchurch. Accordingly the following invitation was drawn up, to be forwarded to all Past- Grand Master Workmen, Master Workmen, District Deputies, Legion Commanders of the Select Knights, and the officers of the Grand Lodge and Legions in San Francisco:—

"You are hereby earnestly requested to be present, without fail, at 32 O'Farrell Street, on Friday evening, the 21st inst., at eight o'clock P. M., for the purpose of making arrangements for a meeting to pay a fitting tribute to the memory of Father Upchurch.   E. DANFORTH,
Grand Master Workmen."

Pursuant to the above notice, delegates from most of the

San Francisco Lodges met at the time and place designated. Grand Master Danforth presided and Past Grand Master Barnes acted as Secretary. After discussing the feasibility of erecting a monument, the matter was relegated for consideration by the Subordinate Lodges, and the following were appointed a committee to make arrangements for a memorial service: Past Grand Master Workman William H. Barnes, Past Grand Master Workman J. T. Rogers, Samuel M. Shortridge, Grand Commander Select Knights, Past Master Workman E. M. Reading and Past Master Workman James N. Block.

MEMORIAL SERVICES.

The committee appointed Sunday afternoon, February 13, and the Grand Opera House on Mission Street, as the time and place for holding the memorial services. Past Master Workman Bro. J. N. Young, of Sacramento, was requested to deliver the eulogy, Past Master Workman Dr. M. S. Levy, of Oakland, to act as Chaplain, and Past Master Workman Sam Booth, of Excelsior, No. 126, San Francisco, as poet of the occasion. In the meantime appropriate action was being taken by Subordinate Lodges in their individual capacity all over the country. Notably by Keystone Lodge, No. 61, of Oakland, and Excelsior, No. 126, of San Francisco. The latter held a regular memorial service in its Lodge hall, January 27, when Past Grand Master J. T. Rogers and Wm. H. Barnes delivered eloquent eulogies, and Bro. E. Knowlton of that Lodge read an original poem.

OAKLAND MEMORIAL SERVICE.

In response to the action of Keystone Lodge, the first to meet, the Lodges of Alameda County held a joint memorial service in the Colosseum, Oakland, Sunday afternoon, February 6.

The stage was occupied by E. B. Marston, Past Master Workman; Hon. W. H. Jordan, Supreme Foreman; Edwin Danforth, Grand Master Workman of the State of California; Wm. H. Barnes, Past Grand Master Workman; Rev. Dr. Akerly, E. F. Loud, Grand Foreman; H. G. Pratt, founder of the Order in California and Grand Recorder; E. M. Reading, Secretary Workmen's Guarantee Fund Association and Past Grand Commander Select Knights; J. N. Young, Past Master Workman of Sacramento, Sam Booth and other members of the Grand Lodge.

The services were opened with singing the anthem, "Trusting," by a double quartette of male voices, under the direction of Bro. W. H. Kinross. A prayer by Rev. Dr. Akerly followed and then the singing of the funeral ode, written for the occasion by Bro. Sam Booth, of Excelsior Lodge, the music having been composed by Brother Kinross.

FUNERAL ODE.

Bowed in sorrow here we come
Round about our Father's tomb,
To bedew his lowly bier
With the tribute of a tear.

Never more his cordial grasp
Will return our loving clasp.
Never more in speech or song
Will respond his tuneful tongue.

Pain and sorrow all are past,
Peacefully he rests at last;
All his toil and labor done,
Gained the crown, the victory won.

Soon, ah soon, we too shall be
In the grave as low as he.
May we too in glory rise
To the bliss beyond the skies.

Hon. Wm. H. Jordan, Supreme Foreman, eloquently delivered the eulogy, from which the following sentiments are taken:—

" It is under peculiar circumstances that I undertake this duty, for besides being intimately associated with the deceased in the work of the Order, he was also a warm, personal friend. As a vessel that has completed a storm-tossed voyage is brought safely into the peaceful harbor to rest, so Father Upchurch has found his rest in the harbor above. All that is mortal of him has been given unto dust. Preeminent among his virtues was his love for humanity, and as of Abou Ben Adhem of old the angels of light above have written that he loved his fellow-men. The story of his life may be quickly told. He was born May 26, 1820, on a farm in Franklin County, Virginia. While a boy he learned mechanics, and when twenty-one was married and went to keeping a hotel. He afterward returned to his trade, and going to Philadelphia became master mechanic in the shops of one of the early railroad companies, when railroading was yet in a rather primitive stage. During a strike on the road there were formed in his mind the ideas which years afterward resulted in the successful foundation of this society. In 1864 the League of Freedom, of which he was a member, resolved to give up its charter and disband.

He seized the opportunity to express the ideas which had so long inspired him and to present the scheme which he believed would lead to a great organization and prove a blessing to his fellow-men. There and then was formed the first Lodge of the Ancient Order of United Workmen. The little society was nearly disrupted by dissensions at the start, but

UPCHURCH REMAINED FIRM.

And from the thirteen who formed that first organization the present vigorous Order has grown. The founder's idea was at first to form a society in which would unite employer and employed; and in which they could talk over their relations and differences and strive for the elevation of labor. For five years the society slumbered, growing but slowly and being disturbed more or less by dissensions. Father Upchurch found it necessary to modify his plans somewhat as he gained experience. He found that he could not bring employer and employed together in the manner he had planned, and he turned his attention to making it a blessing to the families of those who were members, engrafting in the plan of the society the beneficiary feature. This has since proved the main corner-stone of the greatness the society has since achieved. His experience, wisdom and counsel were always at the command of the Order, and he was always ready to sacrifice self and honors for the good of the society. On the 18th of January a telegram reached this city announcing his death. A few days after, in the city of St. Louis, his body was laid away in the cemetery of Bellefontaine, and among the wealth of floral tributes which buried and surrounded his casket none were as beautiful and magnificent as the one sent by the Grand Lodge of California. His loss is mourned to-day by one hundred and eighty thousand men who compose this Order, and by two million families whose lives have been brightened by the light he created. We shall miss him for years to come; we shall listen for the kindly tones of his voice and hear them not; we shall look for the simple form of the grand old man and shall feel for the warm clasp of his kindly hand, and miss them both, and as I think of him come to my mind the beautiful words of the poet:—

Break, break, break,
    On thy cold gray stones, O sea!
And I would that my tongue could utter
    The thoughts that arise in me.

Oh well for the fisherman's boy,
    That he shouts with his sister at play!
Oh well for the sailor lad,
    That he sings in his boat on the bay.

And the stately ships go on
    To their haven under the hill;
But oh for the touch of a vanish'd hand,
    And the sound of a voice that is still!

Break, break, break,
At the foot of thy crags, O sea!
But the tender grace of a day that is dead
Will never come back to me.

At the close of the eulogy the choir sang the beautiful anthem, "Not Dead, but Sleeping." Grand Master Workman Edwin Danforth followed in a brief but eloquent address, in the course of which he said:—

"Of all the beautiful floral tributes which were sent on the occasion of the funeral of Father Upchurch, the one from California was selected by the widow to take with her to her desolate home. Father Upchurch, like many others, did not reap the full reward of his labors in this world and his widow was left in a degree destitute. We in California are expected to respond liberally at some future time, in aiding in the erection of a fitting monument to the deceased and in rendering substantial aid to the widow."

Past Grand Master Workman Wm. H. Barnes was then introduced. He commenced with the beautiful lines:—

"There is a reaper whose name is Death.
And with his sickle keen,
He reaps the bearded grain at a breath,
And the flowers that grow between."

"To-day we are in grief. Let memory go back and think if ever in the history of the world such a tribute has been paid to any citizen as that which is being paid to the memory of John J. Upchurch to-day. The world delights to honor such men. As the changing cycles of time revolve, there will be found engraven upon the eternal tablets of memory the name of John J. Upchurch. You can raise monuments of bronze to the memory of man, but Time, with his corroding finger, will crumble them. If you write upon the hearts of the people you write upon monuments which shall endure until earth reels in the wreck of matter, and crumbles into dust. Upchurch has written an epitaph for himself which shall never fade while time shall last. Who will ever think of Upchurch as dead? Our Legislature did one of the most grateful and graceful acts in the history of the State upon the day when, hearing that John J. Upchurch was dead, and recognizing him proudly as a man who loved his fellow-men, they passed a resolution and adjourned in respect to his memory. When Father Upchurch was in California he won the hearts of all, and in a letter after his return he said: "When you go to see the boys, bear to them my good wishes and good-will. Everybody treats me so well, and with so much kindness, but there is only one California and I hope to spend the last of my days there." We all know how reluctantly he left us, and we have been planning to bring him here to end his days among us. But our desires have been frustrated. It has pleased the Grand Father to take him home. We bid him farewell, but not good-bye, for men like him never die. He leaves behind him that fraternal affection which will survive all time, and we feel almost as though he were with us still.

"Only gone on, only gone on a little ahead of us, and we shall all soon follow. He has been welcomed at the great white throne and even now is looking down upon us with his old sweet smile, sweeter than when he was with us here on earth.

"Good-bye, old friend, so far as this earth is concerned. Good-bye, genial, old man; good-bye, father of our Order. One hundred and eighty thousand men remain behind you pledged to the work you left behind, and we will work and toil, following in your footsteps until there shall be no more sorrow and no more want to relieve, no broken hearts to bind up, no tears to dry; living in the beautiful creed of our Order and practicing to the best of our ability its precepts of Charity, Hope, and Protection."

At the close of Mr. Barnes's address the choir sang the beautiful song, "Rest, Spirit, Rest;" the services commemorative of one of the noblest of God's creatures came to a close and the vast audience quietly dispersed.

SAN FRANCISCO'S TRIBUTE.

According to the arrangements made by the Committee on Memorial in San Francisco, the Grand Officers and those invited to participate in the services, met in the office of the Grand Recorder at half past one o'clock Sunday afternoon, February 13. From thence they were escorted to the Grand Opera House by six legions of Select Knights under the command of W. H Graves, of Oakland Legion, No. 3, who acted in place of Grand Commander S. M. Shortridge, who was sick, Past Grand Commander E. M. Reading being Commander of the day. Arriving at the theater, the Grand Officers and their escort filed upon the stage.

The spacious auditorium and boxes were filled by Workmen, their wives and families, of the various Lodges of the city and neighboring towns; and the services opened by the orchestra playing " Nearer my God to Thee." Past Grand Master Workman William H. Barnes, in his capacity of Chairman of the Committee of Arrangements, conducted the services and introduced Grand Master Workman Edwin Danforth, who spoke as follows:—

" MR. CHAIRMAN, LADIES AND GENTLEMEN, AND FEL-LOW-WORKMEN: Death is always an unwelcome visitor in our homes. During the past year he has entered ten thousand homes within the national jurisdiction of this Order. One who was beloved by all of us now lies in the city of the silent dead on the other side of the continent; and we are here to pay respect to his memory   His death has brought sorrow to the hearts of Workmen, but we know that he has gone to his rest. When the news of his death was flashed across the country, some Lodges favored the erection of a monument to his memory, others thought that such action should be taken by the Grand Lodge, and others were inclined to leave this matter of respect to be provided for by the National Order. But whatever may be done in this direction, it is for us to remember that in death he still speaks to us and admonishes us to do our full duty as Workmen, and to follow the noble example that he has given us."

Dr. M. S. Levy, in a most earnest and eloquent prayer, invoked the Divine blessing. The choir of Calvary Church then sang with exquisite taste and feeling the ode written by Sam Booth to music composed for it by Prof. Gustav A. Scott. Bro. J. N. Young, of Sacramento, was then introduced and pronounced the eulogy as follows:—

"MR. PRESIDENT, LADIES AND BRETHREN:—

·   " 'To live in hearts we leave behind, is not to die.'

"John J. Upchurch was born March 26, 1820. The early part of his life was devoted to acquiring an education and a knowledge of mechanical arts.

"At the age of twenty-one he married the companion of his life, to whom he was fondly devoted.

" A short time thereafter we find him a skilled mechanic in the railroad shops of the Pennsylvania Railroad Company. appreciated and highly respected by his employers and fellow-workmen.

" From there he went to take charge of the mechanical . department of the Schuylkill Railroad Company, where he also distinguished himself by his skill and ability in his employment, by his considerate treatment of his fellow-laborers, and by his marked fidelity to his employers.

"When at the beginning of the late war the employés of the Schuylkill company struck and were obstructing the governmental use of the road, the United States Government ordered J. J. Upchurch to take charge of the road and to conduct its affairs. Under his administration the men almost immediately returned to their employment, and heartily seconded his every known effort.

"From there he went, in 1868, to take charge of the railroad shops at Meadville, Pennsylvania.

" For years he had been painfully impressed with the·

idea that employers were not sufficiently interested in the wants and welfare of laboring men. He now determined to devise some plan to bring employer and employé into closer and more friendly relations with each other.

"He accordingly acquainted the men under him with his wishes and plans in that direction. As a result of their conference, on the 27th day of October, 1868, the *first Lodge* of the Ancient Order of United Workmen was formed. Its membership consisted of thirteen men, many of whom had but the crudest notion and the slightest appreciation of the objects and aims in view.

"It was an experiment at best. To bring about the desired mutuality between labor and capital from opposite poles of interest was as physically impossible then as it is now. Upon this rock many of the leading statesmen of the most civilized nations of the world have wrecked their fondest theories. It remained for the subsequently adopted beneficiary feature of our Order to demonstrate to the world that this much-to-be-desired object may be attained by mutual co-operation. And to-day, the most advanced minds of political economists are fast coming to the conclusion that in the mutual interest arising from co-operation lies the solution of the difficult problems which to-day agitate the political and commercial world.

"Five years of experience and close observation fully convinced the founder of our Order of the failure of his then first purpose. These were five years of great mental anxiety. Dissensions among men who had not yet learned the value of mutual concessions and fraternal relations greatly retarded the growth of the Order, circumscribed its influence and at times even threatened to disrupt the organization.

"With ever changing fortunes, but never disheartened, our brother tenaciously clung to his purpose of permanently establishing our Order, which *he knew*, even if he could not unite the desired classes, would, in time, become one of the greatest blessings to mankind.

"His large heart and generous impulses did not, however, stop at the Lodge room, nor end with the members of the Order. When he saw the widows and orphans of deceased brothers, deprived of their stay and support, in their sadness struggling with poverty and want, he determined that they too should be cared for. For this purpose he devised the beneficiary feature of the Order by which, upon the death of a brother, his family, or those dependent upon him, should immediately receive, without abatement or expense, the sum of two thousand dollars, free from all claims against the estate of the decedent.

"In this feature of our beloved Order, the soft-winged angel of mercy came to suffering and sorrowing humanity with words and works of comfort and cheer, which command the richest blessings of Heaven, and go up as sweet incense before Almighty God. Verily, when the good deeds done upon earth shall come to be gathered into the granaries of the saints, that of Father Upchurch, however great its dimensions, will be filled to overflowing.

"From that little Spartan band of thirteen, who less than twenty years ago met in their crude hall with their yet cruder notions, this, our Order, has so grown in influence, wealth, and power, that to-day, like the mighty banyan tree, whose wide-spreading branches sending down their numerous supports form a natural shield and protection for the flocks and herds which congregate beneath its ample umbrage, its supporting Lodges are planted all over this fair land, and beneath its protecting Ægis it numbers not less than one hundred and eighty thousand active members, while it extends its Heaven-born talisman of Charity, Hope, and Protection over more than a million of beneficiaries to whom it now annually dispenses more than three million dollars, exclusive of charities and fraternal amenities.

"And to-day, all over this land, wherever a weary and worn Workman looks for the last time upon his sorrowing wife and soon to be bereaved family, conscious that he, their stay and support, is bidding them a last farewell, realizing that the brethren of his Lodge will shield and protect his widow and orphans, and that that policy lying there in full view will provide for their present wants and necessities, and enable them to cling together at least during the sad, yes saddest period of a family's existence, satisfied he rests his aching head and fevered brow upon that pillow of death, and from the depths of a heart overflowing with gratitude, thanks Heaven for giving to the world a J. J. Upchurch, and through him to us so beneficent an Order.

"On the 18th day of January, 1887, the electric spark with lightning speed conveyed the sad intelligence all over the continent that " J. J. Upchurch is dead."

"'God's finger touched him and he slept.'

"'A sleep that no pain shall wake,
Night that no moon shall break,
Till joy shall overtake
His perfect calm.'

" Such in brief, are the principal events connected with the life of that great and good man.

" When we turn to the pages of mythology, or history, sacred or profane, we find stamped upon almost every page the unmistakable Ishmaelitish character of the human race, " His hand against every man, and every man's hand against him." Whether we reflect upon the fratricidal conduct of Cain; the age of great men of valor and mighty men of war; the Trojan, Palestinian and Athenian epochs; the Babylonian, Median and Assyrian strifes; the Persian, Grecian, Roman or Carthaginian high-handed and reckless decimation of human life, or the Macedonian rivers of blood; the sanguinary contests of the Cæsars; the slain millions of the Crusades or more reprehensible butcheries of the Roses; the clash of arms or the roar of cannon at a Cressy, Poictiers or Waterloo, or the more speedy devastation of more modern warfare, all—all proclaim in unmistakable terms the brutal antagonisms of man unrestrained.

" But to-day I behold, as in a vision, emerging from this murky cloud of devastation and ruin, a mighty army clothed in the habiliments of peace, upon their banners, emblazoned in characters of living light, that divine precept of justice : 'As ye would that others should do to you, do ye even so unto them,' in their practice encouraging in lustry, stimulating mental and moral culture, promoting philanthropy, rendering mutual aid and assistance to each other, and guarding their families from suffering by want. I see their numbers increasing until by thousands and tens of thousands they spread out over all the land. All nations, tongues, and kindreds feel the benefit of their influence and power. An aromatic halo lights up the horizon of their progress and sends forth a sweet incense both healing to man and pleasing to God.

"As this mighty army of peace, exerting its beneficent influences, passes by into future ages and generations, need I ask you whether he who has borne so important a part in bringing about these salutary results ought to be written down in the history of the human race as a great and a good man?

"He was unconsciously great. His frank, open expression of countenance, and modest, unassuming demeanor, especially under embarrassing circumstances, were calculated to leave the impression upon the mind of the casual observer of child-like simplicity bordering upon mental inefficiency. Such, however, was not the true status of the **man.**

" It was only when he was free from the gaze of admiring brothers seeking to do him honor, or other distracting surroundings, that his true depth of soul, his broad and comprehensive scope of mind, were permitted to do justice to his solid judgment, his generous nature, and his fine executive ability.

"One thing which especially impressed itself upon my mind was the tenacity with which he clung to whatever he believed to be right. Living to see the full fruition of his labors, life to him was one continuous stream of joy. For him to live was happiness; to die was gain. How fittingly may it be said of such a man:—

> " 'An old age serene and bright,
> And lovely as a Lapland night,
> Shall lead thee to thy grave.'

"Contrast with his, the life of a man whose objects and aims all terminate in self, and who, becoming surfeited with the pleasures of this world, looks upon death as an escape from vanity and vexation of spirit, or as Hamlet more aptly puts it:—

" ' To die,—to sleep,—no more; and, by a sleep, to say we end the heart-ache, and the thousand natural shocks
" ' That flesh is heir to, 'tis a consummation devoutly to be wish'd.'

" In 1885, as our guest we welcomed him. He reluctantly took his departure from us. Thereafter his heart never ceased to yearn for California. But his journeyings on earth are past. His labors of love are ended.

" ' His soul is landed on that silent shore
Where billows never break nor tempests roar.' "

The choir then sang, " Beyond the smiling and the weeping," with fine effect, and " I know that my Redeemer liveth," after which Brother Barnes read the poem written for the occasion by Bro. Samuel Booth:—

With head bowed low and solemn step and slow,
And heart subdued beneath its weight of woe,
Like orphaned children to their father's bier,
We come to pay the tribute of a tear.

Low lies the head which was so wise to plan
Relief and comfort for his brother man.
And pulseless now the good, great heart, and still,
That beat for others' good and thought no ill;
Closed now the kindly eyes whose cheerful smile
Indexed a spirit that was free from guile.
Still, too, the cunning hand, which deftly wrought
The generous impulse of his kindly thought—
A heart so big that it could comprehend
Mankind as brothers and each one his friend—
The hand whose honest grasp we'll ne'er forget,
For in our own it seems to linger yet.

Not like a warrior borne upon his shield
From slaughtered foes on bloody battle-field,
With all his shining trophies on his breast,
Was he consigned unto his final rest,
With roar of gun and roll of muffled drum
And martial dirges sounding o'er his tomb.

Not like a statesman to his rest he passed,
Whose words roused nations like a trumpet blast,
And o'er whose dust resounds the grand *Te Deum*
Along the vault of mighty mausoleum.

But though his birth was humble and obscure,
And though his life was spent among the poor,
And though no king-at-arms proclaimed his fame,
Nor wealth nor titles dignified his name,
And though no kindly hands upon him laid
With knightly sword, the knightly Acolade,
Grander than all the names by kings conveyed
Was the good name which for himself he made;
And no distinction doth transcend, nor can,
The simple grandeur of an Honest Man.

Though knowledge to his longing was denied,
And his book learning not profound nor wide,
His battle with the world, its wrongs and strife,
Made him acquainted with the Book of Life.
He saw the follies of mankind with pain,
And strove to lift them to a higher plane.
He saw them suffering, and their own worst foes,
And pity swelled his great heart for their woes.
He saw how, front to front, in hate they stood,
And strove to weld them all in brotherhood.
"Each for himself," he saw the world did teach;
He taught them "Each for all, and all for each."
Though little skilled in creeds and 'ologies,
His heart brimmed o'er with kindliest sympathies,
Though knowing naught of churchly discipline,
His clean soul shrank instinctively from sin;
And though unorthodox, he spent his days
Modestly walking in the Master's ways.
Like a ripe sheaf of corn the reapers come,
He passed in triumph to the Harvest Home.
As a good workman lays his tools aside,
His work well done, good Father Upchurch died.

And so, with solemn chant and funeral bells,
We strew his grave with blooming immortelles,

In token that his life, though ended here
Is still continued in a holier sphere,
Thanking the great All Father that he gave,
To be our guide, a friend so true and brave.
Though in the body dead, may he still be
In all our souls a living memory,
To animate in every heart and mind
A larger love for all of human kind.
And may the precious seed, which he did sow
With so much pain and loving labor, grow,
As years roll on, to such proportions vast
That all mankind shall brothers be at last.

Doctor Levy then pronounced the benediction, and thus concluded the last sad rites sacred to the memory of him beneath whose name

The recording angel's pen could trace,
" He was the benefactor of the race."

ADDENDUM.

It has been deemed advisable to compile as an appropriate addendum to this book, a list of the officers elected at each annual session of the Supreme Lodge of the Ancient Order of United Workmen since its organization; a list of the various Grand Lodges in the order of their institution, together with a page of important incidents in the history of the Order, the whole forming a tabulated epitome of such information as would be useful for reference to members of the Order.

SUPREME LODGE MEETINGS.

First Supreme Lodge met at Cincinnati, Ohio, February 11, 1873. Three Grand Lodges, Pennsylvania, Ohio, and Kentucky, represented by fifteen delegates. Officers elected: Past Supreme Master Workman, W. H. Comstock, of Pennsylvania; Supreme Master Workman, W. W. Walker, of Pennsylvania; Supreme Foreman, John I. Becktol, of Ohio; Supreme Overseer, R. D. Handy, of Kentucky; Supreme Guide, J. W. H. Searles, of Kentucky; Supreme Recorder, ·J. B. Steeves, of Kentucky; Supreme Receiver, Louis Koester, of Ohio; Supreme Watchman, J. M. McNair, of Pennsylvania. Total membership about eight hundred.

Second Session Supreme Lodge met at Pittsburg, Pennsylvania, March 10, 1874. Six Grand Lodges represented: Pennsylvania, Ohio, Kentucky, Indiana, Iowa and New York. Officers elected: Supreme Master Workman, R. D. Handy, of Kentucky; Supreme Foreman, G. F. Cookerly, of Indiana: Supreme Overseer, W. S. Black, of Pennsylvania; Supreme Guide, H. N. Berry, of Iowa; Supreme Recorder, Wm. Martindale, of Indiana; Supreme Receiver,

17   (257)

L. C. Squires, of New York; Supreme Watchman, S. B. Lowenstein, of Ohio; Past Supreme Master Workman, W. W. Walker, of Pennsylvania. Total membership about two thousand.

THIRD ANNUAL SESSION OF SUPREME LODGE met at Indianapolis, March 16, 1875. Six Grand Lodges represented: Pennsylvania, Ohio, Kentucky, Indiana, Iowa, and New York. Officers elected: Supreme Master Workman, J. M. McNair, of Pennsylvania; Supreme Foreman, S. F. Griffey, Indiana; Supreme Overseer, S. B. Lowenstein, Ohio; Supreme Guide, Edwin Elmore, New York; Supreme Watchman, L. Koester, Ohio; Supreme Recorder, J. B. Steeves, Kentucky; Supreme Receiver, Ben. Davis, Indiana; Supreme Trustee, C. Shryock, Kentucky; Past Supreme Master Workmen, R. D. Handy, Kentucky.

FOURTH ANNUAL SESSION OF SUPREME LODGE met at Covington, Kentucky, March 24, 1876. Six Grand Lodges represented, Pennsylvania: Ohio, Kentucky, Iowa, New York, and Illinois. Officers elected: Supreme Master Workman, C. Shryock, Kentucky; Supreme Foreman, O. J. Noble, Iowa; Supreme Overseer, Thos. Curry, Ohio; Supreme Recorder, Edwin Elmore, New York; Supreme Receiver, B. Davis, Indiana; Supreme Guide, O. P. Titcomb, Illinois, Supreme Watchman, A. J. Francis, Kentucky; Supreme Trustees, D. L. Stephenson, Iowa, and A. R. Link, Indiana; Past Supreme Master Workman, J. M. McNair, Pennsylvania.

FIFTH ANNUAL SESSION OF SUPREME LODGE met at Chicago, Illinois, March 20, 1877. Ten Grand Lodges represented: Iowa, Indiana, Illinois, Kentucky, Minnesota, Missouri, New York, Ohio, Tennessee, and Wisconsin. Officers elected: Supreme Master Workman, Samuel B. Myers, Pennsylvania; Supreme Foreman, Thos. H. Curry, Ohio; Supreme Overseer, Chas. O. Thomas, Tennessee; Supreme Recorder, Henry N. Berry, Iowa; Supreme Receiver, S. S. Davis, Ohio; Supreme Guide, O. P. Titcomb, Illinois; Supreme Watchman, A. J. Francis, Kentucky; Supreme Trustees, A. R. Link, Indiana, D. L. Stephenson,

Iowa, and Ben. Davis, Indiana; Past Supreme Master Workman, C. Shryock, Kentucky.

Sixth Annual Session Supreme Lodge met at St. Louis, Missouri, March 19, 1878. Thirteen Grand Lodges represented: New York, Michigan, Iowa, Indiana, Minnesota, California, Illinois, Ohio, Wisconsin, Pennsylvania, Missouri, Kentucky, Tennessee. Officers elected: Supreme Master Workman, M. W. Sackett, Pennsylvania; Supreme Foreman, Leroy Andrus, New York; Supreme Overseer, Wm. C. Richardson, Missouri; Supreme Recorder, Henry N. Berry, Iowa; Supreme Receiver, S. S. Davis, Ohio; Supreme Guide, O. P. Titcomb, Illinois; Supreme Watchman, H. C. Heath, Wisconsin; Supreme Trustees, D. L. Stephenson, Iowa; Benj. Davis, Indiana, and Monroe Sheire, Minnesota; Past Supreme Master Workman, Samuel B. Myers, Pennsylvania.

Seventh Annual Session Supreme Lodge met at Nashville, Tennessee, March 18, 1879. Eighteen Grand Lodges represented: Pennsylvania, Ohio, Kentucky, Indiana, Iowa, New York, Illinois, Missouri, Minnesota, Wisconsin, Tennessee, Michigan, California, Georgia, Kansas, Ontario, Massachusetts, and Oregon. Officers elected: M. W. Sackett, Past Supreme Master Workman; Supreme Master Workman, John Frizzell, of Tennessee; Supreme Foreman, Roderick Rose, of Iowa; Supreme Overseer, M. W. Fish, of California; Supreme Recorder, M. W. Sackett, of Pennsylvania; Supreme Receiver, S. S. Davis, of Ohio; Supreme Guide, H. C. Heath, of Wisconsin; Supreme Watchman, E. W. Boynton, of Illinois; Supreme Trustees, Benjamin Davis, of Indiana, Monroe Sheire, of Minnesota, and Leroy Andrus, of New York. Total membership sixty-two thousand four hundred and ninety-three.

Eighth Annual Session of Supreme Lodge met at Boston, Massachusetts, March 16, 1880. Twenty-one Grand Lodges represented: Pennsylvania, Ohio, Kentucky, Indiana, Iowa, New York, Illinois, Missouri, Minnesota, Wisconsin, Tennessee, Michigan, California, Georgia, Kansas, Ontario, Oregon, Massachusetts, Maryland, Texas,

and Nevada. Officers elected: Past Supreme Master
Workman, John Frizzell; Supreme Master Workman,
Roderick Rose, Iowa; Supreme Foreman, M. W. Fish,
California; Supreme Overseer, Theo. A. Case, New York;
Supreme Recorder, M. W. Sackett, Pennsylvania; Supreme
Receiver, S. S. Davis, Ohio; Supreme Guide, Hugh
Doherty, Massachusetts; Supreme Watchman, R. H. Flan-
ders, Georgia; Supreme Trustees, Monroe Sheire, Min-
nesota; Leroy Andrus, New York, and Alex. McLean, Illi-
nois. Total membership, March 1, 1880, seventy-eight
thousand four hundred and fourteen.

NINTH ANNUAL SESSION SUPREME LODGE met at
Detroit, Michigan, June 7, 1881. Twenty-one Grand
Lodges represented: Pennsylvania, Ohio, Kentucky, Indi-
ana, Iowa, New York, Illinois, Missouri, Minnesota, Wis-
consin, Tennessee, Michigan, California, Georgia, Kansas,
Ontario, Oregon, Massachusetts, Maryland, Texas, and
Nevada. Officers elected: Past Supreme Master Workman,
Roderick Rose; Supreme Master Workman, Wm. H. Baxter, Michigan; Supreme Foreman, M. W. Fish, California;
Supreme Overseer, Theo. Case, New York; Supreme Recorder, M. W. Sackett, Pennsylvania; Supreme Receiver,
S. S. Davis, Ohio; Supreme Guide, R. H. Flanders, Georgia; Supreme Watchman, R. M. M. Patton, Ontario; Supreme Trustees, Leroy Andrus, New York; Alex. McLean,
Illinois, and John D. Vincil, Missouri. Total membership
of the Order, March 1, 1881, ninety-four thousand two
and twenty-two.

TENTH ANNUAL SESSION SUPREME LODGE met at
Cincinnati, Ohio, June 6, 1882. Twenty Grand Lodges
represented: Pennsylvania, Ohio, Kentucky, Indiana, New
York, Illinois, Missouri, Minnesota, Wisconsin, Tennessee,
Michigan, California, Georgia, Kansas, Ontario, Oregon,
Massachusetts, Maryland, Texas, and Nevada. Officers
elected: Past Supreme Master Workman, J. J. Upchurch;
Supreme Master Workman, Wm. H. Baxter, Michigan;
Supreme Foreman, M. W. Fish, California; Supreme Over-
seer, Theo. A. Case, New York; Supreme Recorder, M.

W. Sackett, Pennsylvania; Supreme Receiver, S. S. Davis, Ohio; Supreme Guide, R. H. Flanders, Georgia; Supreme Watchman, R. M. Patton, Ontario; Supreme Medical Examiner, Wm. C. Richardson, Missouri; Supreme Trustees, Alex. McLean, Illinios; John D. Vincil, Missouri; Leroy Andrus, New York. Total membership of the Order, one hundred and one thousand six hundred and eighty-five.

Eleventh Annual Session Supreme Lodge met at Buffalo, New York, June 5, 1883. Twenty-two Grand Lodges represented: Pennsylvania, Ohio, Kentucky, Indiana, Iowa, New York, Illinois, Missouri, Minnesota, Wisconsin, Tennessee, Michigan, California, Georgia, Kansas, Ontario, Oregon, Massachusetts, Maryland, Texas, Nevada, and Colorado. Officers elected: Past Supreme Master Workman, Wm. H. Baxter; Supreme Master Workman, M. W. Fish, California; Supreme Foreman, M. E. Beebe, New York; Supreme Overseer, Wm. G. Morris, Illinois; Supreme Recorder, M. W. Sackett, Pennsylvania; Supreme Receiver, S. S. Davis, Ohio; Supreme Guide, T. H. Pressnell, Minnesota; Supreme Watchman, Wm. R. Graham, Iowa; Supreme Medical Examiner, Wm. C. Richardson, Missouri; Supreme Trustees, John D. Vincil, Missouri; Leroy Andrus, New York, and Samuel Eccles, Jr., Maryland. Total membership of the Order, one hundred and eleven thousand three hundred and seventy-eight.

Twelfth Annual Session Supreme Lodge met at Toronto, Ontario, June 3, 1884. Twenty-two Grand Lodges represented: Pennsylvania, Ohio, Kentucky, Indiana, Iowa, New York, Illinois, Missouri, Minnesota, Wisconsin, Tennessee, Michigan, California, Georgia, Kansas, Ontario, Oregon, Massachusetts, Maryland, Texas, Nevada, and Colorado. Officers elected: Past Supreme Master Workman, M. W. Fish; Supreme Master Workman, Leroy Andrus, New York; Supreme Foreman, Wm. G. Morris, Illinois; Supreme Overseer, Geo. W. Badgerow, Ontario; Supreme Recorder, M. W. Sackett, Pennsylvania; Supreme Receiver, S. S. Davis, Ohio; Supreme Guide, G. R. Keller, Kentucky; Supreme Watchman, Wm. R. Graham, Iowa;

Supreme Medical Examiner, Wm. C. Richardson, Missouri; Supreme Trustees, S. B. Berry, Ohio, Samuel Eccles, Jr., Maryland, and John D. Vincil, Missouri. Total membership in the Order, March 1, 1884, one hundred and thirty thousand six hundred and sixty-two.

THIRTEENTH ANNUAL SESSION OF SUPREME LODGE met at Des Moines, Iowa, June 2, 1885. Twenty-two Grand Lodges represented: Pennsylvania, Ohio, Kentucky, Indiana, Iowa, New York, Illinois, Missouri, Minnesota, Wisconsin, Tennessee, Michigan, California, Georgia, Kansas, Ontario, Oregon, Massachusetts, Maryland, Texas, Nevada, and Colorado. Officers elected: Past Supreme Master Workman, Leroy Andrus, New York; Supreme Master Workman, John A. Brooks, Missouri; Supreme Foreman. Geo. W. Badgerow, Ontario; Supreme Overseer, Wm. H. Jordan, Cal.; Supreme Recorder, M. W. Sackett, Pennsylvania; Supreme Receiver, J. H. Lenhart, Pennsylvania; Supreme Guard, Geo. R. Keller, Kentucky; Supreme Watchman, Wm. R. Graham, Iowa; Supreme Medical Examiner, Hugh Doherty, Massachusetts; Supreme Trustees, Sam Eccles, Jr., Maryland; John D. Vincil, Missouri, and S. B. Berry, Kansas. Total membership in the Order December 31, 1884, one hundred and forty-two thousand one hundred and twenty-two.

FOURTEENTH ANNUAL SESSION OF SUPREME LODGE met at Minneapolis, June 15, 1886. Twenty-two Grand Lodges represented: Pennsylvania, Ohio, Kentucky, Indiana, Iowa, New York, Illinois, Missouri, Minnesota, Wisconsin, Tennessee, Michigan, California, Georgia, Kansas, Ontario, Oregon, Massachusetts, Maryland, Texas, Nevada, and Colorado. Officers elected: Past Supreme Master Workman, John A. Brooks; Supreme Master Workman, Geo. W. Badgerow, Ontario; Supreme Foreman, Wm. H. Jordan, California; Supreme Overseer, C. M. Masters, Wisconsin; Supreme Recorder, M. W. Sackett, Pennsylvania; Supreme Receiver, J. H. Lenhart, Pennsylvania; Supreme Guide, W. R. Graham, Iowa; Supreme Watchman, John A. Child, Oregon; Supreme Medical Examiner, Hugh Doherty, Mas-

sachusetts; Supreme Trustees, John D. Vincil, Missouri; S.
B. Berry, Kansas; H. B. Loomis, New York. Total membership of the Order May 1, 1886, one hundred and sixty-two thousand seven hundred and seventy-six.

ORGANIZATION OF GRAND LODGES.

The following are the dates of the organization of the different Grand Lodges: Pennsylvania, July 14, 1869; Ohio, August 31, 1872; Kentucky, January 7, 1873; Indiana, August 5, 1873; Iowa, November 27, 1873; New York, January 27, 1874; Illinois, June 28, 1875; Missouri, April 25, 1876; Minnesota, January, 24, 1877; Wisconsin, February 2, 1877; Tennessee, February 22, 1877; Michigan, February 27, 1877; California, November 13, 1877; Georgia, July 16, 1878; Kansas, February 5, 1879; Ontario, February 18, 1879; Oregon and Washington, March 4, 1879; Massachusetts, March 25, 1879; Maryland, New Jersey, and Delaware, January 19, 1880; Texas, January 23, 1880; Nevada, May 19, 1881; Colorado, New Mexico, and Arizona, October 10, 1882, Nebraska, June 8, 1886.

PAST SUPREME MASTER WORKMEN.

1873—J. J. Upchurch, Pennsylvania (founder of the Order), by vote of Supreme Lodge. Post-office address, Steelville, Missouri.

1873—W. H. Comstock, Pennsylvania, elected first session Supreme Lodge. Post-office address, North East, Pennsylvania.

1886—William G. Morris, Illinois, elected by vote of Supreme Lodge. Post-office address, 835 West Lake Street, Chicago.

1873—W. W. Walker, Pennsylvania; post-office address, Chicago, Illinois.

1874—R. D. Handy, Kentucky; post-office address, Covington, Kentucky.

1875—J. M. McNair, Pennsylvania; post-office address, Pittsburg, Pennsylvania.

1876—C. Shryock, Kentucky; post-office address, Lexington, Kentucky.

1877—Samuel B. Myers, Pennsylvania; post-office address, Franklin, Pennsylvania.

1878—M. W. Sackett, Pennsylvania; post-office address, Meadville, Pennsylvania.

1879—John Frizzell, Tennessee; post-office address, Nashville, Tennessee.

1880—Roderick Rose, Iowa; post-office address, Jamestown, Dakota.

1881—William H. Baxter, Michigan; post-office address, Detroit, Michigan.

1882—William H. Baxter, Michigan; post-office address, Detroit, Michigan.

1883—M. W. Fish, California; post-office address, Oakland, California.

1884—Leroy Andrus, New York; post-office address, Buffalo, New York.

1885—John A. Brooks, Missouri; post-office address, Kansas City, Missouri.

SUPREME MASTER WORKMAN.

1886—George W. Badgerow, Canada; post-office address, Toronto, Ontario, Canada.   .

PUBLICATIONS IN THE INTEREST OF THE ORDER.

Overseer, St. Louis, Missouri.
Pacific States Watchman, San Francisco, California.
Wisconsin A. O. U. W. Advocate, Milwaukee, Wisconsin.
The Protector, Baltimore, Maryland.
The Canadian Workman, Orillia, Ontario, Canada.
The Anchor and Shield, Paris, Illinois.
The New England Workman, So. Boston, Massachusetts.
Kansas Workman, Minneapolis, Kansas.
Ohio A. O. U. W. Journal, Cleveland, Ohio.
Indiana Recorder, *A. O. U. W.*, Evansville, Indiana.
A. O. U. W. Guide, St. Paul, Minnesota.
The Canadian Overseer, Toronto, Ontario, Canada.
The A. O. U. W. Argus, Buffalo, New York.
The Loyal Master Workman, Des Moines, Iowa.
The Fraternal Guide, New York City.
The A. O. U. W. Recorder, Hampstead, Texas.

www.ingramcontent.com/pod-product-compliance
Lightning Source LLC
Chambersburg PA
CBHW020356030726
47496CB00007B/2171